my big nose

and other natural disasters

BY SYDNEY SALTER

Houghton Mifflin Harcourt
Boston   New York   2009

Library of Congress Cataloging-in-Publication Data

Salter, Sydney.
My big nose and other natural disasters / by Sydney Salter.
p. cm.
Summary: In Reno, Nevada, seventeen-year-old Jory Michaels is self-conscious
because she does not fit in with her "beautiful" family, so while her two best
friends plan on a summer spent discovering their passions before their senior
year of high school, she gets a job and saves money for plastic surgery.

ISBN 978-0-15-206643-7 (pbk.)

[1. Self-esteem—Fiction. 2. Self-acceptance—Fiction. 3. Individuality—
Fiction. 4. Beauty, Personal—Fiction. 5. Friendship—Fiction. 6. Dating
(Social customs)—Fiction. 7. Mothers and daughters—Fiction. 8. Reno
(Nev.)—Fiction.] I. Title.
PZ7.S15515My 2009
[Fic]—dc22
2008048427

To the amazing women with whom
I created so many Reno High memories.
When's our next girls' weekend?

Chapter One

JUNE: SUMMER OF PASSION?

It all comes down to my nose.

Good old Great-Grandpa Lessinger's famous nose. The one they used to joke about until it turned out that I didn't "grow into my nose" like they'd all hoped, and probably prayed, even though we're not exactly a churchgoing family. My parents worship at the Caughlin Club—you know, the gods and goddesses of good golf swings, cute tennis skirts, prestigious addresses, and beautiful, gifted progeny.

I don't fit in.

My eyes are muddy brown while everyone else in the family has eyes that rival the color of Lake Tahoe. Sure, I've got the blond hair, but mine is curly and more brown than blond (though Mom insists I'm blond like the rest of them). Mom's is more a Platinum #305, but she'll never admit to it. "It's just a conditioning rinse," she always says. Right.

And it's just a nose.

If only I were some brilliant scholar who'd written six novels, created my own Web-based business, and spoke fluent Chinese. But no. I didn't even take any AP classes junior year, and I still have a B average.

I'm ordinary.

Evidence: last night's annual Reno High Awards for Students Who Are Actually Doing Impressive Things. I'd sat with my parents, craning my neck so I could see Tyler Briggs—who received an award for his charity work—sitting three rows behind me. My younger brother, Finn, popped up for his seven hundredth award of the night, Most Excellent French Student. He'd already won Most Soccer Goals Scored by a Freshman, Best Freshman GPA, and the Freshman Citizenship Plaque. Swoons, sighs, and giggles echoed all over the auditorium; the girls sitting next to me decided Finn should get awards for Best Legs, Best Smile, and "like Biggest Studliest Cutie ever." Like *that* makes any sense! Then Buddy Dickenson, Dad's Mr. Country Club golfing partner, leaned forward and said, "Are you sure Jory isn't adopted? She hasn't been up there once." He broke into his ex-smoker guffaws. My dad laughed, but my mom pursed her lips and glanced at me real quick. I buried my nose—my long, lumpy nose—in the program. Mr. Dickenson and his stupid booming voice. Had Tyler heard him?

I looked up only when Tyler received some ski team honor.

Afterward, I stood in the auditorium with my friends, nibbling a stale sugar cookie and sipping too-sweet punch, while my parents lingered near the stage accepting congratulations for having birthed the truly amazing Finn Michaels.

"It's going to be the best summer ever." Hannah's short blond pigtails bounced like an anime character's. "We have no worries." She fanned herself with her certificates for Outstanding Community Service, Super School Spirit, and Best Poetry. "We can relax and really discover our passions."

"Like getting into college? Getting real work experience?" Megan had already taken her SATs, twice, and talked nonstop about early-admissions this and AP-credits that. Plus, she'd lined up an internship with the U.S. Attorneys' Office. Tonight she'd dressed like a TV lawyer—silky blouse tucked into a short skirt, long dark hair pulled into a messy bun.

"No, silly." Hannah flapped her certificates at Megan. "Fun stuff!"

Both of us were a little sick of Megan's I'm-so-done-with-high-school attitude, especially when we still had a whole year left. Megan had changed a lot since the three of us had bonded on the first day of freshman year, sitting on the cement steps, eating homemade sandwiches, watching the kids who knew better head off campus for lunch. Yup, we were quite the trio:

Megan with purple orthodontia, zero boobs, and acne; Hannah with a back brace for her scoliosis; and me with the Nose. We spent hours dreaming up popularity ploys—the worst resulting in disastrous sophomore-year cheerleading tryouts (Megan got stuck halfway into her splits; Hannah couldn't stop giggling; I fell during a lift and had to wear a Band-Aid on my nose for an entire week).

"Well," I said, "I know my passion. His name is Tyler Briggs." I looked around real quick to make sure he hadn't heard me. Oblivious, as usual. Despite the ninety-degree heat, Tyler wore a starched buttoned-up shirt, an art deco tie, and the butt-hugging khaki pants that had once distracted me so much I'd slammed my forehead on Hannah's open locker. I watched his mother rake her long red nails though his wavy blond hair in a way that I'd only fantasized about. A giggling group of sophomores—the ones who frequently fawned over Finn—hovered nearby.

"I mean passion in the *creative* sense of the word." Hannah shook her head at me. "Meg's right. You do have boy issues."

"Duh." Megan cut her eyes at me, then Tyler.

"You have to love yourself first, you know." Hannah put her hand over her heart as if pledging allegiance to herself—something she actually *does*. I tried it once, but Finn and his friends saw me; I endured *weeks* of Pledge Allegiance to Jory jokes.

4

"No need to go all peace, love, and yoga on me." I glanced over at Tyler, who smiled all sweet, shy, and adorable as his dad clapped him on the back. "I totally have a plan."

Megan gave me the Look that my mother must have taught her. Too bad they didn't give out certificates for that kind of thing; instead, Megan had gotten a stack of academic awards. I was surprised they hadn't given her a certificate for tutoring me in Algebra II.

"I have an *amazing* plan."

I sort of had a plan: to catch up on my beauty sleep. God knows I needed some. Beauty, that is. Although I had to admit that eight hours of sleep a night for a year had done *nothing* for my beauty—if anything, it had made my brain simply more alert and aware that I lacked beauty or any other distinguishing features, skills, or appealing qualities.

And so there I was on the first day of summer vacation. Awake. With a big nose, no passion in my life—in the creative sense of the word—and all signs still pointing to me dying a virgin. *Guinness World Records'* entry: Jory Michaels, World's Oldest Virgin. Or maybe it would be for World's Most Unlovable Human. Or both.

In the kitchen, my parents argued at a few decibels above

any possibility of ignoring them, and the smell of roast chicken with wild rice and broccoli wafted into my room. Ah, yes. Day 6 of Mom's Dinner For Breakfast diet. You see, you can eat anything you want, only in reverse. In reality, you eat almost nothing except a big bowl of cereal at night because roast meat just about makes you want to hurl at seven o'clock in the morning. I groaned and pulled my pillow over my head, but I could still hear them arguing. So much for sleeping in. I kicked my comforter off, rolled out of bed using Hannah's yoga-inspired healthy-back method, and stretched. Like *that* would make me feel any better.

"Great start to summer vacation." I pulled my pajama bottoms out of my butt and padded down the hallway, past framed photos of Finn posing with a soccer ball, Finn sitting on a boulder at Lake Tahoe, Mom holding baby Finn, Mom and Dad's wedding, Mom and Dad grinning on a cruise ship, and one little five-by-seven photo of me in first grade. I don't do anything worthy of the family hall of fame. Or maybe it's just that I'm not photogenic enough. Or it might be because I've destroyed most of my school pictures since George Grobin called me "elephant nose" in the second grade.

I plopped myself down on a kitchen stool. "Oh, Mom. But I wanted lasagna for breakfast."

"Don't you even start with me." Mom opened the oven and grimaced as she read the meat thermometer. "I might be late for my first client because I've been up since five A.M. preparing you a delicious din—" She stopped.

"Ha! Caught you! You were going to say *dinner*." I flipped my hair back and forth. "You said *dinner*. You said *dinner*."

Mom shot me the Look while Dad gathered his briefcase, keys, pager, planner, and cell phone. "I'll grab something at work," he said, smiling at me. "Great reason to get a summer job, Jory: office doughnuts."

"Evan, you can't eat doughnuts! You said you'd support my new family-eating plan." Mom shook her wooden spoon before wiping her sweaty forehead with the back of her oven mitt. "Oh, fine. I'll save the chicken for dinner. Just this once."

Dad squeezed my shoulder and whispered, "We *will* triumph over this one, honey. She's breaking. Won't be long." He kissed my forehead, then blew a kiss to Mom.

After the door to the garage slammed shut with an echoing thud, I jumped up to grab a box of cereal.

"No, you don't. We can have the leftover pizza Finn and his friends ordered."

I spread the Living section of the paper out in front of me and glanced over the comics. "Mom. Pizza is not a diet food."

"It's not a *diet*. It's a family-eating plan." Mom slumped down on a stool and put her head on her arms. "Oh, God, I'm exhausted. Whoever invented this die—I mean, eating plan—was a damn insomniac."

I shoveled a spoonful of crunchy delicious-for-breakfast cereal into my mouth while watching Mom wrinkle her perfect little nose. "You look good, Mom. You look like a mom."

She pouted. "I don't want to look like a mom. Oh, never mind. I'll have grapefruit for breakfast."

"Ahh, yes. Sweet, or should I say, sour, memories of wacky diet number forty-seven." I scooped up another bite but slopped milk down my chin onto the newspaper. Mom dieted like Greg LeMond had trained for the Tour de France.

"Jory, you have no idea what it feels like to—" Mom looked away. She must've remembered the Nose. "I'm just tired." She rummaged for a grapefruit in our overstuffed fruit-and-veggie bin. "Your dad's right, you know. You should get a job this summer."

"Finn doesn't have to get a job."

"Finn keeps busy with soccer. Besides, his coach is already talking about his scholarship potential. And after last night—"

I get it. Super Schnozz has to work harder than the Nice Noses. A cartoon popped into my head, captioned: "Super Schnozz. Unable to awe people with her beauty. Unable to wow them with her intelligence. But if you need to identify an unusual odor, it's Super Schnozz to the rescue." Ah, that could be my passion. I could become a clever comics mogul. Hero to the proboscisly overendowed everywhere. Except I can't draw.

"Jory? Are you listening?" Mom whapped the classifieds on the counter. "You might find a summer job quite rewarding." As if she didn't constantly complain about her "rewarding" work as a mortgage specialist!

"I don't know where to start." I glanced down at all the itty-bitty squares of print. "Aren't these all for old people?"

Mom grabbed a handful of cereal out of the box and munched it noisily as she poured a cup of coffee. "Start with things you like to do."

I flipped to the *T*s for "Television Critic" but there were only ads for telemarketers. While fifteen dollars an hour sounded pretty good, having people call me nasty names and hang up on me all day would do nothing for my self-esteem. Although, maybe some cute guy would like the sound of my voice and fall deeply in love with me over the phone . . .

"What about baby-sitting?" Mom stirred a spoonful of sugar into her coffee, a sure sign that any dieting attempt was over for at least three days.

"Uh, no. I'm not spending my summer washing sticky hands and watching kiddie TV without even the possibility of seeing a cute guy." Unless the guy they paid to cut the lawn was totally hot and he saw me and, you know, *had* to have me. Can the desire to lose your virginity be a passion, in the creative sense of the word? I could totally see not-until-I'm-married Hannah taking a deep cleansing breath and closing her eyes if I even asked.

"I could work at the mall. Except not at the food court. Yuck. Maybe I could sell shoes? I love shoes. I'm always noticing people's shoes. And then I'd get a discount. How great would that be?" I looked through the "Retail" section of the classifieds, but everything said "experience required."

"This is so stupid. How hard could it be to grab a size seven and tell someone they look fabulous?" Hard enough for me, I guess. I try really hard not to lie. Ever (if possible). It's the Pinocchio thing. I can't take any chances.

"Well, what else do you like to do? Work with me, Jory. Please."

"Sleep. Maybe there's some sleep study up at UNR that I could enroll in?"

The Look.

I flipped past the automotive, bookkeeping, casino, and construction jobs. "Here's something." I read it aloud (don't ask me why).

DRIVER. Local deliveries.
PT + some weekends. Clean
MVR. Competitive hourly
wage. Katie 555-4653.

"Jory *driving?* That's pretty hilarious." Finn strutted into the kitchen, texting one of his girl-fans, looking like he'd gotten all of my beauty sleep.

"Honey, you know"—Mom crinkled her nose—"I'm not so sure it's a good idea."

"Why? It was an *accident*. That's why they call them accidents!"

Chapter Two

THE JOB INTERVIEW

Dappled sunshine sparkled through the trees as I drove my mom's minivan down by the river looking for Flowers and Cakes by Katie. I made two wrong turns before I finally found the little pink and blue house near the McKinley Arts and Culture Center. It looked like something Hansel and Gretel would wander into, except it was in a rundown neighborhood, not a scary woods. I pulled up in front of an accountant's office a couple of buildings away; I didn't want anyone to see that I was parallel-parking challenged. After all, I *was* applying for a job in the driving industry.

I was still slightly shocked that Mom had let me drop her off at work early and borrow the minivan. Like I keep saying, it was an accident! I thought I was hitting the brakes, but I was hitting the gas instead. It was only in the movie-theater parking lot, and I totally blame the guy for looking like Tyler

Briggs. Really, it was no big deal. Except that I lost my car. One little mistake and my car becomes too expensive to insure. (You'd think the Mercedes I hit would've had a sturdier bumper!) All I have left of my sweet-sixteen dream is the personalized license plate: JORRIDE. I also have to put up with the joy-ride jokes my dad makes every time I get behind the wheel—even when I drive up the hill to the grocery store or Starbucks.

Parallel parking in seven easy steps. In the middle of the steering wheel, I'd stuck the sticky note with the instructions I'd copied off the Internet. Usually it's pretty easy to avoid parallel parking in Reno, which is nice for those of us who'd failed that portion of our driving tests more than three times but fewer than five.

SIX EASY STEPS TO PARALLEL PARKING, JORY STYLE

1. Signal. (Of course!)
2. Make sure your back bumper is even with the other car's bumper. (Simple.)
3. Back up slowly, cranking the wheel toward the curb. *Lurch.* (*Slowly* being the key word.)
4. When your front door is even with the rear bumper, turn the wheel away from the curb. (No problem, unless your rear tire is stuck against the curb.

Scrape. Ignore the violent beeping from the rear sensors Mom had installed just for you. Repeat steps 1 through 4. Again. Third time is the charm, or something. Maybe it's the fourth. Give yourself more space. Okay, try a different parking place—this one is cursed. Master steps 1 through 4.)

5. Slowly back into the space.
6. Straighten the wheel and center the car. You should be less than a foot from the curb.

It was only after I'd jumped out and clicked the locks that I noticed the minivan stuck far into the street; I also noticed that the car behind me had a nice paint job, so I just walked away.

"Okay, time to look calm, cool, and collected." I took in a big, deep breath like Hannah always does, but I still felt all twitchy. With a businesslike stride, I walked down the block to Flowers and Cakes by Katie.

My parents wanted me to get a job so I could learn to be responsible and all that blah, blah, blah. They thought I could buy another used car and pay for my own insurance. What they didn't realize was that I had another kind of insurance I wanted to purchase: I wanted to *ensure* I'd have a better life by buying a brand-new nose. If I got this job, I could become a member of the Nice Nose Club in time for senior year. All I needed was approximately five thousand dollars and two weeks of recovery time, according to all the new-nose sites on the Internet. If I used my own money, Mom couldn't say, "Absolutely not. You're beautiful just the way you are." (Her standard line whenever I mentioned plastic surgery.) She'd have to let me do it.

Super Schnozz would be defeated. One last sniffle, then bye-bye.

"Okay, focus," I told myself as I walked through the white gate to the bright green door. A little bell tinkled as I walked into every kid's fantasy world. Flowers, teddy bears, kittens, puppies, knickknacks, bubbling fountains, and balloons in all shapes and colors surrounded me; gauzy fairies hung from the ceiling, and silk flowers bunched together in painted vases on the floor; roses in a rainbow of colors decorated a glass case. The whole place smelled sweet and sugary, like someone had baked a million birthday cakes. (I guess they had.) I breathed in deeply, wondering if even the air had calories. Mom would *never* come into this place.

A woman came from the back through some swinging doors, wiping her hands on a towel. "What can I do for you?"

I noticed that her hair was tied up in a net, showing off her big brown eyes, sweet round face, and cute little pug nose. A white apron that said "Katie Bakes!" was tied around her plump waist. I figured that was the hazard of making cakes for a living. Or maybe the air *did* have calories.

"I'm here for the job interview." I tried not to do that nervous nose-touching thing that Megan says I do before every school presentation or even when a cute guy talks to me.

The lady cocked her head and looked at me. "The driver position?" She spoke slowly, as if I were kind of stupid and had walked into the wrong place to ask for a job.

"Yeah." *Way to sound confident.* I looked down at her scuffed-up loafers. She had a glob of pink frosting on her right foot.

"Well, okay." She sighed. "You're not exactly what I had in mind, but I guess you can apply."

I watched the frosting wobble on her foot as she walked toward the cash register at the front of the store. A bunch of helium balloons floated in a basket on the ceiling. I half wished I could take the whole strange collection of ladybugs, smiley faces, high-heeled shoes, turtles, dolphins, and miscellaneous *Happy* messages and float into the sky. What did she mean by "not exactly what I had in mind"? Had she been hoping for some gorgeous showgirl type who could dance and sing with the deliveries, and Super Schnozz didn't fit that image? She gave me the application, then went back to the kitchen.

The application had a bunch of little boxes for previous job experience. I tried to make myself sound impressive without really lying. I put down *pet sitter* because I once fed Hannah's cat when she went out of town. *Child care.* I counted back on my fingers. I've baby-sat occasionally since I was about eleven, if you count the times I kept an eye on the neighbor's baby while she mowed her lawn. That gave me six years of experience. But I didn't have any so-called delivery experience. (Though I did run up to Scolari's every time my mom forgot some strange ingredient necessary for her wacky diet of the week.) Technically, I delivered groceries. I printed *grocery deliveries* in the first box and wrote *Scolari's* in the next box that asked for location, but I skipped all the phone number and address stuff.

Now I needed something to give me a little edge. Something to show that I was good with people. But somehow *Spanish club member* didn't sound too impressive, plus I'd dropped out when I realized that no cute guys had signed up. Just that one freshman, but he'd been Finn's best friend in third grade and I'd watched him eat his boogers one too many times.

I thought about how Megan and I had stood at the bottom of the chairlift exit up at Mount Rose all last winter and greeted at least three cute guys (ones who were not wearing goggles, matching ski attire, or smoking) before each run. I wrote *greeter* in the first box, then *Mount Rose Ski Resort*. I added *volunteer position* in the salary box to show that I wasn't doing this just for the money, even though I totally was.

While I waited for Katie Bakes! to come back from the kitchen, I sat on the twirly chair by the cash register and spun from side to side as a pink bear with a white ribbon stared at me with complete disdain. The phone rang and Katie Bakes! bumped through the swinging doors.

"Flowers and Cakes by Katie," she answered in a singsong voice. "Mmm. Hmm. What's the address? Phone number?"

Something in the back started making a grinding noise followed by *whap, whap, whap, whap.* It sounded like some kind of heavyweight boxing match going on. Katie put her hand over the receiver and called to me, "Will you run and turn that mixer off?

"That does sound lovely," she said into the phone. "Would you like to include a message?" She motioned to me with her hand to hurry.

I pushed through the swinging doors to the kitchen.

In the center of an island countertop, a big mixer whacked at a huge lump of thick white frosting stuff. The mixer had levers and buttons. But which one made the thing stop? With a constantly dieting mother, I had absolutely zero baking experience. I panicked for a moment before reminding myself that I was applying for a driving position. I watched the white stuff roll in violent waves. *Rrrr. Rrrr. Rrrr.* The mixer sounded like an old car trying to start on a cold day.

Push a button, I told myself, any *button.* I moved a lever forward and the mixer yowled, sending the white stuff swirling through the air like feathers during a pillow fight. Little bits thwacked me in the face and stuck to my clothes as I searched for the off button. Panicking, I flapped my arms around like a sick duck, then pulled another lever.

Bump. Bump. Thwack. The top of the mixer bounced up and down in the bowl, sending bigger chunks soaring onto a long shelf filled with clean cake pans. And one cooling sheet cake. Very little was left in the mixing bowl; I reached up and tried to grab some of the larger hunks in midair. No luck. *Smack.* A chunk struck my cheek, sticking for a moment and then bouncing off my shoulder and onto the floor. Was I ruining some poor kid's birthday cake? White streaks covered the black marble counter like crazy zebra stripes.

Grrrr, the machine growled. *Thump, thump, thump* went my racing heart, while the mixer went *whap, whap, whap,* smacking me with sugary globs. Finally I noticed a big red power button on the side. Duh. I'm such an idiot.

"I'll have it to you by three o'clock," I heard Katie's cheery voice say from the front. "Bye-bye."

Oh, God. What had I done now? The counter was covered with white formations that made it look like Mono Lake. I scooped a handful of the bits together and scrunched them into a ball that I used to try to pick up the other stuff, the way you use your gum to pick up the bits of a bubble that explodes all over your face. Except it takes much longer to clean up a kitchen.

My sneakers were sticky as I moved, quickly flinging the white stuff back into the bowl. Sweat poured from my armpits; I turned my face to avoid the blended odor of stinky gym locker and cupcakes. Unfortunately, the ceiling fan whirling above me did nothing to stop the burning in my cheeks. Can someone get fired before she even gets hired?

I was down on my hands and knees trying to pluck some of the stuff off the previously clean tiles when Katie pushed through the doors. Her mouth hung open. "How—"

"I accidentally turned it higher." *I'm so not getting this job.*

"Great. I've had that ad in the paper for two weeks and the only person to apply is an accident-prone minor with extensive —what was it? Greeting experience?"

I looked down at her shoes. Only a greasy smudge remained of the pink frosting, but her shoes made a sucking sound as she shuffled her feet. I tried to take a deep, calming breath but instead made a strange wheezing sound.

"Do you often have these kinds of accidents?"

"No. No. I swear." Except for in sports, school stairwells, buffet lines, while talking to cute guys, and when driving in movie-theater parking lots.

"You *can* drive?"

As I nodded, I noticed a little white gob wiggling on the end of my nose. Looking down, I wiped my hands across my face. Sticky.

"You can drive a *van?*"

"Yes, I do deliveries in a van from the grocery store."

"For your mother, I imagine. Please don't tell me it's a minivan."

That nervous never-tell-a-lie feeling gurgled deep in my stomach. "Well, it is." I picked at a fleck of white stuff on my hand. "But it's practically all I've ever driven." When Mom actually lets me drive.

I watched Katie Bakes! smoosh a big white chunk with her foot. Accidentally, I might add. She threw her hands in the air. "I may be crazy, but you're hired. I need the help and I can't afford to pay the going rate. You okay with nine dollars an hour, plus occasional overtime?"

"Sounds great!" I smiled. Mentally I tried to multiply 72 times 5 divided into 5,000 to figure out how many weeks I'd need to work for el nose job.

"I've got help through the weekend. You can start Monday. Six o'clock sharp."

"It's a deal!" My hand stuck to hers after I shook it.

"You really know how to drive a van?"

"Uh-huh." I wished my voice sounded a tad more confident. And that I didn't have so much white stuff stuck in my hair. Or on my shirt. To avoid Katie's discerning gaze, I looked out the screen door.

I saw the van: a multicolored, custom-painted behemoth squatting in the driveway like a hideous floral toad, itty-bitty windows in the back, side mirrors like a semitrailer's. It made Mom's minivan look like a Porsche Roadster. Would I actually have to back the thing out of *that* skinny driveway?

Chapter Three

GRADUATION NIGHT

Two nights later, we sat in the nosebleed seats at Lawlor Events Center watching the Reno High graduation on the jumbo screen, along with a bunch of giggling underclassmen girls and third-cousin-once-removed-type relatives who couldn't score the good seats.

"Ahh, he's so sweet," Hannah cooed as Dave Richards walked across the stage to accept his diploma.

"Need I remind you? Valentine's Day? Vomiting incident?" Megan said. "He's got drinking issues."

Dave reminded me of my first big die-when-I-saw-him-in-the-halls crush—Zane Zimmerman. I went to every basketball game freshman and sophomore years just so I could watch Zane run around in his baggy shorts, his blond hair flopping over one eye. Afterward, I'd beg Hannah and Megan to stick around so I could hear him say, "Hey, Jory." We waited all year for him to ask us to a party. Never happened. Finally, Valentine's Day sophomore year, we skipped out on the school dance (none of us had been asked) and headed up—slightly uninvited—to a party at Dave Richards's house. When we arrived, Zane said, "Hey," patted my head like a puppy's, and continued to spend the night playing a drinking game with a bunch of seniors. Near curfew, Dave Richards hurled all over Megan's shoes. Thus, the Valentine's vomiting incident.

"I still miss those suede clogs," Megan said as wild applause broke out when Dave high-fived the principal. She rolled her eyes. "*So* mature."

"But he's always so nice to *me* now." Hannah giggled.

"Because he thinks he ruined *your* shoes," Megan said.

"I know. It's so cute how he's got us all mixed up." Hannah sighed. "Remember how he asked me on a shopping date? But I was seeing that guy from yoga."

Ever since she'd ditched the back brace, Hannah has had to use two hands and one foot to count her boyfriends. My hands *and* feet could get amputated in a terrible car accident (not my fault, someone else's) and I'd still be able to count my boyfriends.

"I'm so invisible." Megan shook her glossy hair around her shoulders.

Not true. Plenty of guys noticed Megan, but she intimidated them. The good grades. The good looks. The not-so-good attitude. Last summer, Megan got her braces off, begged her mom to pay for contact lenses, grew four inches, and then developed "major issues with the pathetic high school social scene," probably because she didn't instantly become Miss Popular. Not that it would be easy to find a guy who met her superior standards—intelligent, ambitious, good-looking, athletic, popular (but not shallow), socially conscientious, politically involved, nice car, good wardrobe, sophisticated taste in movies and music, avid reader . . . Her list went on and on, plus she kept adding to it. Hannah had her standards, too, but they mostly revolved around a fuzzy combination of religious morality and touchy-feely stuff like vibes and kindness to trees and animals—oh, and good looks. Basically, she dated anyone with great dimples, lean muscle mass, and cool-looking hair who attended church more than twice a year and owned a shelter dog.

Several senior girls tottered across the stage in high heels. I was going to have to practice for hours to avoid making a total fool of myself next year. I could practically hear all of Lawlor erupting into big guffaws as I tripped down the steps. My diploma would roll down the aisle, but then Tyler Briggs would catch it. Our eyes would meet and he'd realize that I was the only girl he'd ever wanted. We'd go off to college together, graduate and come back and buy one of those big Caughlin Ranch mansions, and live happily ever after with our gorgeous little babies that looked like him and not me. On second thought, maybe I'd buy six-inch stilettos and *not* practice walking in them.

"Sleepy's coming up." Megan nudged me with her elbow. "Then we're leaving."

"Come on, we have to stay for the whole thing." Hannah pouted.

"Whatever." Megan sat back and searched her hair for split ends. She doesn't have any.

Everyone called Zane Zimmerman "Sleepy" because of the ZZ thing and because he had a tendency to fall asleep in class. Even his license plate said SLEEPY Z. (I used to love watching him rest his head on his arms in geometry. Once he winked at me before he closed his eyes.) From where we sat, Zane looked like a little black dot, except for a splash of white-blond hair glowing in the big overhead lights. People started yelling "Sleepy" even before the girl in front of him received her diploma. Several groups of students started fake snoring like they used to do at basketball games right before he'd shoot a free throw.

After shaking hands with the principal, Zane did three cartwheels across the stage. Then after one more not-short-enough speech about an Exciting New Journey into the Unknown, the whole senior class tossed their mortarboards into the air.

"Only one more dreadful, boring, immature year before we're free," Megan said.

After the ceremony we hung around to see if anything was going on, but the seniors were all headed up to a grad-night party at Tahoe, and even *we* weren't going to be caught dead at Matthew Doogan's video-game fest. I looked around for Tyler so I could say something not too stupid about us being seniors now, but I didn't see him anywhere. I hoped he wasn't going on some big family trip all summer. He was going to be the main ingredient in my Summer of Passion. At least, that was the plan.

"We need to celebrate," Hannah said. "We're seniors now."

"I don't want to stay out too late. I've got orientation tomorrow," Megan said.

"Oh, come on, Meggie." Hannah leaned her head on Megan's shoulder. "You can't turn into a high-powered attorney's summer-helper thingy yet. We're having our last free summer. Next year we'll all be heading off."

"*You'll* be heading off," I said. "I'll be heading to Truckee Meadows Community College to raise my grades." Staring at Zane for two years hadn't done much for my GPA. Neither had Tyler Tracking this past year; I kept getting hall passes to the bathroom so I could walk by his classes.

"Where's the positivity? We've got to do something. We're young, we're sexy, we're seventeen, we're new seniors." Hannah clapped her hands together. "Plus, tonight is day number one of my new midnight curfew. Yes, folks, the Johnstons have given their little girl a whole new half-hour of freedom."

"I'll do something involving nachos." Megan has a total junk food obsession, except she calls it "study munchies," like that makes it healthier or something.

"I'll do something involving boys." I swung my long hair from side to side. "I'm going to major in Boys 101 at TMCC."

Me and my future Nice Nose.

"You don't give yourself enough credit," Megan said. "You could get good grades if you'd focus. You could even get an internship if you'd simply figure out what you want to do with your life." I hated the way she liked to channel my mother.

I smirked. "FYI, I got a job."

"Doing what?"

I hesitated. All week I'd avoided the topic of jobs. Not that I wasn't excited about having a job and looking responsible and all that. I just wanted to postpone the inevitable teasing, especially after Dad's one-man comedy show: *Joy Ride Does Deliveries*. Very funny. Not.

I spoke fast. "I'm the new delivery person for Flowers and Cakes by Katie."

"Wait a minute. Your job involves *driving?*" Megan drew out the word *driving* longer than necessary.

"Is that a good idea? I mean, do they know about, you know—" Hannah paused.

"I can totally drive!" I put my hands on my hips. "Okay, I changed my mind. Forget nachos. Forget boys. Tonight I want to do something involving cars."

"You're not laying a finger on Bugsy," Megan said.

Megan's two great loves: her 4.0 GPA and the Volkswagen bug she had saved for since she was ten. She had even banned me from riding in Bugsy for a week after I spilled a Diet Coke during lunch last March. (Accidentally!)

"I've got it!" Hannah squealed. "We can do all three! This is going to be great."

Two hours and a platter of nachos later, we were sneaking up the walking path toward a certain desirable address on Long Knife Road, wearing jeans and black shirts and armed with whipped cream, mustard, ketchup, and chocolate sauce. Our shadows led the way in the moonlight.

"What if a car comes?" I whispered.

"We'll hit the dirt." Hannah smacked her hands together, dropping a can of whipped cream and making a huge hey-notice-me echoing sound.

"Shh!" Megan hissed. Something rustled in the bushes along the side of the road.

"What if coyotes are stalking us?" I asked.

"Hello? We're in a fancy-schmancy housing development." Megan rolled her eyes at me; I could tell even though it was totally dark. I could *feel* it.

"People report coyote sightings all the time in the *Caughlin Rancher*." We were one of the only neighborhoods in Reno with our own newspaper; people bragged about their fancy parties, newly decorated family rooms, job promotions, children's GPAs/athletic accomplishments/excesses of talent/ college admissions. And any wild-animal sightings. Great stuff. It was my mom's favorite reading material.

"Now that's pathetic." Megan walked ahead, muttering to herself as if to remind us—yet again—that this was *not* her idea. Reflections from a streetlamp shimmered in the man-made pond, and a pair of sleeping swans bobbed in the water.

"Car!" Hannah squealed. We slammed ourselves down on the paved path as headlights wound around the corner. The low-growing drought-resistant landscaping barely hid us. I inhaled the spicy scent of sagebrush as I pressed my arms against the still-warm asphalt.

"This is so juvenile," Megan said. "I'm going to regret this tomorrow when my alarm goes off at six-thirty."

I kind of recognized the *boom, boom* techno beat of LCD Soundsystem echoing down the street—so what if I'd started listening to the bands that Tyler advertised on his T-shirts? Maybe I could have a Tyler's-music passion or something. "It *is* him! Omigod!" I felt my cheeks glowing like a flashlight. "Could he see us? Did he see us?" I could totally read his personalized plate: PLAYER 5.

We lay on the pavement while the red taillights on Tyler's Jeep turned onto Long Knife Road. I prepared for Megan to launch into a speech that was a combination of how we were wasting her precious time and how Tyler Briggs was a spoiled rich boy who used people, especially girls. To top it off she'd repeat some anecdote from their shared AP English class—probably the one she'd heard about how Rachael Beal read *Rebecca* out loud to him while he lifted weights—to further prove his unworthiness. Hannah would counter with something about his cute smile and the nice vibe he gave off when he spoke up in their shared AP history class, but she'd agree with Megan about his "girl issues."

"That was close." Hannah giggled. "How long should we wait until we attack?"

"Maybe we should just forget about it." I sat up and brushed a bit of grit off my chest. "We're going to get caught." *Caughlin Rancher* headline: "Jory Michaels, Secret Stalker, Stopped."

"Yeah," Megan said. "He probably parks in a fifteen-car garage anyway."

"No, he parks in the driveway." I scrunched my eyes closed. And waited.

"Now, that's *truly* pathetic. I suppose you simply happen to jog all the way up here from your cozy little abode in The Cottages. Or maybe you lost the dog you don't even own. Or maybe you absolutely *had* to sell something as a fundraiser for a club you don't even belong to. Or—"

"Shut up, Megan. My mom walks up here all the time and sometimes I keep her company." I looked at Tyler's roof through the trees. "I can't help it if she's in love with Tyler's house." Tyler's dad paid for their humongous house by working as a big executive-CEO-president of something or other at the Atlantis Casino.

"How romantic," Hannah said. "You could totally marry Tyler, and your mom could live with you, and her dream of living in that house would come true."

I pictured waking up next to Tyler. Nice. But then Mom would be in the kitchen making meat loaf for breakfast. "That's sick."

"That's what I've been trying to tell you," Megan said. "You're sick. I don't get your Tyler obsession. He's pretty immature."

"Like you would know."

"Let's count." Megan held out her hand and put down her fingers one at a time. "I had three classes with him and you had—hmm?"

"One."

"And it was PE," Hannah said, as if I didn't know.

The last thing I wanted to think about was being the slowest one around the jogging track, whiffing the softball, scoring a goal for the opposing team in soccer, and getting hit in the head with a volleyball. No wonder Tyler never asked me out. Plus, the coach made me wear my long hair tied back so I was *all* nose. Super Schnozz! Able to humiliate herself during any sport.

"Quiet, quiet." Hannah walked up toward Tyler's house.

Tyler had parked his Jeep at an angle across one of the driveways of his six-car garage. Hannah made yellow-mustard smiley faces that showed up really nice against the forest green paint, while Megan drew ketchup hearts with chocolate sauce arrows across the windshield. I was supposed to write *RHS Seniors Rule!* with whipped cream on the windows. I sprayed *Seniors* across the back and *Rule* on the passenger window.

"Duck," Hannah whispered as a light went on in the house. So that's where Tyler slept. Second floor, above garage number three. I watched his shadow pull his shirt over his head. *Omigod! What if he sees me?* I started breathing fast as my heart thump-bumped wildly. Would he be totally mad? Or totally flattered?

"He's naked!" Hannah squeal-whispered. Her mouth bunched up like she was trying to hold in giggles.

"I do not need to see this." Megan choked on a laugh. "Jory, hurry up with the whipped cream already."

I put my foot out as if to flee down his dark driveway, but I couldn't take my eyes off the shadowy figure in the window. All that après-ski-season weightlifting.

"Not now!" I whispered.

Both Hannah and Megan nodded vigorously. Hannah clapped her hand over her mouth and made little squeaking noises.

Tyler's light switched off, but I'm pretty sure that I still glowed able-to-be-seen-from-outer-space neon red. I ran to the driver's-side window, squeezed the nozzle, and sprayed an *R* shape.

"Oh! Crap!" The window was open. Whipped cream flew across Tyler's nubby upholstery. I leaned my head through the window and tried to scrape some of it up with my hand. What a sticky mess!

He'll be pissed for sure. At me. Unless he never finds out.

Hannah and Megan burst out laughing. Tyler's light turned back on, and his shadow walked toward the window.

"Run!"

Chapter Four

THE BONFIRE

Saturday night, I sat scrunched in the back of Bugsy as we wound up a dusty road into the hills, searching for the ex-seniors' bonfire party. So far, we'd found nothing. Megan cranked up Sleater-Kinney on her stereo, in spite of Hannah's begging to listen to something more "now." Between the bumpy road and the music, the whole car rattled, along with my stomach. I totally hoped to see Tyler. I wanted to talk to him in a way that didn't involve apologizing for my lacking softball/volleyball/soccer skills. I hated not being in school and not hearing about his reaction to our decorations. Had he seen us? Would he guess it was us? And if so, would he be glad? Or mad? Maybe he thought it was guys from the ski team—though probably not, with the hearts and stuff. So many girls liked him. He'd never really dated anyone, but there were rumors about the gorgeous senior he'd escorted to the McQueen prom. Rumors

I chose to ignore. Yesterday I thought I saw his car pulling away from Starbucks as I was coming out of Scolari's with my mom, but I wasn't sure. No one had reported any vandalism in the *Caughlin Rancher*. That was a good sign. At least he wasn't call-the-police angry or anything.

"Read the e-mail again," Megan said. I did.

diploma, Ring. ahead Road unseen. I's not 80. don't Drive me 2
far East. let's Exit where Sage fills View. we Go, forgetting Past,
our Skeleton selves, Houses familiar onto Unpaved, untaken
Roads. changing, Watch me Glow. old Senior identity Inferno. a
Fairy godmother If i Needed one. pass this on to those you love.

"I don't get it," I said.

"Mrs. Muir would definitely fail this idiot poem," Megan said. "I'm surprised that whoever wrote it actually graduated. Why don't we skip the party and go get some cheese fries?"

Megan acted so uninterested, but she'd worn her tightest jeans and a blouse that would've been a dress-code violation if she'd worn it to school. Plus, she'd practically begged me to get directions. I wasn't about to mention that I'd gotten the directions by sneaking into Finn's e-mail; his password is always his favorite soccer player. How pathetic is it for a new senior to have to get party details from a sophomore? Almost as pathetic as Megan pretending she has no interest in high school while still struggling to become popular.

"Let me see it." Hannah grabbed the paper from me and flipped on the overhead lights. Her bare shoulders shone with glitter spray that perfectly accented the sequins she'd sewn onto her shorts.

"I can't exactly see where I'm going with that light on." Megan sounded tense. A rock popped up and hit the windshield. "Oh, Bugsy!"

"Give me a minute to feel the message." Hannah mumbled as she read through the e-mail. "This is important."

"Not as important as surviving," Megan said. "I have bigger plans than high school parties . . ."

Ignoring Megan's rant (so predictable), I leaned back and once again questioned my choice in T-shirts. Did light green truly show off blond hair? I should've dressed up more, like Hannah and Megan, but part of me wanted to look casual, as if I'd just stumbled upon the party, in case someone made a fuss about our slightly uninvited presence. I smoothed my new jean mini over my thighs. Mom had taken me pity shopping after the disastrous awards ceremony. At least my bottom half looked decent.

"Okay," Hannah said. "It has weird capitals. Let's only read those words. Ring Road."

"Duh. We took McCarren." Megan gripped the steering

wheel hard as she turned downhill. Gravel crunched and the tires squealed as she hit the brakes over and over again. And people complain about *my* driving!

The car slid a few feet. I imagined slipping into some ravine. It would take weeks for searchers to find my dead, virginal, too-pathetic-to-find-the-biggest-party-of-the-year body. At least I had on clean, never-before-worn underwear (red, for good luck).

"I's not 80," Hannah repeated over and over again. "That's strange."

"It means we should take I-80," I said. "I told you guys that the party would be out that way." Maybe I should admit that I stole the directions from Finn. We could go get cheese fries or whatever, head home, and watch a movie. I'd continue my safe, if not quite fulfilling, fantasy relationship with Tyler. No. This is the summer before senior year; my last chance to make high school mean something more than mediocre grades, unrequited crushes, and complete Super Schnozz–induced insecurity. Could I make it happen?

"Okay, okay." Hannah switched off the overhead light. "We go two miles—well, two somethings—on I-80, take the Sage View exit, go past some skeleton—maybe new—houses, and watch for the senior inferno."

"Senior inferno?" I asked. "Did they change the name or something?"

"Maybe they're trying to be clever," Hannah said.

"Yeah, this is all so clever." Megan shook her head but then smoothed her hair back into place. "Poor Bugsy's never going to be the same."

I flew back against the seat as Megan sped up on McCarren, driving toward the freeway. I have to learn to take chances. I wished I could be more like Hannah, not caring what people thought. Guys seemed to love that about her—as if the fact that she liked herself made it okay for them to like her too. All those years of wearing a scoliosis brace and dealing with nasty Hunchback Hannah comments gave her *more* confidence. Utterly perplexing!

"Are we sure we still want to do this?" Megan asked.

"Yes!" Hannah and I said simultaneously. Megan didn't say much as we drove out of town; she took the Sage View exit and rumbled along on another, slightly less bumpy, dirt road.

"Up there!" Hannah pointed to a glow in the distance. "Do you think the cops will bust it again this year? I hope not. I mean, since this is my first time and all."

I looked around at all the nearly finished houses. "We aren't going to have any hills left for our party when we graduate," I said.

"Oh, come on, Jory," Hannah said. "Live in the moment." Hannah moved her hands to the *duh-duhduh-duh* beat blaring from the speakers. "You're right, Meg, these guys are great."

Megan checked her lip-gloss in the rearview mirror. "Classic."

"Do you think Tyler knows it was us?" I asked.

"For the zillionth time," Megan said, "I don't know, but you'd better hope so since you've been trying to get him to notice that you're alive for over a year now."

"He knows I'm alive."

Proof that Tyler Briggs knows I'm alive:

- At the Dickensons' Fourth of July barbecue, he mistook me for a girl in his English class.

- He apologized every time he hit the volleyball anywhere near me in PE.

- On March 16 he said, "Great sweater," when I passed him in the hall.

- May 6, he said, "Nice choice," when he stood behind me as I ordered a strawberry frappuccino at Starbucks.

I shook my head so my hair fanned around my shoulders. My nose itched, but I couldn't scratch it because I'd wipe off my special nose-minimizing makeup. Mom had taken me to her favorite makeup lady at Dillard's and bought me two hundred dollars' worth of special "enhancing products." It took me a half-hour to shade my nose, as if I were some kind of Renaissance painter. Actually, I think it just made me look smudgy. When I came downstairs, Mom said, "You look great," but her mouth looked a little tight. Maybe she'd gotten another Botox treatment and hadn't told Dad. Or maybe I looked like a zebra nose, with dark lines going down the sides. The lady swore it was the same makeup used by magazine models. Yeah, right! The whole time she worked on me I imagined Super Schnozz flying from building to building shading everything with a giant "enhancing pencil." When she was done, all the downtown buildings would look really tall and skinny. Next she'd go shade all the fat ladies at the health club so they looked slender. No need for unsightly bulges of any kind; enhance it away.

Megan stopped and stared at the steep hill in front of us. "There's no way I'm driving Bugsy up that."

A few other cars had also stopped at the bottom of the hill. We parked next to a shiny graduation-present Honda (license plate: PRD O U) and climbed out of the Bug. No one else was around and it was pretty dark without the headlights. I looked up at the stars shining above and tried to find some kind of destiny there, some kind of message that this summer would be different. That tonight would be different. Better.

"Do you think we have to walk up there?" Hannah asked. "I'm wearing my sparkly ballet flats."

"I've got flip-flops on." I imagined my dusty feet with little rocks between my toes. So much for my Dragon's Breath nail polish and going for the casual-yet-sexy look. (I read in some magazine that most guys like feet.) I saw myself all sweaty and dusty after walking up that hill. My "enhancing makeup" would be dripping onto my upper lip like a chocolate-milk mustache. Yeah, I'd be a real winner.

Headlights appeared at the top of the hill. A green (green!) Jeep rumbled down.

"Omigod!" I screamed. "Is that—"

"Good old Player 5," Megan said. "Stay calm. Maybe this is what the note meant about a Fairy godmother. A play on words with *ferry*."

"I'm going to die laughing." Hannah covered her mouth.

The Jeep's gears rumbled, and my stomach felt bubbly when Tyler stuck his head out the window. "Need a lift, ladies?" His voice sounded low and sexy.

When Megan opened the passenger door I noticed a little smudge of yellow mustard in the crease of the side mirror. Hannah giggled as she climbed into the back after Megan.

They saved the front seat for me. Looked like my luck might be changing after all. Was this a sign or *what?*

Tyler wore a snug, muscle-enhancing My Morning Jacket T-shirt with a bulldog on the front, and long shorts that highlighted his calves. He had on flip-flops—just like me. So cool!

He turned and looked at me, arching his perfect eyebrows, nodding. "You'll be happy to know that there is absolutely no volleyball being played up there." He tossed me a dimpled smile.

"That's good." My voice sounded squeaky and weird. I touched my nose, and immediately remembered the makeup. Oh, God. Had I smeared zebra stripes all over my nose? Did my nose look like a nasty old plaid sofa now?

The Raconteurs—another Tyler T-shirt band—blared through the speakers.

"I love these guys," I lied. Tyler grinned and turned the music up even louder.

"Still have that four-point-oh, Meg?" he asked above the music.

"Yeah, whatever." Megan always sounded casual about her grades. Most people never saw how she stressed and obsessed about test questions. What did you get for number three? What about number seventeen? She'd go on for hours.

"Pieretto screwed me on the final." Tyler ran his hand

though his spiky, dark blond hair. "I got a three-point-five, and my dad threatened to send me to summer school."

"That's so not supportive," Hannah said.

"Want to be my mom?" Tyler asked.

We all laughed, though I totally felt jealous. Tyler shifted, and his hand brushed against my bare knee. Little shocks pulsed through my body. No one said anything as we climbed up the hill. At times it seemed like we would tip over backward. The whole experience made me woozy: the loud music, his hand near my knee, his deep voice, the steep hill. But I didn't want it to end.

"It's getting kind of wild up here," Tyler said as we climbed out of the Jeep. "You ladies be careful."

"Thanks," I said.

"Anytime, Jory." He winked. He *winked*. He said my name and he winked (at me!) before turning the Jeep around and heading back down the hill.

We could feel the bonfire's heat from where we stood. Dave Richards got up and screamed, "Cheers!" Everyone, including Hannah, yelled back, "Cheers!" Dave chugged a beer, crushed the can, and tossed it into the fire. Loud indie electronic music played from speakers in a shiny graduation-present truck. No license plate yet.

"Why did I let you talk me into this?" Megan drew her long brown ponytail into a bun.

"Because you're still a teenager." Hannah reached up and pulled Megan's ponytail out of the bun. "Come on, let your hair down."

"You're such a hippie." Megan shook out her hair.

Hannah pushed a hunk of stiff-looking hair behind her ear and ran her tongue across her teeth; Megan had absolutely freaked when Hannah started flossing her teeth in Bugsy. Hazard of having a dentist daddy: Hannah had major dental-hygiene issues.

"Hanegan!" Dave Richards noticed us. "I mean, Han. No, Meg. Hanegan!" He started laughing. He was pretty wasted, as usual. Megan stepped away from him as he tried to put his arm around her. He stumbled into Hannah, who stumbled into me. Next thing I knew, we were all on the ground.

"Get off me. Yuck!" Hannah shoved Dave off her so that he fell on me. He smelled like a drunk ashtray.

Suddenly, a big, warm hand pulled me off the ground. Zane Zimmerman smiled at me. His blond hair flopped over one eye. So cute!

"Sorry about Dave," he said.

"No biggie." I looked down at the blue stripe on Zane's high-tops and at the bulge of his calf muscle.

He reached over and touched my hair. "Stick." He showed me the twig he'd pulled out. Great. Tyler was going to come back and I'd look like I'd been rolling around in the dirt with the whole basketball team. Well, the starting forward, anyway.

I shook my hair as Zane smiled his lazy smile. "See ya, Jory." He squeezed my shoulder and walked back over to a group of just-graduated ex-seniors.

"Ooh, Jessica Milton is totally giving you the evil eye," Hannah said.

"So," Megan said. "Do we go hang out with the potheads, get drunk with the basketball team, or—"

"Meg." Hannah pouted. "We're going to have fun."

Right then Rachael Beal stumbled toward us holding out a small silver flask. "Want some? I stole it from my mom." She laughed, but it sounded like she was trying too hard. "Crème de menthe. It'll make your breath smell good. Just in case." She made a kissing sound.

"No, thanks." Megan turned around and pulled Hannah with her.

"I'll try some." I tilted the flask into my mouth. It tasted minty at first, but I gagged as liquid fire scorched my throat. "It tastes a lot better on ice cream." I coughed.

"You gotta sip it." Rachael took a big swig.

I took a few more tiny sips. It wasn't so bad. My face felt

warm, but I didn't feel any better about talking to Tyler, rolling around on the ground with Dave Richards, not looking Zane in the eye, or the fact that we were standing close enough to the fire that my Super Schnozz was probably emerging from my enhancing makeup like some mythical beast.

"Tyler!" Rachael yelled. I hadn't noticed Tyler getting out of his Jeep. Rachael ran up and flung her arms around his neck. He patted her back but looked over her head. At me? I drew my hair over one shoulder and tried to look alluring in the firelight, but Tyler only nodded at me as he joined a group of new and ex-seniors passing a bong around.

Megan appeared next to me like a sudden conscience. "One bad choice is enough for tonight."

"I don't have to try the drugs or anything," I said. "We could talk. Or something."

"Oh, Carlos is over there. He's totally cool," said Hannah. "He knows my body is a temple."

Megan shot her the Look.

"Not like that. We've just talked about how I like to make healthy choices." Hannah rolled her eyes. "We *are* at a party."

"Fine." Megan walked ahead of us to the group. "But you both owe me cheese fries."

Like that's a healthy choice!

People sat around on two-by-fours stolen from the construction site. Did they use the same wood for the bonfire? Was that legal? Oh, God. *Don't be so practical. You're here. You're a new senior in high school. You're at a party. Tyler Briggs is sitting not five feet from you. The mood lighting is great, plus he's in an altered state. Oh, God. That's pathetic thinking!*

"Let's try to get Tyler to talk about his decorated car," Hannah said.

"No! Don't." I took off my flip-flops and squished my toes into the cool dirt.

Hannah shrugged and plunked herself down between Carlos and me. She shook her head when he offered her the bong. The rest of us did the same.

"Cool." He nodded real slow.

Tyler sat across from me, wearing Rachael Beal like a scarf. She flung one of her long skinny legs over his and wrapped one arm around his neck. Tyler sucked on the bong for a long time before passing it to Rachael. She started giggling and couldn't hold the smoke in. She leaned over and started whispering in his ear, but his expression didn't change. He merely stared straight ahead. Straight at me, but he didn't seem to be seeing me.

"You're staring." Hannah nudged me. "She's just a tease." She tilted her head as Zane Zimmerman sat down on the other side of Megan.

"Sleepy, what up?" Carlos handed Zane the bong.

He shook his head. "I gotta pee in a cup Monday."

"Casino job?" some older guy asked—one of the guys who still hangs out at high school parties years after graduation. He probably bought the keg.

"Naw, I'm helping out with the Wolfpack Junior Basketball Camp before I leave for school."

"Rugrats. Cool." Carlos nodded.

"Hey, Tyler, how come you don't have to pass a drug test to work for your daddy?" the same guy yelled. "I guess you get special treatment when Daddy's the big boss."

Tyler focused a hard stare on the guy.

"I'm not working for my father." He stood up so fast that Rachael lost her balance and fell over backward. Tyler left her there and walked toward his Jeep; Rachael jumped up and followed him.

"Wait for me, Tyler," she whined. They both got into his car.

Tyler ground his gears, made a sharp, dirt-spraying turn, and sped down the hill too fast. Was he okay to drive? He seemed pretty wasted. And what the hell was Rachael Beal going to do with him, *to* him?

"Touchy!" the older guy said. "I tried to work for his daddy but couldn't pass the drug test. The Atlantis sucks anyway. But those casino jobs pay good." The guy laughed. "God, I miss high school."

I'd never been so happy about Hannah's curfew. We had spent the last forty-five minutes listening to people debate the merits of crunchy versus puffy Cheetos. Zane had left with Jessica Milton in his shiny new truck, taking the music with him. My makeup started feeling itchy, and a breeze pushed smoke from the dying bonfire over us.

"That was kinda fun," Hannah said as we inched down the steep hill.

"I can't wait to get to college," Megan said. "I'm *so* done with high school."

"Do you think he, like, actually *likes* her?" I stopped to pick a pebble from between my toes. "It's not like she's gorgeous or anything. Is she? And she's kind of dumb and he really cares about his grades, doesn't he, Meg?"

"Ahh, Jory. He was pissed, stoned, and she was drunk. Do the math," Megan said.

"That was kinda weird." Hannah stopped. "He completely freaked about his dad."

"*Serious* father issues," Megan said.

"Maybe he just needs an understanding girlfriend." I imagined how we'd drive back to Caughlin Ranch in his Jeep, walk along the path to the pond, and watch the swans float around in the moonlight. I'd listen as he talked about his dad; he'd listen as I talked about Mom. Then we'd kiss. And he'd walk me home.

"You've *got* to find something to do with your life," Megan said.

"Remember, this is the summer for finding our passions," Hannah said.

"In the creative sense of the word," Megan and I said at the same time.

"Actually, I have a plan," I added. "You just wait."

Chapter Five

FIRST DAY ON THE JOB

For the millionth time, I stifled a yawn as I swung the heavy van door shut. I might have to start drinking coffee. The fact that my bike was my only transportation to work only made it worse. I had shown up for my first day with my hair all wild from blowing out behind me as I cruised downhill. Stinky sweat marks darkened my shirt's armpits, and now I looked completely bored, or lazy, yawning all the time. Great first impression, Jory.

By seven o'clock, we'd filled the racks in the van with pies and cakes for the Monday-morning casino deliveries. With the frosting smell and the humongous flowers painted all over the van, it was like driving the entire cake and flower shop around town. Pretty embarrassing.

"If you don't mind, I'll drive," Katie said. "That way you can take notes." She handed me a yellow notebook. "Write down the address and the order. I've been doing this for so long that I've got it memorized."

She pulled the long skinny gearshift to reverse. I kind of grimaced; Mom's minivan was an automatic. I'd never *technically* learned to drive a stick after that slightly disastrous experience in driver's ed. Smoke. Melted gears. I made Kyle Cartwright swear never to tell anyone. And no one ever saw car #647 again. I'd obviously have to practice. By tomorrow.

"How is this going to work if you won't even pay attention?" Katie asked.

"I'm listening. I swear."

"Well, write it down. The Fitzgerald takes sixteen pies: four apple, four lemon meringue, four chocolate cream, and four berry pies." Katie pulled into the service entrance. "You can park here, but you have to be fast."

I helped Katie pull her delivery cart out of the van, loaded the pies, and wheeled them through the casino. Some drunk guy who'd obviously been playing video poker all night staggered past us and said, "Won't you give me some pie, honey?" He laughed—lots of missing teeth.

"Ignore the riffraff," Katie said.

Katie introduced me to the food-service manager, an older Chinese man who nodded a lot and showed me how to write a receipt, and then we moved on. Next stop: the Sands. We delivered a dozen pies to the buffet place and followed that up by dropping off six small plain white wedding cakes to the casino wedding chapel.

"Any changes to tomorrow's flower order?" Katie asked.

"Naw. Some gal asked for three dozen roses in three different shades of pink, and I told her she'd have to sober up and drive back to California and find a wedding planner for that one." The lady laughed. "She ordered your Forever Bouquet for nineteen ninety-five instead."

Two hours later, we'd restocked the van three times and I'd filled up several pages in the notebook. I glanced at my watch. Only an hour until lunch break. I was going to hate Mondays, and Wednesdays, and Fridays. My head ached with the smell of stale cigarette smoke, crazy casino carpets, and the names of more wedding chapels than I even knew existed in Reno: Beautiful Beginnings, Agape Love, Antique Angel, Candlelight, Celebration, Chapel of Bells, Heart of Reno, Silver Bells, Starlight, Strawberry Fields, White Lace and Promises, Drunk Night O' Passion. Okay, I made up that last one.

"Now we check the flower orders for today." Katie held the shop door open for me. I breathed in the sweet scent of roses and frosting; Katie found another notebook over by the cash register.

"Two baby bouquets at St. Mary's, and a birthday bouquet in the Northwest. Not bad." Katie looked me in the eye. "You think you can handle these on your own?"

I nodded as she told me how to go to the front desk in the hospital lobby.

I waited until Katie had gone into the kitchen and started making noise with her mixer—didn't want her to hear me grinding the gears—before grabbing the keys and running down the front steps.

"Let's just get this over with." I hopped onto the front seat. Nice and springy. Sliding the gear into neutral, I peeked at the secret notes I'd taken while watching Katie drive. I turned the key, pressed my foot onto the clutch pedal, latched my seat belt, and moved the gearshift into first. Or what looked like first. So far, so good. I eased my foot off the clutch as I pressed on the gas. *Lurch!* The van died. I did it all again, a little bit slower. The van eased forward. I drove away from the shop going about ten miles an hour. I didn't want to risk having Katie watch me.

I tried shifting to second as I drove down Vine Street, but the van died again. Oh, God. I couldn't ruin another car by shifting wrong. I glanced at my watch: 11:45 A.M. Megan had mentioned something about meeting for lunch since she worked so close. Maybe she could teach me to drive a stick?

Then I could make the deliveries. After all, the ladies with babies probably wouldn't be going anywhere, and the birthday person would have to work until at least five. There must be a law or something about having to give your employee a lunch break, right? I pulled the van over to the side of the road, got out, and ran to the path along the river. I huffed and puffed all the way to the U.S. Attorneys' office, right across the street from good old Reno High.

Megan pushed through the front doors right as I arrived all sweaty, wiping mascara smudges from under my eyes. Not a great idea to go running in eighty-five-degree weather at noon.

"Meg!" I breathed.

"What's wrong?" She rushed over to me. "Are you okay? You look all red."

"I need you to teach me—" I looked up to see Tyler Briggs standing next to Megan. Wearing those khaki pants and a blue shirt with a tie. What was he doing here? Did he get arrested for a DUI? He smiled and said, "Hey, Jory."

Megan shrugged. "Guess who's interning with me? Isn't that funny?"

I felt dizzy. "That's great."

"Why don't you sit down," Megan said.

"I'll grab you a water," Tyler said, running back up the steps.

Once he was gone, I turned to Megan. "Why didn't you tell me?"

"I just found out. He missed orientation. We're totally having fun, even though we're stuck in this refrigerator of an office with no windows, making copies." Megan smiled. "He's kind of a nice guy, actually."

Oh, no, you don't! He's mine. I've been pining for twelve months, eleven days, and about six hours.

"So he's no longer immature?" I smoothed my hair.

"Relax, Jory," she said. "I'm saving myself for college. No distractions."

Tyler arrived with a cold bottle of water. "It's one of our perks. Cold water for the kids working in the freezer."

Megan laughed like he was hilarious. Right, saving herself.

"Hey, let's all go to lunch. I'll drive." Tyler jiggled his keys.

"Actually," I said, "can I drive? Or rather, can you teach me to drive a stick?" My face felt hot again; at least I was already red. I put the bottle of water against my cheek. "I'm kind of having trouble."

Tyler drove us over to Vine Street.

"Thanks, Tyler." I stood by the now extra-embarrassing flower-covered van. "There are only two seats. The rest of it is all set up for the cakes and pies and stuff."

"If Tyler is cool with it"—Megan smiled at me—"I'll drive over and get us subs for lunch while he teaches you."

"I trust you, Chill Pill." Tyler tossed his keys to Megan. "Get me an Italian with everything, a bag of Doritos, and a surprisingly chilly Coke." He and Megan laughed again. I grimaced at the likelihood of a whole summer of private jokes between them.

"You know what I like," I said. "No onions." I felt relieved not to have to eat another PB&J. Day 2 of the Peanut Butter Diet. Peanut butter on toast for breakfast, PB&Js for lunch, Chinese chicken salad with peanut butter dressing for dinner. Peanut butter mixed with vanilla yogurt for dessert.

Megan gave me the Look. Just like Mom. But I couldn't really feel too irritated since she had figured out a way for me to get some Tyler time. Alone. (Yet, unfortunately, involving driving.)

"Okay, let's drive this dream machine, baby." Tyler rapped his knuckles against the blue lilies painted on the passenger door.

I sat in the driver's seat, and Tyler told me how to let the clutch out slowly while I pushed on the gas. He taught me how to listen to the engine so I'd know when to shift. I could barely focus as he went through all the gears, his hand on mine. The van still died the first time I tried to drive away from the curb.

"No problem. Just try again." *He's so sweet!*

He pressed his hand down on my knee as I pushed down on the gas.

"Now let out the clutch real slow," he said.

I did it! The van jerked down the street.

"Now put the clutch in and out fast while you shift."

Why did everything sound so dirty all of a sudden? I fought back a major case of giggles.

"You're doing it," Tyler said. "Where's our first delivery?"

"The hospital," I said. "You really want to come along?"

"I don't want you to get fired on your first day of work." Tyler glanced at his watch. "I've got time."

Tyler watched the van while I pulled up right in front and ran the two bouquets to the front desk. We even had time to deliver the flowers to the birthday person at an accountant's office nearby. Good thing I hadn't waited until five; I liked making someone so happy. The lady thanked me a million times, as if *I'd* sent her the flowers.

"You're a fast learner," Tyler said on the way back to the U.S. Attorneys' office.

"No, I'm not."

"It took me a few days to get the hang of driving my Jeep.

My dad even threatened to take it back to the dealership before I did permanent damage."

I thought of the damage I'd done to my sweet little JORRIDE. Only a couple of thousand dollars, but I'd permanently scarred my parents. And their insurance guy.

"No, really. You're a good teacher," I said. Maybe if my mom hadn't shrieked in mortal terror so much while teaching me to drive . . .

"Thanks, Jory. That means a lot."

We walked over to the river and ate our sandwiches on the grass. I raised my eyebrows at Megan after Tyler gave his Doritos to a homeless guy sitting under a tree.

I know. I know, she mouthed. *Nice guy.*

"So do you guys get to work on any big cases or do you make copies and file and stuff?"

Megan licked orange Cheetos dust off her fingers and started to say something about hoping to write summaries for the law clerks.

"Actually, I've got a big case I'm working on this summer," Tyler interrupted.

Megan's face changed like she'd just found out that someone had scored better than she did on a test.

"It's a vandalism case I call *Whipped Cream on Upholstery versus Giggling Girls.*"

I choked on my Diet Coke.

"Any evidence?" Megan couldn't keep the laughter out of her voice.

"A single strand of long, curly blond hair."

Tyler looked right at me.

I could've died.

Chapter Six

JUST ANOTHER DAY AT WORK?

I pulled up in front of the Jewel Café in the middle of one of those older southwest Reno neighborhoods that had slowly become more dentists', accountants', lawyers', and insurance offices than homes. I had three specialty cakes to deliver: Black Forest, lemon poppy seed, and carrot. Katie had frosted tiny orange carrots all over the top of that cake so each slice would have one. I slid the van door open and picked up one cake in its pink box.

Violin music filled the air when I opened the door of the café, but it didn't sound like a recording. Large tables covered with small boxes of beads crowded the whole room; beads hung on strings along one wall, and more boxes of beads cluttered floor-to-ceiling shelves along another wall; and overgrown houseplants crowded every corner, giving the place a real earthy jungle smell. A striped orange cat came and wrapped itself around my ankles, meowing.

I looked around, but I didn't see anyone.

"Hello?" I called out. "Delivery!" I tried to sound official. Should I go out and lock the van so that my other cakes didn't get stolen? How long would it take them to melt in this heat?

The violin music stopped.

"Hello?" I called out again.

"Just a minute," a deep voice answered. A guy my age came through a swinging door hidden near some shelves. He was tall and thin—a mass of dark curly hair clouded around his pale face. He had huge brown eyes, full lips, and a big, wide nose. I suddenly felt really stupid standing there holding a cake box, even though it was my job.

"How did you know it was my birthday?" he said. "This is so sweet of you. Are you going to sing, too?"

"It's not a—This is fourteen-oh-five, right?" I looked down at his bare feet sticking out from under the frayed bottoms of his faded jeans. Curly little black hairs grew on top of his big toes. He wiggled his toes as if he knew I was staring at them. I looked up to see his deep brown eyes looking straight into me like he could read my mind.

"I'm just messing with you." His fingers brushed against mine as he took the cake box from me. "Come on, I'll show you where to go." I followed him back through the swinging door, which he held open for me. He wore a black T-shirt but it looked faded compared to his hair.

"Don't stare at my ass," he said just as I *was* totally staring at the way his butt fit perfectly into his jeans.

"I—I—"

"Only kidding." He laughed. We walked through a big empty room with long tables. Plants hung near the windows. A gray and white cat snoozed along the top of a faded old sofa. Paintings hung on the walls with little price tags next to them. I tried to look at anything and everything besides his butt.

"Oh, Mother dearest," he called as we entered a small 1950s-looking kitchen. "Your delicious pastries have arrived."

A woman with long gray and brown hair, wearing a peasant skirt, a fitted shirt, and several beaded necklaces, came into the room.

"You must be Katie's new girl." She squeezed my hand. "I'm Helen." She lifted the lid of the cake box and inhaled dramatically. "Isn't Katie fabulous? Her baking inspired me to do this whole little café experiment. I simply had to have an excuse to buy her cakes more than twice a year for birthdays. So voilà: the Jewel Café."

"Helen is living out all of her passions at once: confections, jewelry, and art." He put his arm around his mom. "Crazy little lady. How many cats do we have now?" He leaned down and kissed her on top of her head. In front of me! I couldn't imagine Finn doing that to Mom.

"Oh, Gideon. Stop it." She pushed him away. "Go help this girl—what's your name, dear?"

"Jory."

"Go help Jory with the other cakes."

"Yes, ma'am." He did a deep servant bow that made his mom laugh. I waited for Gideon to lead the way, but he motioned for me to go first.

"For the record, we have four cats, not forty," Helen called after us.

"It's my turn to check out your ass," he whispered. "Fair is fair."

I surprised myself by turning around and walking backward, looking him straight in the eye. I guess I figured since he was in the Super Schnozz club, he could handle my nose. Or maybe I wanted to look into those big eyes of his. He was so bold—so different from other guys. Even older guys like Zane Zimmerman.

"Watch out for the—"

I bumped into the edge of a table in the front room, jabbing my hip with a sharp blast of pain. A box of beads fell and clattered onto the hardwood floor, rolling in every direction.

"Oh, no. I'm so sorry." I got down on my knees to scoop the little heart-shaped beads back into the bin. Gideon crawled around with me.

"No apologies necessary. You've made a boring morning quite interesting." He dropped a few beads into my hand. "And you have a great ass."

I sat on the floor and just looked at him. Amazed. Did he actually expect me to say something? Megan would've given him the you're-sexually-harassing-me evil eye. Hannah would have giggled, batted her eyelashes, and said, Thanks, you too. I just sat there. On my butt. Hiding it.

"That was what we guys call a compliment," he said.

My cheeks felt as warm as fresh-baked cherry pie. "I better go get those other cakes."

We each carried another cake back into the kitchen. His mom had left to go organize something out back, and Gideon leaned against the kitchen sink. "You go to Reno?"

"About to start senior year." I tilted my head up and down like one of the World Cup bobbleheads Finn had collected back in fourth grade.

"Thought so." He kept looking right at me. "You hang out with Megan Moore. Pretty girl. Smart as hell. A little—"

"Intimidating?"

Gideon did a cute little shrug thing.

I'd had this conversation before. He obviously had a huge crush on Megan. Probably wanted to use me to get closer to her. No guy ever asked Megan to do anything without checking with me or Hannah to make sure she wouldn't cause a ginormous scene, like she had the time Jonah Swenson asked her to homecoming in sophomore year (she *had* thought it was a prank).

"So, how do you know Megan?"

"I 'transferred' to Reno High a few weeks ago." He made air quotes around the word *transferred*. "After a little 'incident.'" Air quotes. "With the school paper at McQueen."

"You're the guy who hijacked the senior quotes and made fun of everyone?"

"I like to think I made everything accurate."

"They kicked you out for that?"

"I like to think that my talents could be better used elsewhere."

I smiled at him for a few seconds before remembering my delivery van and the flowers wilting in the heat. "I gotta go. More deliveries and stuff."

"I will await next Wednesday with bated breath, my lady." He bowed and kissed my hand. "Nice meeting you, Jory."

I looked down at his feet and mumbled, "Yeah."

His lips felt soft on my hand. But what a weirdo!

"Interesting foot fetish thing you've got going on," he said.

Chapter Seven

WOOSTER GUYS AND GREASY FRIES

I set the tray of miniature tiered wedding cakes in front of the taste-testing couple. Groom Guy chose the chocolate buttercream, tenderly feeding it to Beloved Bride as she made noises like on late-night premium cable.

I stammered something about letting them sample the other flavors in private and escaped to the kitchen to call Megan again. I'd left messages all afternoon about the Rodeo Carnival—we'd gone together every year since ninth grade, when Hannah had gotten her back brace off and could ride roller coasters again.

"Please pick up."

Megan answered just as the couple started kissing each other's frosted fingertips.

"Uh. Yeah. Rodeo C-carnival," I stammered, not really

hearing Megan until she said Tyler's name, something about a movie and just the two of them.

"But—tradition." Engaged Couple morphed into Tyler and Megan look-alikes, groping the cakes, each other. I saw it: first a movie, then senior prom, followed by cake testing and a summer wedding. Sad, virginal me would deliver and set up the cake.

"Tyler and I have to see it tonight. It's a legal thriller and the main character totally looks like Barnes!" *Barnes?* I snapped out of my miserable fantasy of Megan and Tyler's wedding. Groom Guy faked a cake smash in the face but then popped the sample into his own mouth, making Beloved Bride giggle until her face turned pink like the frosting roses. Megan rambled on about Tyler and lawyers or something.

"Fine. Go to the movie." I snapped my phone shut, forced a sugary smile, and went out to check on the happiest couple on earth (until Tyler and Megan usurped the title).

Three hours later, overcompensating, cheerful Hannah and mopey me walked around the Rodeo Carnival. Hard rock blasted through the air, along with the rattle of the rickety carnival roller coaster and its shrieking riders. I did not want to be at the stupid Rodeo Carnival. I wanted to be at home, suffering. Megan *knows* how much I like Tyler! How could she let him take her to the movies? On a real date! Wasn't that like one of the unbreakable rules of friendship?

Traitor!

"You're thinking about it," Hannah said. "I can tell by the way you've scrunched up your nose."

The last thing I need: a major nose-highlighting quirk whenever I freak out. I should just go live in a convent with a bunch of nuns. I already have the chastity thing down.

"I don't know why you aren't mad. You're the one who started the tradition, so she's completely letting you down too," I said.

Hannah took a deep breath, straightening her spine. "Sure I'm a little disappointed—" A frown flickered across her face. "Okay, more than a little, but Jory, we've got to try to live in the moment. And tonight we're here to find us some real live cowboys!" Hannah's gaze followed an older guy built solid as a stallion. "Or cowmen."

"This is not a moment I want to live in." I watched a tattoo-covered carny ogle Hannah's yoga-enhanced curves, eyes roaming up her frilly cowgirl blouse and down her tight Wrangler's. I'd dressed like Hannah's city cousin: flouncy mini, layered tees, and vintage cupcake-pattern Vans. I had bought them with my first paycheck and saved the rest for el nose job. With a couple of hours of overtime, and minus taxes and Vans, I'd saved $314.65. In only one week!

Then again, what was the point if Tyler was falling for Megan? Right at this moment, Megan was probably whispering big words from her SAT prep course to her date, getting him all hot and horny: *perspicacious, volition, antediluvian, sagacious, turncoat, tramp.*

"I think you need some cotton candy." Hannah adjusted her cowboy hat and headed toward the concession stand. We stood in line behind a group of boys having a burping contest. Tyler would never act so crude! *Stop. Don't think about him.*

But why couldn't he like *me?*

Of course he likes Megan. Not only does she share his lawyerly ambition, she'd suddenly grown into the girl every college puts on the cover of its brochure: gleaming smile, shoulder-length dark hair, big blue eyes, no-nonsense style, and the cutest little perky nose. She and Tyler shared the same level of attractiveness. They matched, the way movie-star couples looked good together. If Tyler took me out, people would probably say that I must be really sweet, or, worse, that I must *do* something really sweet.

Hannah handed me a towering fluff ball of pink cotton candy. I pinched off an airy chunk and let it melt in my mouth to take away the salty taste of the tears I'd choked back.

"You're so cute!" Hannah swiped at a strand of cotton candy stuck on my cheek.

Cute! That's all anyone says about my looks. I'm cute the way those creepy Cabbage Patch dolls are cute, the way those little hairy trolls are cute. The way scruffy old dogs are cute, the way a newborn baby—all smooshed-looking and red—is cute. Even a kid who has just smeared grape jelly all over his face gets called cute. I don't want to be cute. I want to be beautiful. Or *gorgeous, ravishing, exquisite, captivating, alluring, resplendent, radiant,* or *pulchritudinous.*

Oh, God, Jory. How sad is it that you've looked up synonyms for beautiful *in a thesaurus? And* that's *what you're thinking about at the Rodeo Carnival.* I scanned the crowd for gorgeous cowboys but saw only whiny kids yanking on their parents' arms, begging for stuff.

"Oh, I love that ride!" Hannah pointed to a swaying pirate ship. "And look." She nodded to a group of guys wearing shorts and matching red Wooster High football shirts.

"They're not exactly cowboys, Han."

"They're the Wooster Colts." Hannah walked ahead of me. "Cowboys ride horses. Close enough."

"I don't know." The smell of hamburgers, gasoline fumes, cigarette smoke, and greasy fries mixed with all the loud music, bells, whistles, and screaming made my head ache. I wanted to go home, hide under my covers, and pretend I had a better life.

"Come on." Hannah grinned her dentist-for-a-daddy smile. "You need to meet someone new."

"Whatever." Megan was probably trying to revise and improve upon the movie's kissing scene with her date. What if they showed up at the carnival? How humiliating. I scanned the crowd but didn't see anyone even remotely as good-looking as Tyler. Or Megan, either.

We stood in line for the pirate ship behind the Wooster guys, who kept punching one another on the arms and making jokes about barfing. When they went to board the last row, Hannah pulled me over behind them.

"Mind if we join y'all?" She tilted her cowboy hat, acting like we were in southern Texas, not the Biggest Little City in northern Nevada.

"You can sit by me, little gal," a gorgeous Hispanic guy said.

Hannah winked at me as I squeezed between two big guys in the middle. The ride clanked and clunked ominously. Would Tyler even feel sad if I plummeted to my death? Or would he bring Megan to my funeral? Everyone would talk about how good they looked together.

"You know, she died a virgin," people would whisper. "It was the nose." Someone helpful would add, "She's in a better place." They'd all agree.

I tightened my grip on the safety bar.

"You from around here?" a guy in a baseball cap asked.

"Yup."

The other guy nodded toward Hannah. "So what's with the cowgirl getup?"

I shrugged.

"José's going to be disappointed," Baseball Cap said. "There goes his rodeo/ranch/cowgirl/horse fantasy." The other guy laughed and reached over my head to hit his friend on the arm. Major wafting pit odor.

Baseball Cap put his huge freckled hands on the bar next to mine. "Inside joke. Sorry."

The ship started swinging back and forth slowly, higher and higher. At first I loved the fluttery feeling in my stomach because it reminded me of how I felt when I saw you know who. Before. Or when that Gideon guy kissed my hand. (So bizarre!)

"Raise your arms!" Baseball Cap lifted his arms high. The dropping force of the ship pressed my face into his stinky, wet armpits. Again the ship went higher. Again the arms rose. Hannah giggled, but I tried to focus on the stars in the sky.

I imagined smelling cold, empty air, drifting weightless into outer space. Just when I didn't think I could take it anymore, the ride slowed down.

"You okay?" Baseball Cap asked. "You look a little peaked."

"Peaked?" The other guy laughed.

"It's something my mom says."

"Oh, little Tommy looks peaked."

"Don't call me that." Tommy smacked the guy on the arm. He looked back at me. "Let me buy you a soda or something. Maybe it'll settle your stomach."

He may have been deodorant challenged, but he seemed like a nice-enough guy, and an icy soda sounded good.

"Nurse Tommy knows how to settle a wee little tummy," the other guy said in a baby voice.

Tommy cuffed the guy in the head. "I'm trying to impress the lady," he said. "Forgive my idiot friend." He put his hand out to me. "Nice to meet you, I'm Tom. And the idiot is Luis."

"Jory."

He shook my hand with a strong, firm, but not bone-crushing grip. He had gazillions of brownish freckles on his pale arms, but he also had impressive muscles on those arms, and green eyes in the middle of the gazillions of freckles on his face, as well as an ordinary, proportional nose.

"Let me guess." He bit his lower lip and looked me up and down, nodding. "Reno High."

"Yeah." I looked at his red and white sneakers with dirty laces.

Luis jumped at the bait. "So, I guess you're spending the summer by the pool, tanning. Or maybe up at your quote-unquote 'cabin' at the Lake."

"No, I'm working."

"Some cushy job Daddy got you at his company?" Luis asked.

"I drive a delivery van." I looked at Tom for his reaction.

"Very unexpected." He nodded. "Let's go get that soda."

Hannah sat on José's lap sharing a cup of Idaho Spud fries while I sat between Tom and Luis sipping a cherry Coke. Tom had thought my blood sugar might be a little low after I'd explained how I'd skipped out on day 9 of the Peanut Butter Diet.

"Tilt-A-Whirl, anyone?" Hannah jumped up.

"I call the middle," Luis said.

"I'm game." José took Hannah's hand.

"I don't know." Just sitting still made me feel like I might vomit.

"We'll sit this one out," Tom said.

Did he like me or was he also feeling kind of sick? We sat

there not really saying anything while I finished my soda. A good-looking cowboy walked by wearing brand-new jeans, an enormous silver belt buckle, shiny boots, and a crisp, new-looking Stetson. A group of tween girls swung around to follow him. Exactly like the gaggle of sophomores always following Finn. And Tyler.

"Those guys look so sharp," Tom said. "You ever been to the rodeo?"

"Just the carnival." I forced myself to look at Tom's face, but he looked straight ahead.

"You should go sometime. They're impressive athletes. And it won't upset your stomach." He smiled at me. "Come on. Let's walk around."

We wandered over to the midway where a bunch of kids gathered around a big guy throwing darts at balloons attached to posters. *Pop. Pop. Pop.* His sleazy-looking girlfriend squealed, "Win the one with the Ferrari, baby." I imagined Megan hanging all over Tyler like that.

Tom fanned his arm out like a game-show hostess. "Okay, pick your prize."

"You're kidding, right?" He actually wanted to try to win something for *me?*

"I haven't invested ten years of allowance money in midway games for nothing."

I glanced around at the stuffed cartoon characters, cheap-looking teddy bears, beer glasses, and raunchy posters. "That one!" I pointed at the Throw the Baseball in the Lion's Mouth game. Big stuffed snakes hung all around the booth, like a made in China jungle.

"Very unexpected," Tom said again. "The girl with cupcakes on her shoes likes snakes." He walked over and paid ten bucks for ten balls. "I have to warn you. Baseball's never been my game." He straightened his shirt, nodded at me, and threw the first ball. The ball smacked the lion's tail.

The carny guy laughed. "Come on, tough guy, you gotta do better than that to impress your lady." He laughed until he coughed. *Hack. Hack. Hack. Smack. Smack. Smack.* Tom missed the next three balls.

"Fifth one will be lucky." *Smack.* Miss.

Tom blushed, making his freckles stand out even more. He almost matched his red shirt. I noticed a little girl staring. Where was Hannah? Would someone I knew walk by and think we were actually together? What if Tyler found out? I stepped back a couple of feet.

"It's okay," I said. "Maybe we should go meet those guys." I didn't like the way he looked kind of angry. A vein in his neck pulsed.

Tom didn't even look at me. He bit his lower lip, closed his eyes, pulled his arm back, and released the ball. *Whoosh*. Right through the lion's mouth. Small snake. *Whoosh*. Medium snake. *Whoosh*. Giant snake.

"We have a winner!" the carny yelled.

Tom grinned at me. "What color do you want?"

I picked out a black snake with red diamonds on its back. Tom gave his last two balls to a little kid standing in line.

"It's a little tilted to the left," he told the kid. "Good luck, buddy. You can do it."

Tom put the snake around my neck. "Goes great with the shoes." When he smiled at me, I saw that his face had turned back to a regular color. I kind of liked the attention. Maybe Tyler *would* find out and get jealous.

As we wandered back toward the rides, Tom brushed his fingers against mine like he was about to hold hands, but then he must have changed his mind. Did he not want to give me the wrong idea? I could kind of imagine myself with a guy like Tom: big, burly, midway stud. But maybe I was so desperate for a boyfriend that I'd take any warm body in the fifteen-to-twenty-five age range. Anyway, he didn't want to hold my hand, probably didn't find me attractive and/or interesting.

As we rounded the corner, I saw Hannah hunched over a garbage can. José and Luis stood back, pretending like they didn't know her.

"Hannah, are you okay?" I ran over and held her hair back, trying not to gag on the smell as my queasy stomach returned with a vengeance. "Hey, remember what happened to Meg—" I paused as Hannah heaved again. "Last summer." All year we'd had a running joke about spinning with fries. I felt mad at Megan all over again—and not just because of Tyler. So what if she was "so done" with high school? She wasn't done with *us*.

"Get me out of here," Hannah pleaded.

"Okay, let's go." I stood still for a moment, looking at Tom, tilting my head up and down in rhythm with the rickety Ferris wheel cars swinging above us. Would he ask for my phone number or e-mail or something? Anything? He *had* won a carnival prize for me. Probably just showing off.

Hannah moaned.

I waited a few more seconds with her swaying next to me. "Guess we gotta go."

"See you around," Tom said, not quite looking at me. Then he turned and joined his friends in their Zipper-versus-the-Scrambler debate.

After making sure Hannah was steady on her feet, I glanced back. But Tom had already disappeared into the crowd. Hannah vomited twice on the way to the car. I had to drive as she hung her head out the window. The fresh air smelled good as we sped up McCarren toward Hannah's house at the top of Skyline, and she never once complained about my driving.

I noticed that Hannah had a phone number scrawled on her hand. She hurls in front of a guy and gets his number. I have a daintily unsettled stomach, sip a soda, wear a stuffed snake around my neck (in public!), and get nothing. How pathetic is that? Current chances of dying a virgin: 77 percent.

"José is totally sweet. Big brown eyes," Hannah murmured as I slammed on the brakes at a stoplight. "And Tom seems to like you." She leaned back and closed her eyes. "Maybe you should move beyond the Tyler thing."

"I don't know. He might be the smash-the-cake-in-your-face type, and I think I like the delicate-feeding type."

"What?"

I started to explain, but Hannah moaned. "Don't talk about food."

Chapter Eight

CHOCOLATINIS AND JUDITH

Finn sat in the family room with a few of his soccer buddies arguing about which action-slasher boy movie to watch first. They planned to rank each movie by number of unnecessary deaths, decapitations, and dismemberments. Real mature!

"They love my peanut butter shakes," Mom said.

"Because they're mixing M&M's into them."

Finn tossed an M&M for me to catch in my mouth. I missed. His friends tossed a few more to me. I missed, missed, and missed again. One slid down my shirt. Apparently, I will not be making an appearance in the M&M-mouth-catching event at the Olympics.

"Well, at least they're getting some good nutrition," Mom said over the roar of the blender. "I've lost seven pounds in two weeks."

"You look beautiful as always."

Mom smoothed her blouse around her hips. "You're saying that to make me feel good. I've got a long way to go before the Dickensons' barbecue on the Fourth."

"Whatever." I grabbed my bag off the counter. "I'll be home at midnight-ish?" I looked at Mom. "I'm just going to the movies."

"That's fine. I support your desire to learn more about foreign cinema."

"You sound like Megan."

Mom smiled. "Well, that's certainly a compliment."

I hadn't clued Mom in to the whole traitorous-Megan incident. Megan had called yesterday to remind me that I'd promised to join the community cinema club with her, since I loved movies and was trying to find my passion and everything. All casual, she had added that Tyler wanted to take us out for dessert first.

She didn't even mention the big date. And I was too wimpy to ask—didn't want to give her the satisfaction, even unknowingly, of crushing my entire fantasy life. Anyway, foreign cinema sounded better than sitting around with a bunch of M&M-tossing, boob-ogling sophomores keeping track of spurting blood and oozing guts. I ran out the door when I heard the car honk.

Tyler's Jeep purred in our driveway. He was alone. *Breathe.*

In. Out. Walk to the car without tripping. Tyler reached across and popped the door open for me; a Richmond Fontaine song played low and growly.

"I told Meg I'd pick you up since you're on the way and everything."

"Great." I climbed into the front seat, wishing I'd worn something more alluring. I had tried to look intellectual with my San Francisco Museum of Modern Art T-shirt, jeans, black flats, and braided hair tucked under a little pink beret; now I wished I'd shown off my legs or at least my hair. I hadn't bothered with much enhancing makeup, since we'd be in the dark or near dark the whole time. But here I was, sitting next to Tyler as the last bit of daylight blazed right onto my face. Squinting could not be good for my nose, but there was no way I'd wear sunglasses and risk looking like one of those big-nose-with-glasses things people wear on Halloween.

"Megan said you could show me how to get to her place."

"Sure." He didn't know how to get to Megan's? Good sign. Giving directions gave me something to talk about, even if "turn left here" wasn't exactly scintillating conversation. Megan lived in a cute, but tiny, old brick house. Her parents were divorced, and her brother lived with their dad. Lucky! I imagined life without Finn around to constantly remind me of my lack of social status. Maybe I could convince Mom that Finn should study abroad in some soccer-obsessed country? Then I could stay home alone, eating M&M shakes and watching brainless comedies.

I climbed into the back seat when Tyler honked for Megan.

"You don't have to do that," Tyler said.

"Oh, I thought—"

Tyler smiled his perfect magazine-model grin. "It was just a movie."

"Oh, yeah. I mean—" Oh, God. Was my face the color of my stupid beret?

Megan ran out to the car and gave me a weird look as she climbed into the front seat. "I know you've moved to the fancy neighborhood and all, but I didn't think you required a chauffeur."

Tyler raised his eyebrows at me in the rearview mirror. "She almost refused to get in because I didn't pick her up in a limo."

"I did not!" I was flung back against the seat as Tyler zipped out of Megan's driveway.

"Let's go to that little dessert place on California," Megan said. "They have the best peanut butter chocolate cake."

"Peanut butter cake?" Between twelve days (probably a new record) of Mom's Peanut Butter Diet and a week of cake deliveries, I'd come up with my own Anti–Baked Goods Diet. Just the smell of fresh-baked cake and frosting made me want to eat celery and carrots.

"They also have coffee, fondue, and a bunch of other stuff."

"Lead the way, Counselor Charming," Tyler said.

Another inside joke. I held on to my beret as the hot summer air blew wispy hairs loose from my braid. For twelve months, however many hours, minutes, blah, blah, blah, I'd been trying to figure out Tyler's mixed signals. Now he flirted with me almost every time he saw me but took Megan to the movies. On a Friday night. That was like a date, right? Otherwise why wouldn't they have asked Hannah and me to come along? Also, he had all these little pet names for Megan, but they *did* work together *and* they had had the same class schedule: AP and all that honors crap. My klutzy self got to have PE with him. He's a studly skier and all-around athlete. I managed to humiliate myself 3.2 times per week during gym.

To pay me back for taking care of her during the vomiting incident, Hannah had tried to find out the truth about the big date, but Megan had never returned her calls. She ignored text-message questions by responding with perky so-not-true-to-herself quips, until even Hannah grumbled something about "nonpersonal technological friendships." I wasn't quite sure what she meant, but I happily commiserated about Megan's friendship flaws.

Tyler parked along the curb on the little side road next to the dessert place—impressive parallel-parking skills. Maybe I could ask him for another driving lesson?

In the café, people wearing business-type clothes sat around little black tables. A couple of guys in suits came over to talk to Tyler and Megan. Law clerks.

I glanced around the room at the groups of ladies sharing a single piece of cake and sipping coffees. Several people drank cocktails; we had to be the youngest people in there. I sat up straight, attempting to look older, while glancing at Tyler's and Megan's clothes. Tyler wore a silky yellow shirt and jeans. Very mature. Megan looked every bit as good in her sparkly blouse and short black skirt. I looked like a child compared to them, plus I could tell my hair had blown around all crazy in the Jeep. I got up to run to the bathroom while Megan told the lawyers about the community cinema club's best-of-Britain review.

I tried not to watch myself in the bathroom mirror as I rebraided my hair. Fluorescent lighting = not good. My nose looked giant and red and blotchy; my whole face was splotchy. Why hadn't I noticed all those blackheads on my forehead? Why hadn't I worn more makeup? Why had I worn this stupid shirt? I looked like a backpacking-through-Europe cliché. I turned around to check out the rear view and noticed a smashed M&M on my butt. Finn's idiot friends!

By the time I got back to the table, our waitress had set chocolate martinis in front of Megan and Tyler. She never drank! And had plenty to say about people who *did*.

"What would you like, sweetie?" The waitress couldn't have been more than five or six years older than me.

"I'll have the same." I tried to sound confident.

"How old are you?" She narrowed her eyes. "Do you have valid ID?"

"On second thought, I'll have an ice water." I shrugged my shoulders. "Dieting."

"Girls," Tyler said. "My, uh, *little sister* is always on a diet, even though she's cute as a bug." He reached over and pinched my cheek. "Mom's going to send you back to the clinic if you keep this up."

I stomped my foot under the table, accidentally crushing Tyler's shoe, but his smile didn't waver. "We'll also have an order of chocolate fondue and a slice of your famous peanut butter chocolate cake." He flipped my foot off his and pressed his foot on top of mine, not too hard, but I'm pretty sure he wasn't flirting.

I turned the little menu cube over in my hands, not reading the words. I didn't look up when Tyler lifted his foot off.

He glared at me. "What was that about, Stompy?"

Not answering, I looked down at my beautifully blurred reflection in the shiny black table.

"Toast." He and Megan clinked their glasses.

"Sorry, Jory." Megan leaned over to me. "But you don't look old enough, especially the way you're dressed. Plus, the law clerks vouched for us."

"What happened to making good choices?"

"Relax, Jory." Megan tipped her glass to her lips. "Nothing wrong with one little après-work drink."

"Isn't it illegal?" Ignored. Just like Hannah's phone calls and text messages.

"We're going to owe them some bigtime copy jobs." Tyler leaned back and sipped his chocolatini. "It *is* a nice way to end the workday."

The waitress clunked my ice water on the table while smiling at Tyler. "So you're a lawyer?" she asked.

"Guilty." Tyler flashed his alluring smile. Everyone laughed, except me.

"That must be great, to have a lawyer in the family," she said to me.

"Oh, yeah. Great."

Did she *honestly* think I'm his little sister? I had to look a teensy bit like a girlfriend. After all, people don't even think I'm my own brother's real sister, and Tyler's even better looking than Finn—to me at least. I pushed my little square cocktail napkin around the table in a circle while Tyler and Megan gossiped about the different lawyers in their office. *No, he left his wife for a law clerk two summers ago. Major scandal. He was going to run for office, but dropped out of the race. Don't dip your pen in the office ink. Ha. Ha. Ha. So-and-So has a thing for murderers. She supposedly flirts with them before putting them on the witness stand. Apparently she wins all of her cases.*

When the waitress came with the fondue and cake, I scraped every bit of frosting off the top just to spite Megan, but she was too busy eating a chocolate-dipped strawberry off Tyler's fork to notice. That sure answered some of my questions. After all, Tyler did meet 99 percent of Megan's superior standards for boyfriend material.

I walked ahead of them as we crossed the bridge over the river to the theater; they had ordered another round and were both slightly tipsy. Anything wrong with *two* drinks, Megan? I had drunk so much water that I'd probably have to pee a thousand times during the movie. I tried to shake my hair around my shoulders, forgetting that I'd tied it up in a stupid intellectual-looking French braid; my beret fell into the gutter behind me.

"My little sister would forget her head if it weren't attached." Tyler picked up my beret and plunked it back on my head, hard. "It's a good thing you don't live in France."

What the hell did that mean? Did I look so terrible in a beret that they'd stop me at the border? Would shops have my picture up like a Wanted poster, saying, "Do Not Sell a Beret to This Woman!" Or was I simply too klutzy to live in *très* elegant France?

The theater was surprisingly crowded, considering they were showing some old British movie that was made before I was born. Another bonus: almost every member of the community cinema club was over the age of thirty. I sat between Megan and some possibly pervy forty-year-old geezer chowing down on popcorn.

Right before the movie started, a woman stood up and announced the premiere of some wonderful French movie next Saturday. "For those of you who haven't already bought tickets, reserve them this week. This one will be very popular."

They probably wouldn't let me in because I'm beret challenged.

During the opening credits, I had to get up to pee, but

Tyler didn't move his legs and I nearly fell into his lap. "Watch the Italian loafers, Stompy."

Jerk!

The movie was about a timid old maid who barely survives by giving piano lessons and spends a scary amount of time talking to a photograph of some old biddy. When she finally thinks she's found love, it turns out the guy is totally using her, so she starts drinking as if booze is her only friend. In one scene she totally freaks out when she spills some whiskey. That's what I had to look forward to: a life like *The Lonely Passion of Judith Hearne*—*depression, sadness, gloom, dejection, discouragement, downheartedness, melancholia, despondency, desolation.* So I've looked up *depression* in the thesaurus. Hasn't everyone? Anyway, I didn't feel like a freak for thinking about all those words after that god-awful movie. The couple in front of us got into a big argument on the way out of the theater; I heard only one disturbingly cheerful person say, "Wasn't Maggie Smith fabulous?"

I didn't say a word on the way home.

Tyler dropped me off first.

I didn't even care.

Chapter Nine

POPCORN AND POSSIBILITIES

The phone rang again. Mom glanced at the caller ID and shook her head. "She's called four times in the last half-hour." She handed me the phone. "What's going on between you two?"

"Nothing." I flopped down on the sofa and crushed one of Mom's fancy pillows to my chest, then picked at an M&M matted in the fringe.

"Does this involve a boy?" Mom got on her I-really-care-about-you-so-you-can-humiliate-yourself-with-juicy-details face and sat next to me on the sofa.

"No!"

"You can talk to me, honey. It wasn't so long since I was there myself." She ran her hand through her newly dyed blond hair, but it got stuck because of all the junk she smeared on her head every morning. Was she aware of that gesture? Like, subconsciously, she knows she's not young anymore, even though she's still trying, as day 17 of the Peanut Butter Diet attests. I'm never eating peanut butter pancakes, peanut soup, nutty noodles, or Chinese chicken salad again. Don't even mention the skinny Elvis: PB and banana on whole wheat.

"I just don't want to go to the stupid cinema club with stupid Megan and stupid Tyler because all they talk about is work this and work that. Plus Tyler thinks—"

"Tyler, as in Tyler Briggs?" Mom's eyes got wide. "Oh, honey. He's such a sweetheart. Did he tell you how his mother recently remodeled their kitchen?"

"Uh. No."

Her voice got low. "I heard a rumor at work that it cost something in the mid–six figures. She did it all because she was hosting the book club in November and couldn't do a tea in her *Sunset* magazine double-page-spread backyard. Apparently, she still hasn't forgiven Cindy Yee." Mom leaned back, clutching a pillow to her chest. "I've been trying to swing an invitation to that book club for over a year. I read all the books just in case I get invited and people talk about previous selections."

"That's kind of sad, Mom. Why don't you start your own book club?"

"Never mind." She shook her head. "We're talking about you. So, you and Tyler—"

"There is no me and Tyler. He thinks of me more like a sister."

I put my face into the pillow and groaned. For five days, eight hours, and twenty-three minutes, give or take, I've heard his voice in my head: "little sister," "Stompy," "Italian loafers." I tried to get Hannah to analyze his statement about my not living in France, but she said it probably meant nothing and I should focus on the present, which just then involved selecting the juiciest melon for her fruit salad. Sometimes I think Hannah's actually a forty-year-old narc on an undercover gig. She wouldn't come to the movies because of some church youth night that her latest crush, Alex from Church, said he "might" or "probably" would attend. She wouldn't analyze that, either. So irritating. I totally envied her live-for-today attitude, though. Wouldn't work for me: today involved Megan, Tyler, and another boring movie.

"But you'd like there to be a you and Tyler." Mom tucked her legs under her skinny bottom. "Is that it?" Too much glee hummed in her voice. She'd want me to date the biggest loser at Reno High if it meant her getting into that book club.

"I'm really tired of the whole thing. I'd love to stay home and watch some sappy romantic comedy, eat junk food, and get nine or ten hours of beauty sleep. God knows I need it."

"Oh, is *that* what this is all about?" Mom said. "Honey, your face has so much . . . character."

Character ranks well below *cute* in the noncompliment department. *Character* is code for "ugly," but in a fascinating watching-a-car-wreck-on-the-freeway sort of way. An old woman with wrinkles on her wrinkles has a face with character. Ugly guys with great personalities and loads of money have character in their faces.

My mom touched my nose, actually touched my nose, as if some kind of magic could spread from her beautiful face through her well-manicured fingernails to my nose. After my $360 paycheck on Friday, I was only $3,326, give or take, from buying myself some magic. Part of me wanted to tell Mom about the surprise nose job, but I didn't want to give her another opportunity to lecture me. Or give me a definite *no* answer. Again.

"Come on, let's go make you look great for an evening of foreign cinema."

"Mom. I don't think I even like foreign cinema. It's all so drab and depressing. People drink way too much. I don't think it sets a good example for an impressionable young woman like myself."

"Nonsense." She led me upstairs into her bathroom, with

its specially installed good lighting. "Tyler likes foreign cinema, so you can like it. How hard is that?"

That sounded so dishonest, or fake, or something. I kind of cringed because it reminded me about pretending to like the Raconteurs' music just because Tyler did. But that really wasn't the same, was it?

"Tyler might just like Megan."

"Megan! She's a fine girl, but nothing like you, honey." Mom ran a brush through my hair. "You look like Rapunzel."

"So lock me away in a tower. Really, I'm fine with that at this point." I could make friends with some big-beaked birds, take up a hobby like rock-wall etching, and die a virgin. Unless some blind woodsman found me first.

"Megan doesn't have your sense of humor."

"Yup. I've got a good personality. Hear that, boys? Jory has a good personality." I put my hand to my ear. "My God, I can hear them lining up already. Mom, you're a miracle worker."

Mom whacked my butt with her brush. "What I wouldn't give for your tight little fanny."

"Mom! Your butt's smaller than mine."

She shook her head and rolled her eyes. "What are you going to wear?"

"Well, since it's about a million degrees outside, shorts and a tank top and my flowered flip-flops."

"Why don't you go for a more intriguing, intellectual look? What about your beret?"

"Been there, done that." Did *all* of her ideas have to suck so much?

Forty-five minutes later, Mom had layered so much make-up on my face that I'd have to wait and leave the house under the cover of darkness or else I'd frighten small dogs. She even made me try on a pair of her capris with some high heels but relented after I told her I'd be able to make some good cash turning tricks on Fourth Street after the movie. Maybe I'd found my career path after all, I joked. Fifty bucks a trick, a hundred for the all-night special. Finn's comment about working as a hooker out at Mustang Ranch clinched it. Mom even redid my eye makeup.

"Goodbye, Dragon Lady Eyes," I said. "I'll see you again when I get my job at a house of ill-repute." I scrunched my lips up and made kissing noises at the mirror.

I heard Bugsy's peppy little honk in the driveway.

Mom kissed my forehead. "Have fun, darling."

"Remember, I get a percentage," Finn called.

"Shut up, Finn!" Mom and I yelled at the same time.

Tyler jumped out and flipped the front seat forward so I could climb into the back. Did that mean anything? His legs weren't much longer than mine; he'd be a flats-only boyfriend.

Just in case, I'd been buying flats exclusively for the last year.

"I tried calling you all afternoon," Megan said.

"Really? Maybe Finn—" I stopped before I told an actual lie.

"Didn't you get my e-mail?"

"I've been really busy, what with work and all."

"Ah, but you haven't had the Copy Job from Hades." Tyler put his hand on Megan's shoulder. What did *that* mean?

"Dante's frozen Hades, that is." Megan and Tyler laughed.

"No, but I have to carry pies past drunk gamblers at seven in the morning," I said. "This one drunk guy at the Gold Dust West always follows me around and tells me the same stupid joke every single time."

"Sounds like Funnyman Richards."

Megan looked at Tyler and smiled. "Nonfunny, you mean."

I gave up, leaned my head far back, and watched the streetlamps above me. Tyler and Megan didn't even notice my silence. *What about that guy who stole all that money from his boss? Daniel thinks he's totally guilty. So-and-So is going to Aruba, but her husband is staying home. Ooh, scandal! Looks like someone has commitment issues.*

Hey, I thought of piping in, I delivered an extra chocolate cream pie to the Sands on Thursday. Not even one person ordered flowers on Friday. Weird, huh? Katie booked a big last-minute wedding on July 2. The guy at the Jewel Café who said he wanted to see me again wasn't even there, but the cat rubbed my ankles like he was in love. I'm thinking a cat would make a great boyfriend. Good listener; likes to cuddle; enjoys beauty sleep; great hair. Plus, I've always been into stripes.

Nope, silence was best.

Megan dropped me off first so I could save seats. Tyler went to keep her "safe" in the parking garage. Mental note: see if she's still wearing all that lip-gloss when they get back. Violin music played as I looked up the steps. I hated looking so desperate, wretched, and beyond hope, walking into a movie theater alone on a Saturday night.

I waited down by the bridge for a minute but worried that Megan would get mad if we had to sit in the front row or all spread out among the geezer film geeks. I shook my hair and climbed up the steps. Gideon, the guy from the Jewel Café, stood near the door, playing his violin behind a sign that said: "Can young people really learn in a big yellow-tiled bathroom? Please donate to remodel the halls of Reno High School."

Several coins sparkled against the red velvet inside his violin case. Even a few dollar bills lay on top. I watched an older guy drop a dollar into the case. "They've had the same yellow tile on those walls for over forty years," he said. "Great idea, young man."

Gideon nodded in thanks, then noticed me and raised his eyebrows. I waved real quick and hurried into the theater, suddenly feeling hot all over. I stopped to buy a jumbo Diet Coke.

I sat by myself in the semidark theater for several minutes, holding the Diet Coke cup to my warm cheeks. I took a couple of deep breaths like Hannah always does, but they made me feel more lightheaded. Finally, Megan and Tyler walked down the aisle, arguing.

"That guy goes to school with us now?" Tyler asked.

"He transferred with like two weeks of school left." Megan set her soda in the drink holder. One soda. Two straws. It was too dark to check her lips. "Actually got *kicked out* of McQueen."

"No surprise there. I've heard rumors he has a juvie record." Tyler sat next to me. "What a freak."

"Didn't you date somebody from McQueen once?" I asked, eager to get Tyler off the topic of trashing Gideon. Plus, I wanted to see if Megan got jealous when I mentioned Tyler's other conquests.

"What? Where did you hear that?" he asked.

"Your prom date?" I reminded him.

He laughed, sounding strangely relieved. "Oh, her. It was just a dance."

Just a dance, just a movie. Maybe he and Megan weren't an item after all.

None of the previews looked good—just another crop of sad stories about lonely people with depressing lives. Fifteen minutes into the movie I still had no idea what was going on. All the characters looked the same, plus I kept missing the subtitles because I was too busy watching Tyler feed popcorn to Megan. I'd sucked down my soda so fast that I had to pee like crazy. Maybe Gideon was still outside. Maybe he'd suggest we run away with the Reno High remodeling fund; we'd go to Europe, live like gypsies, and eat crusty bread and cheese near old fountains and big rosebushes.

I carefully stepped over Tyler's and Megan's feet.

Megan shrugged.

"Bathroom," I whispered.

She nodded while looking past me at the screen. Would they even notice if I never came back? Tyler reached over and plunked another kernel of popcorn into her mouth. I hurried up the aisle and ran to the bathroom. Afterward, I wandered out to the concession area and watched a couple of bicycle cops talk to Gideon. Tyler had muttered something about "loitering laws" right as the movie started. So much for my European escapade. I bought a pack of Red Vines, but they only reminded me of the time Hannah, Megan, and I conducted a Red Vines versus Twizzlers survey at 7-Eleven after a football game last year (77 percent of cute guys prefer Red Vines).

Before heading back into the theater, I watched the cops walk Gideon down the steps. Did he actually get arrested? Maybe he did have a humongous criminal record like Tyler hinted.

Bam!

I banged into a guy carrying a jumbo tub of popcorn.

"Watch it!" he yelled.

Popcorn cascaded over the top of my head and into my tank top. I leaned over to pick up the bag of M&Ms the guy had dropped. I'm such a klutz!

"I am so sorry." I handed the guy the bag. Familiar shoes. Red-striped Adidas sneakers. Filthy laces.

"Oh, it's you." Tom kind of shook his head and relaxed his hands. "Jory? Right?"

"Hi—" I watched his face turn from pink to red.

"Tom."

"I knew that."

He pushed a piece of popcorn off my shoulder. "So I suppose you're here on some hot date?"

"Not hardly," I said. "For some stupid reason I joined the community cinema club."

"So you like to read your movies?" Tom picked a piece of popcorn out of my hair and ate it. Was that gross? Super weird? He found three more pieces. *Munch. Munch. Munch.*

"Not really. I'm trying to discover my—you know, something I like to do this summer, and I like movies, so I thought—" Stop babbling. "The movie is really depressing." The movie actually might have been a comedy. People were laughing. Watching Tyler and Megan, however, was totally depressing.

"I'm not into my movie either." His freckled complexion reminded me of Katie's orange poppy seed cake. "I promised my little sister I'd take her to this girlie piece of crap for her birthday." He looked at the empty popcorn container. "I guess I'd better get a refill on this."

I fumbled for my wallet. "It's my fault. Let me pay for it."

"Naw, you don't have to pay for refills." Tom bounced his toes up and down, crushing popcorn into the rainbow squiggles on the carpet, looking bored.

"I guess I'd better get back," I said. "Or else I'll never figure out what's happening."

"Sure. Yeah. See you around." Tom nodded at me.

I wanted to know if he watched me walk away, but I didn't want to turn around; he was seeing my best side, after all. He still hadn't asked for my phone number. José had e-mailed Hannah a few times, which gave her double-date fantasies. Maybe I should inform Hannah that she needed a better-looking friend.

Chapter Ten

HARD LEMONADE AND THE GREEK ALPHABET

Hannah drove slowly, peering at the big old houses set back from the street to find some Theta Pi Phi Omicron Omega Zeta Nu Sigma Epsilon Gamma Delta Mega Mojo frat house at UNR. One of the guys from Hannah's church youth group had invited her, and Alex from Church had kind of raised his eyebrows. Maybe that meant he might show up. Or maybe he disapproved of frat parties. Could he possibly be jealous? I relished the opportunity to analyze Hannah's love life because fair is fair, right? She'd have to at least *pretend* to be interested in my situation, beyond our ongoing why-is-Megan-avoiding-us discussion.

After a whole five minutes of analyzing my Tyler-Megan dilemma, Hannah decided that I needed to find more mature men—or at least guys who didn't go to our school.

"Meggie's the one always saying that girls mature faster than boys," Hannah said.

"So?"

"So dating a twenty-three-year-old is like dating a seven-teen-year-old, so if she *is* in fact dating Tyler and not simply belonging to the film club with him, she's really dating an eleven-year-old." Hannah grinned.

After I wiped up the Diet Coke I'd sprayed all over my shirt, I agreed.

College guys would appreciate my inner beauty and my love of—well, I hadn't figured that part out yet. I know: my love of mature college guys. People like talking about themselves, right?

We finally found a house with funny Greek letters that was all lit up like it was Christmas. People hung out on the front porch, smoking and drinking, while music blared from super-sized speakers. Hannah and I walked up the path to the front door. I wore jeans with my Pillsbury Doughboy T-shirt and my flower flip-flops; I didn't want to look like I was trying too hard, because frankly I'd given up, but Hannah had put up with twelve months, twelve days, and fourteen hours of Tyler Talk, so I figured I could help her with Alex from Church. Hannah looked adorable in a tight tank top tucked into a jean skirt she'd sewn herself—it had a zillion little pockets—and her sparkly ballet flats. She shook her short hair.

"Can you still see the glitter?" she asked. "Or is it too dark? Is there *too much* glitter?"

"Quit worrying about your hair."

Hannah gave her hair one last shake, ran her tongue across her recently flossed (in the car!) teeth, and said, "Let's go."

A guy standing by the door handed us each a jumbo plastic cup in exchange for five bucks. No one else seemed to notice us as we squeezed through the crowd toward the kitchen.

"We need something to drink to make us look older," Hannah said. "Do you think they have sodas and stuff? Since I'm driving and all?"

"I think they have beer and other illicit items." I looked into a dark room with a lava lamp where people were passing around a joint. A guy gave me a blank stare and then shut the door right in my face. As we stepped into the kitchen, someone bumped into me and sloshed beer on my shoulder; he hadn't even noticed me because he was too busy leering at Hannah.

"Oh, gross. Did you see that guy?" Hannah frowned in the way that makes her button nose squinch up even cuter. I'd never attempt such a maneuver; I try to keep my face pleasant and neutral at all times.

"He looked like he was forty!" By that she meant twenty-five.

"Do you see anyone from your church?" I looked around at the guys—some with actual facial hair—talking to girls who looked like they could buy their own beer. I overheard one group arguing about environmental policy. Another girl waved a cigarette around and talked real loud about the Paris subway.

I didn't see anyone I knew.

Hannah surprised me by walking over to the keg and having the guy fill her cup with beer. I did the same. Not that I actually liked beer, but I felt so young and stupid, standing there not knowing anyone. We screamed *high school*. I thought I recognized a guy who had been a senior at Reno when I was a freshman, but he was latched on to some girl. A couple of guys attached this big bottle to a tube and one guy drank it all as the others yelled, "Chug! Chug! Chug!"

"Was that a beer bong?" I asked.

"I don't know, but it looks better than drinking this stuff slowly." Hannah sipped her beer, getting foam on her lips. She crinkled her nose again. "Yuck! I'm going to go outside and pour this out."

"Why don't you toss it on the floor?" I stepped over a puddle of beer. "That's what everyone else seems to do."

I followed Hannah back out to the porch. No way was she leaving me alone in there. A guy noticed her spilling her beer into the bushes even though she made a big production of pretending to stumble.

"Not a big beer drinker?" he asked.

"No, I prefer other things like—" She tilted her head like she was thinking.

"How about lemonade? I've got some up in my room."

"That sounds great." Hannah bounced along after the guy. "I had a lemonade stand one summer, but my dad made me stop because he's a dentist and completely freaks about sugary drinks."

"Han—" I tried to tell her that it wasn't going to be that kind of lemonade, but it was no use.

The guy unlocked his door and let us into his little room: mattresses covered the entire floor, except for one corner that had a desk, bookshelf, and mini fridge. The place smelled like lemon air freshener mixed with cologne. My nose twitched.

"Take your shoes off and make yourself comfortable." He kicked off his own flip-flops and bounced over to the fridge, then he handed Hannah and me each a bottle of hard lemonade.

"Thanks so much," Hannah said. "This is so refreshing!" She took a long drink. Did she even realize it was alcohol?

I sipped mine and looked at all the different patterns on the guy's sheets: racecars, bold stripes, plaid flannel, Scooby-Doo.

"You like my sheets?" he asked.

"They're interesting." I looked at him real quick, but he was staring at Hannah and bouncing on the mattresses.

"I'm the only guy in the house with a true *bed* room. Get it?" He laughed. "Everyone calls it the orgy room."

Hannah snapped back to herself. "That's *so* funny. Well, we should go find our friend George Eliot."

"Like the author?" The guy stopped bouncing on his mattress. "That's a lot to live up to."

"He has crazy librarian parents," Hannah said.

"But George Eliot was a woman—"

"Uh, it's a—a nickname." Hannah backed out of the room. "Thanks for the lemonade and all."

"Yeah, thanks." I turned and followed her.

"Wait, guys. I haven't showed you the best part."

Hannah ran down the hallway laughing, and we took the stairs two at a time to the living room.

"Can you believe that guy? And how silly am I? The only name I could think of was George Eliot—it's on my summer-reading list, but I obviously haven't started the thing. Ugh!"

"You know you're not drinking lemonade, right?"

"I figured that out. I'm so stupid, duh, but I'm also super thirsty. Just this once?" She took a deep cleansing breath as if that made up for breaking her no-alcohol rule. "We'll stay for a long time."

"Oh, goody." I gathered my hair into a ponytail and fanned my neck. So much was changing this summer—Megan downing the chocolatinis, and now Hannah gulping hard lemonade. Not that they'd gone crazy-wild, but I could suddenly see them becoming popular senior year—invited to all the parties, proms, and stuff—and leaving me behind. My friends had blossomed big and bold like the flowers on the Katie Bakes! van, while I struggled like the weeds in the middle of a cracked driveway.

We stood in the crowded living room watching other people party. I wanted to go back home, mope about Tyler, and maybe watch out of my mom's bedroom window for his car to drive past after the cinema club's Italian romance night. Megan hadn't even tried to convince me to come with them, but she did manage to mention that they were going to the Macaroni Grill for dinner first. Like on another real date.

I was on the verge of giving up on Tyler. Who needed the aggravation? But I didn't have anyone to take his place. Wooster Tom acted nice, winning that snake and everything, but he never asked for my phone number or even my last name. And Gideon. I hadn't seen him during my last delivery; I heard him playing the violin and his mom had said something like "Gideon loves the German chocolate cake." Maybe I could disguise myself as a German chocolate cake and let his lips nibble me all over. Okay, that's sick.

"The band's on in five minutes," some guy yelled.

People filed downstairs to the basement, so Hannah and I shrugged at each other and followed. Some guy squeezed my butt on the stairway; I turned around to give him the Look, but he turned his head away fast like he hadn't done anything. Mature college guys, my ass. Literally!

"Alex loves music. Maybe he'll be down here." Hannah shimmied through the crowd and disappeared into the darkness while I kept my back to the wall in case Ass Grabber lurked nearby. The basement smelled like the inside of an alcoholic's stomach with the added stench of stale cigarette smoke. I set my lemonade on the floor; I wanted to have all my faculties in this situation or else I'd end up in the orgy room making it with some guy who still had Scooby-Doo sheets. Not my idea of a first romantic experience. Orgy-Room guy definitely did not make it on the worthiness scale! I'd rather die a virgin.

I stood on my tippy-toes and found Hannah near the stage talking to someone, hands flying about like they do when she's excited. Had she found Alex from Church? Ass Grabber stood a few feet in front of me, talking to some older girl's boobs. Is this what I had to look forward to? Maybe I'd just skip the college scene and go straight to living in some depressing Irish hotel, giving piano lessons, and falling in love with a bottle of whiskey. Orgy-Room Guy came down the stairs and handed hard lemonade to a girl with curly red hair. She reached up and kissed his cheek. Who could be that desperate? She even had a great nose!

Someone shoved me aside as he made his way to the stage, making me stumble into the wall; lukewarm lemonade spilled over my toes. The lights went out. The speakers whined with a high-pitched squeak.

"Sorry about that," a deep voice said.

I felt the music booming in my chest like a heartbeat on steroids. Sound vibrated throughout the room, and a spotlight shone on a disco ball spinning from the ceiling. The guy with the deep voice started singing about feeling alone and looking for love—a basic anthem of angst. Where the hell was Hannah? Did she ditch me? I couldn't exactly call my mom and ask her to pick me up at a frat party. She'd freak. And my summer of passion would be over. Maybe it was already over. Maybe getting grounded could give me a good excuse for being so lame in love. I could spend all my evenings with Tommy the Rodeo Carnival snake. *Oh, God, Jory. That sounds so phallic.* I inched along the wall toward the stage, knocking a few more beverages onto my feet. My flip-flops stuck to the floor with every step. Sexy!

The song ended and soft red lighting lit the stage.

"Our next song is about a girl," Deep-Voice Guy said.

A guy playing an electric violin walked onto the stage. Gideon! His hair flopped over his closed eyes as he whipped his bow back and forth over the strings. I felt all fluttery inside as the violin mixed with the drums and guitar. The singer's voice purred seductively as he told a story about a girl who made him warm just by smiling but didn't realize it. I closed my eyes, swayed to the rhythm of the violin, and pretended that Gideon played the song just for me.

Someone grabbed my butt.

"Hey, there." Ass Grabber blew yeasty beer breath into my face. He reached over to grab my boob, but I smacked his hand away. "What's wrong?"

I didn't say anything but tried to squeeze past him to get away.

The song ended and Deep-Voice Guy said something about Gideon. People clapped. Ass Grabber loomed over me, trapping me against the wall. "Isn't this why you high school girls come to frat parties?"

I stomped on his foot, but he wore thick sneakers. Or may-

116

be he was too drunk to notice, or to care. He clamped his hand on my arm. "What's wrong? Aren't I enough of a pretty boy for you, girlie?" He put his face near mine and wiggled his tongue out. I turned away, tears in my eyes. Oh, God. Was this really happening? An icy shock of panic streaked through my body. I wanted to scream for Hannah, but she wouldn't be able to hear me. No one seemed to notice me.

People jumped up and down to the fast song the band played next. A spotlight flashed around the room, blinding me every few seconds. The guy wouldn't move. I struggled against him, but he pressed into me harder. I closed my eyes tight and screamed as loud as I could, barely hearing myself above the music, laughter, and talking. My whole head filled with noise.

Someone shoved the guy away from me. Ass Grabber whipped around with his fist held high. "What the—"

"Leave my friend alone!" Hannah yelled.

Ass Grabber scowled.

Hannah pulled back her hand. "Move or I'll karate chop your balls."

"You pathetic little tease." Ass Grabber shoved me against the wall before he walked away.

I started crying with blubbery, snot-producing sobs. "I'm so stupid."

"I shouldn't have left you alone." Hannah put her arm around me. "I'm so sorry. I wasn't thinking. Let me run and tell Alex that we're leaving."

I wiped my nose with my arm and nodded. "Promise to hurry?"

"Of course."

As I watched Hannah maneuver toward the stage, I saw Gideon talking to a group of girls in front of me. One of them draped her arm over his shoulder and talked right into his ear. I sucked a bunch of snot back into my nose and tried to look normal; I smiled, as if that could mask feeling so dirty. I still felt that guy's hands all over me, and I rubbed my arms hard to feel something different.

Gideon noticed me and raised his eyebrows. I waved. Just barely. I wanted to look friendly, but I didn't want him to talk to me. *I'm too disgusting,* I thought.

The room went dark again, but the band flipped on some black lights. The Pillsbury Doughboy on my shirt glowed. So did a smear of snot on my arm. I wiped it against my jeans as Gideon walked over to me. The band started another slow song. Orgy-Room Guy danced as close as you can get with the red-haired girl. I turned away, glancing quickly at Gideon before focusing on a glowing spot on the wall behind him.

"You sounded great," I said in a fake cheerful voice that sounded way too much like Mom's.

Gideon shrugged. "Having a good time?" He stared at me, but the black lights made it impossible to read his expression.

I didn't trust my voice, so I nodded my head up and down in time to the music, then stared at the floor. Little bits of things glowed all over the place. A torn beer label. A smooshed piece of gum. The white threads on Gideon's jeans. His toes. Toes? I looked at my feet. The little white flowers on my flip-flops glowed, but not my toes. I looked back at Gideon's feet. He wore flip-flops, too. And his toenails definitely glowed, like casino lights. All ten of them!

"So you and that guy—"

I glanced up at his face, still so hidden in the dark. Was he talking about Ass Grabber?

"Guy?" Again I moved to the beat of the music, wanting to pretend the whole Ass Grabber thing had never happened. "What guy?"

Gideon turned his head toward the wall as he said something, but the music overpowered his voice, so I focused on his toes. As he spoke, his glowing toenails wiggled up and down, flashing like a marquee advertising showgirls or has-been lounge singers.

I started giggling.

"What?" Gideon asked.

"Your toenails are glowing!" Laughter bubbled through me.

Our heads kind of bumped as we both looked down at his feet. Gideon stumbled, trying to cover one foot with the other, making me laugh harder.

The black lights clicked off with the last note of the song, and even though I caught a hurt look on Gideon's face before the room darkened again, I couldn't stop laughing about his glowing toes. I received more than a few nasty stares when my guffaws continued to echo around the room while the singer started in on a slow ballad.

"I hope you're not the one driving." He kicked a cup, splashing beer against the wall.

All I could think to say was "I haven't been drinking. Much. And I'm a good driver. Sort of."

Gideon tossed his hair as if sweeping away dirt. "See you around."

Hannah finally showed up and hunched her shoulders questioningly as she looked from me to Gideon, who shot away like a kicked beer cup. I just shook my head.

I'm such a loser. Only drunk guys like Ass Grabber and the Gold Dust West Stalker Guy could like me.

Chapter Eleven

JULY: DOWN DOGS AND CABBAGE SOUP

Hannah unrolled her pink yoga mat on the shiny wooden floor. She practically vibrated with excitement about my desire to try yoga as my newfound passion. She'd been into yoga since she first got diagnosed with scoliosis.

"It *saved* me, Jory. All that teasing, you know. I totally *found* myself with yoga. You will learn to *love* your body."

I held my sticky blue mat from the free-for-you-to-use basket and wondered when it had last been cleaned. Who had sweated all over this thing?

People, mostly old people, in comfy yoga pants and snug tops wandered into the room. I wore my stupid RHS gym shorts and a baggy Monterey Bay Aquarium T-shirt with a whale wrapping around the back of it. I felt kind of like a whale. One small bowl of Mom's Cabbage Soup Diet concoction had packed me with so much gas that I could probably float.

"So, you're being evasive." Hannah stretched her arms above her head. "Do you like that guy with the big nose or what?"

"Gideon. He has a name, you know." I hate it when people describe someone as having a big nose. Freshman year I had a major argument with Megan over Barbra Streisand's nose. And elephants are my favorite animals.

"Well, do you? Like him?"

"I don't know. He seems nice, but he's most definitely not interested in me." I snapped my mat down on the floor and stepped onto it. "Ew. I think I'll get another mat. This one is all sticky."

"They're supposed to be sticky, silly." Hannah sat on her mat cross-legged. "So you don't slide around during the poses."

Hannah took a few deep breaths.

"Oh." I sat down on the mat and decided I would shower again after class.

"So how many times have you seen him? And didn't he, like, get kicked out of school?"

All of a sudden she's interested in analyzing my lack of a love life! If this yoga thing worked out, I planned on travel-ing to the headwaters of the Ganges, wasting away to ninety pounds, living alone with my spiritually awakened self, and being okay with dying a virgin after I turned 117. Only a hundred years to go.

"Jor—"

"We've had exactly two conversations, but I've heard him play the violin three times, including, you know, the other night." I closed my eyes and shook away the memory without even thinking.

"Oh, Jory. Yoga will totally help you release all the tension from the other night." Hannah rolled her head in a slow circle. "What did your mom say?"

"About the Ass Grabber? I didn't exactly tell her." I hadn't even let myself think about it because it felt so dirty. I wanted to forget the whole thing. Nothing really happened anyway, right? Still, I kept waking up in the middle of the night after dreaming about being trapped in a fire; I never dreamed about Ass Grabber, but it was like I knew he was lurking in the flames. Yesterday I felt all panicky when I had to deliver a bouquet of flowers up near UNR. Maybe I'd have to study harder senior year so I could go to school out of state after all. No matter what, my new nose would have a big brute of a boyfriend who wouldn't let anyone near my butt.

I could tell that Hannah was working on some kind of speech, but the yoga teacher came into the room, dimmed the lights, turned on some weird chanting music, and told us to stand at the front of our mats.

I let a tiny bit of gas escape.

"Bring your hands to your heart center and find your breath." Find my breath? A bunch of people started gasping as if suffocating. I glanced at Hannah to make a joke, but she did it too. No way was I making that noise in public. Instead, I farted. Quietly.

Next, Yoga Lady had us face toward the windows and do sun salutations to, quote, "honor the beauty of the day." Sun salutations apparently involve a lot of toe touches. My big T-shirt kept flopping over my nose, making my giant nostrils blow hot air all around my face. Hannah's body practically bent in half, but my fingers barely touched the mat. Even this old geezer man next to me placed his hands flat on the ground.

We went up and down a few times, moving into this position called Down Dog. It looked easy to put your hands and feet on the ground and stick your butt in the air, but I wanted to die. *Let us stop*, I wanted to scream. My hands and arms hurt as I pressed into the mat.

Yoga Lady complimented everyone on their beautiful poses but came over and lifted my hips up. A little puff of gas escaped. Could she smell it? *Oh, God, this is so embarrassing.*

"Is that better?" Yoga Lady kind of turned away. *Oh, God, she smelled it. Serves her right for singling me out in front of everyone as the sucky new student.*

I tilted my head and looked at the geezer next to me. His giant, hairy bare feet stood flat on the ground! The guy was my grandpa's age probably. Finally Yoga Lady told us to walk to the front of the mat and touch our toes again. My legs wobbled with weakness and I felt like crying, for some strange reason. Hannah had told me yoga would relax me. Liar! She had gone on and on about how professional athletes and movie stars did yoga. So how come everyone in *this* room looked like they lived in a retirement village? How could my passion be something that made me feel weak and extra klutzy and didn't even involve cute boys?

Next, we did balancing poses. I teetered on one leg, tipping over as I tried to do the flamingo thing called Tree. Even the old ladies could do it!

"Sometimes we blow in the wind." Yoga Lady, or, rather, the Sunny Sadist, looked right at me. "We're working toward rooting ourselves in the ground."

Everyone knew she was talking about me. Blowing in the wind. Worst of all, I was still blowing wind—little puff-puff farts poisoned the air around me. I hoped people were thinking that Hairy-Feet Geezer had done it, but then he scooted his mat up a couple of feet from me. Even Hannah gave me a strange look. I could just see it. *Caughlin Rancher* headline: "Yoga Class Evacuated After Jory Michaels Fumigates the Place with Cabbage Soup Gas; Three People Hospitalized." Okay, maybe not.

I fell on my butt when the Sunny Sadist told us to do this pretzel-type move. No one laughed, but almost everyone looked at me. Hannah gave me one of her sympathetic closed-mouth smiles. I'd show her! Squeezing my butt gas-trapping tight, I made myself do the twisty thing even though my leg shook as if hurricane-force winds blasted through the room.

The Sunny Sadist told us we could retreat into Child's Pose at any time. She came over, tapped me on the shoulder with her light-as-a-feather touch, and told me to find my breath. I let out a gasp of air; I hadn't realized that I'd been holding it in. She plopped down on the floor and showed me how to fold up like a sleeping baby. Everyone else did the pretzel pose on the other leg. No one looked at me.

"Breathe," she whispered.

Two big tears plunked down on the mat and I had to stifle one big snuffle before I started thinking about how I should've punched that damn Ass Grabber in the balls.

"Focus on the breath," the Sunny Sadist said. "Keep your mind clear as you do the inversion pose of your choice."

I peeked over at Hannah, who stood on her head with her feet up in the air, totally still. A few other ladies balanced their legs against the wall. Cheaters.

"Remember, we learn from our failures," the Sunny Sadist said.

What a load of stinky cabbage gas! What had I learned today?

- Never, ever do yoga again.
- Never, ever eat cabbage *anything* again.
- Make peace with dying a virgin.
- No one decent will ever want a Super Schnozz.

The Sunny Sadist spoke in a soft voice. "Now, release your pose, keeping your mind clear. Breathe."

Huddled in a cloud of my own smelly gas, I tried not to breathe. How could I keep my mind clear? Ass Grabber never would've done that to a prettier girl. Ugly girls are supposed to be easy, right? I should've been grateful. Gideon probably noticed me only because my big red-from-crying nose shone in the lights; he probably figured he should talk to a member of the big-nose club. Just to be nice. The way Tyler always says flirty things to be nice but goes off to every single movie-you-have-to-read with Megan. And feeds her popcorn.

I skipped the next three poses, but when the teacher told us all to roll over on our backs, I happily complied. Plus, no one would be able to tell that I'd been crying. The Sunny Sadist told us to balance our legs in the air with our shoulders off the mats. My abs burned like my bellybutton had caught fire. I looked over at Hannah, who had bent her body into a graceful V shape. Long, perfect, tan legs. If Alex from Church didn't go for her, he must be planning to be a monk. She even smiled.

I tried to lift my legs straight but crashed down with a thump that hurt my back.

"Remember, this is not a competition," the Sunny Sadist said. "We're always striving toward something, pushing at the edge of sensation but not pain."

Pain walloped every part of my body as we lay in a cleansing twist, wringing out our organs. I pictured my heart as a sopping-wet rag. *Focus,* I told myself, but I kept feeling bad about being the worst one in the room in the over-two and under-ninety-nine category. Put me up against an infant or a 120-year-old woman, and I'd show you some yoga! I also had the biggest nose in the room, with the exception of Hairy-Feet Geezer.

The Sunny Sadist pulled down the shades on the windows and switched to weird, wordless *wa-wa-thwang* music. We lay flat on our backs with our hands facing the ceiling and our eyes closed. Corpse Pose. Or, in my case, Dead Virgin.

"You may repeat something inspirational to yourself if you wish," the Sunny Sadist said.

My nose tickled. I tried to make the feeling go away by doing strange contortions with my mouth and nose. Everyone had closed eyes, right? I peeked at the teacher, who was lying still with her eyes closed, smiling serenely, but then she picked a wedgie. I sucked in air instead of laughing out loud. I turned my head and looked at what other people were doing. One old lady's giant boobs oozed down the sides of her chest like lava. I sucked in another giggle. I watched Hannah mouthing *Alex* over and over again. I sucked in a huge gulp of air. *Do not laugh. Do not laugh.*

I let out a rip-roaring, make-my-little-bro-proud belch, followed by a big guffaw and a Nevada nuclear-test-site atomic fart.

Kaboom!

At least the Sunny Sadist stopped smiling.

Chapter Twelve

DICKENSONS AND WIENERS

One week of the Cabbage Soup Cleanse + Snobby Rich Caughlin Ranch Families + the Dickenson Lake House + an Old-Fashioned Bunk-Bed Sleepover = the Fourth of July.

I tossed some clothes into a duffel bag. Mom, in a fit of über-excitement about losing six pounds on the cabbage cleanse and daring to wear her bikini with a heavy-fabric sarong, let me borrow the minivan to drive up to the Dickensons' quote "cabin," aka "mansion bigger than our house" at the lake. She and Dad headed up early with friends to enjoy the full day of festivities—rich people fawning over one another's possessions and drinking too much.

I'd been up since six helping Katie with a Fourth of July wedding. She'd made this cake with red, white, and blue fondant decorated to look like the stitching on an old American quilt. Who gets married on the Fourth of July, anyway? Guess the bride had a thing for fireworks and old quilts. She looked pretty old—gray hair and the whole bit. Was she still a virgin? Had it really taken her an entire lifetime to find someone who actually loved her? Groom Dude had a weird beard, long ponytail, beer belly, and laughed too hard at his own jokes. Did she actually love him? Or did she just get too desperately lonely?

I imagined myself decades in the future, withered with age yet still virginal, designing my own quilted wedding cake. I shuddered. All week I'd dyed white carnations blue and red for this wedding. The only good thing about working the Fourth: time and a half. It added $108 to the nose fund, for a grand total of $1,100-ish.

After work, I raced home to pack my cutest shortie PJs, favorite bikini, and new casual but sexy mini, just in case a certain flirtatious someone happened to be there. He was last year. That's when the obsession began: fireworks, the beach, my first-ever margarita.

He had smiled at me and uttered the immortal words, "Weren't you in my English class?"

No, but I still fell into a crush deeper than Lake Tahoe. A year of "Hi, Jory" smiles in the yellow-tiled hallways of good old Reno High only deepened my feelings. Even Hannah's family didn't socialize with the Dickensons, so I knew Megan and her schoolteacher mommy wouldn't have scored an invitation—maybe that's why she'd called Hannah (as if I wouldn't find out!) last night to ask how much I *really* liked Tyler. Ha! She *should* worry. Jory's back! I'd blast into Tyler's consciousness like an M-80. *Whammo.* I'd do whatever it took. *Prepare to have your world rocked.* I turned up the stereo and sang along with Vampire Weekend, changing the words to "Jory's got a new face."

I took the freeway instead of the scenic route. Cops pulled several people over, but no one ever notices speeding in a minivan, so I made good time and caught my first view of Lake Tahoe—a deep Tyler's-eyes blue—right as the cocktail hour started.

Mom's minivan looked out of place in the Lexus/Mercedes/BMW dealership–looking driveway. I glossed my lips, fluffed my hair around my shoulders, and strode up the driveway. I noticed a bit of red fondant under my fingernail as I rang the doorbell. No one answered, so I let myself in. Mom's high-pitched laugh echoed from the kitchen across the cathedral ceiling. Cocktail hour must have started *much* earlier.

"Oh, stop it," Mom said. "I look the same as always."

A blender whirred.

"You truly are the mix master, Barbara."

Barbara? As in Barbara Briggs? Excellent. I took a deep, cleansing yoga breath, but not one of the strange noisy ones.

"Hi, Mom! Hi, Mrs. Briggs."

"Jory, don't you look cute, as usual." Mrs. Briggs scraped salt off the rim of her margarita glass with a long red-white-and-blue polished fingernail. "Tyler and the kids are down on the dock."

"Uh, great. Where can I change into my suit?" I held up my duffel.

"You youngsters are up on the sleeping porch," she said. "We grownups get the bedrooms." Barbara clinked glasses with Mom, who looked at me with a blissful, slightly tipsy grin.

"So, I'll be sure to pick up that book tomorrow—I'm sure I can finish it in time." Mom winked at me and gave me a subtle thumbs-up. *Looks like she finally swung an invite to the book club.*

Upstairs, I examined each duffel bag and suitcase carefully to figure out which bunk belonged to Tyler. I peeked inside one and saw Tyler's LCD Soundsystem T-shirt. Bingo! I put my duffel on the bunk next to his, changed into my bikini, gave my hair a good flip-over brushing, and headed down to the water.

As I stepped down the path to the Dickensons' private dock, I soaked in the pine-scented air and enjoyed the tickle of my hair against my bare back. Anything can happen! Drew Dickenson's ski boat pulled a wakeboard out past the rocks. Only one person sat on the dock sticking his feet in the water. *Yes!*

"Happy Fourth," I sang out. Tyler wore red and blue swim trunks and nothing on his fabulously tan upper body; his skin was the color of caramel pie.

"Jory," he said. "I wondered if you were going to come up. Your mom's trying to outdrink mine. Quite a challenge." He held up a pitcher of margaritas. "But she might be winning because her judgment was impaired enough to give me this. Want one?"

"Sure." I sipped the watery limeade with not much tequila. "Mmm. Good."

"Naw, they're watery as hell." He pulled out a bottle from a beach bag. "That's why I borrowed this." He tilted his head at me. I nodded, happy that Megan wouldn't be around to make some totally hypocritical drinking comment.

The burn of the tequila in my throat made me gasp. "That's better."

We stood up as the ski boat roared closer to shore.

Tyler laughed. "Your face is so red. Want me to dunk you in the lake?" He tugged on my arm.

"No!" I squealed. "I'm not hot enough yet."

"Oh, you need to get hot?" He stood so close, the tie from his swim trunks poked my stomach. "How hot?" I felt his breath against my ear, smelled his coconut suntan lotion.

I somersaulted into the icy water. *Splash!* My chest constricted. The outline of Tyler and his red and blue swim trunks wavered above me like a mirage. I pushed out of the water and pulled myself back onto the dock.

"I'm so going to get you." I moved toward Tyler, tugging on his arm, but he dug his feet in.

Drew waved to us as the boat slowed to no-wake speed.

"No messing with the hair." Tyler didn't smile. "Why do you think I'm sitting here instead of in the boat?"

"Fair is fair."

"Don't, Jory." He gave me the Look. Had Megan taught him that?

I swung my hair, but it only smacked against my back in one wet rope. I lay down on my beach towel and closed my eyes, feeling massive quantities of freckles popping up on my mountain of a nose. Would he have let me throw him in if I looked better? He'd been so flirtatious, but all of a sudden it had stopped—like someone had pressed the off button. Maybe with my wet hair, I looked too disgusting to even acknowledge.

I heard the *glug-glug* of Tyler pouring more tequila into his cup and the sound of water lapping against the dock, but he didn't say a word to me. We lay like that while Drew and the others tied the boat to the dock.

"Jory! When did you get here?"

Megan. The traitor times ten. She hadn't said *anything* about coming up to the lake when she'd called Hannah!

"You should go out on the boat. It's so fun. You should've seen Finn and Luke. Major enema, right, guys?" Megan wrung out her long dark hair and let it fall back against her dark tan skin. Her eyes matched the lake, just like Tyler's.

"Megan's a total sport," Finn said. "I'm surprised she's friends with such a klutz." Finn kicked my thigh with his clammy foot.

"Why are you here?" I regretted my bitter tone. "I mean, I wasn't expecting to see you."

"Yeah." Megan adjusted her uncharacteristically skimpy bikini. "Tyler invited me."

Maybe it didn't mean anything. Maybe it was a coworker thing, not a dating thing.

"Hey, guys. Want to go kick the ball around before dinner?" Drew toweled off his hair.

I'd forgotten that Drew, Finn, and Luke all shared the soccer-geek passion. I snuck a peek at Luke's toned legs as he walked by; usually, Kayla Neal hung all over him, and I half expected her to rise out of the water like a mermaid.

Megan squeezed between Tyler and me; he watched the soccer geeks race up the path, not acknowledging Megan, but her leg touched his knee in a comfortable, familiar way.

"This is going to be so fun," she said. "I can't believe we get to stay the night and watch the fireworks and everything. This will be the best Fourth of July ever."

I gave her the Look, but she didn't take the hint. The Look probably requires a small nose. How could she flaunt her coziness with Tyler right in front of me? Hannah had told her that I *did* like Tyler. A lot.

"I know. I'm acting like a dork, but this is the most fun I've had all summer." She hugged her arms around her long, lean legs.

"What about your great job? And all your hilarious nicknames? And inside jokes?"

"I thought I'd get to work on real law cases, but I'm stuck making copies."

"Well, what about all those movies you've been seeing?" Or *not* seeing.

"That's mostly to add diversity to my résumé." She bumped Tyler with her elbow. "Should we tell her?"

"We snuck into an action flick during German-drama night." Tyler's voice sounded flat.

"It was so much fun! I felt totally rebellious. I never knew how good a car chase could be compared to a guy drinking himself to death." Megan laughed, and a blue jay answered back as if she were a Disney-movie princess.

"I'm going to go change," I said.

"I'll go with you." Tyler wobbled as he stood. "I need to drink more if my dad's going to insist on singing the national anthem like he usually does. But goddamnit, I'm not playing the piano."

"Guess I'm coming too." Megan folded her towel into a neat square.

When Megan and I got back to the sleeping porch, Kayla Neal lounged on a bunk bed, reading a gossip magazine and kicking her legs up behind her. Red-white-and-blue toenail polish.

"Hi, I'm Kayla. Luke's GF." She waggled her finger at me.

"I know you! You're Finn's sister. He's such a sweetie. And you're Tyler's . . . ?" she said to Megan.

"Yeah." Megan combed her hair.

Yeah? What did that mean? Kayla hadn't asked a specific question. But the implication was definitely *girlfriend,* right? Had Megan and Tyler started dating officially? I glared at Megan for a few seconds, but she didn't look at me.

"The boys are out playing with their balls," Kayla said.

Megan laughed.

"What?" Kayla looked at us with Bambi eyes. "They're doing it on the grass out back."

I could see Megan biting her cheek. Hard. Not amused, I shuffled through my duffel. My clothes suddenly seemed so plain, plus I'd forgotten to bring anything warm to wear at night. Maybe I'd just stay inside and hide under the covers. No one would notice. I didn't need to impress anyone, right? Everyone was already taken; well, except for Drew, but he wasn't exactly into girls.

We endured dinner with the parents—including Mr. Briggs's worse than off-key rendition of the "Star-Spangled Banner" (Tyler *did* play piano)—before walking down to the beach to watch the fireworks. I wore my red mini with a white T-shirt, even though Drew teased me about wearing Wooster colors. Major soccer rival. Drew made me bring his blue Reno High sweatshirt in case I got cold. He and Finn talked about some Brazilian soccer goalie while Kayla publicly fondled Luke. Ah, the beautiful people. Tyler and Megan walked far behind us. Doing what? Kissing? More? A few minutes later, Megan stomped up next to me.

"Something wrong?" I didn't disguise my sarcasm.

Megan brushed under her eyes. Smeared mascara? Tears?

Tyler ran ahead of us, scooped Kayla—squealing—into his arms, and disappeared into the darkness. I couldn't stop myself from smiling.

"Meg. What's going on?"

"Nothing. Apparently, nothing. Always, nothing."

Drew brought a big beach blanket. I lay down next to Finn. Not quite the romantic vision I'd had. Current chance of dying a virgin: 98 percent.

Megan plopped down next to me, exhaling loudly but not saying anything. I imagined her giving the Look to the stars. Tyler sat next to Drew, while Luke walked around to the rocks with Kayla. Luke had a bit of a reputation, from what I'd overheard Finn and his friends say. Would anyone cute with half a personality ever want to take me to the rocks? Drew opened a cooler and handed me hard lemonade, but I refused it. I felt too confused already—as if someone had taken my life and flipped it over like a pineapple upside-down cake. Were Tyler and Megan together or not? Hannah sure thought they were, based on their phone conversation and the "vibe" Megan had given off in a recent text message. Whatever.

Soon fireworks flashed overhead—red, yellow, green bursts that reminded me of the volvox we'd studied in biology class. People all around me oohed and aahed. I kept looking over at Tyler, who stared straight ahead. Not at the sky. Not at the water. Just straight into the blackness. He guzzled from a flask. *Why does Tyler make me feel so insecure? Why do I let his actions make me feel ugly? Who needs all his drama anyway? Megan can have him.* Almost as if reading my thoughts, Megan sat up and glanced at Tyler. Then she lay back down with a huff. "He's a mere speckle in the vast quantities and qualities of males available to me," she said. "I'm done with him."

I thought maybe I was too.

Chapter Thirteen

DICKENSONS AND DOUGHNUTS

All the rustling around made it sound like raccoons had invaded the sleeping porch. Right after I crawled into bed, I overheard Kayla whispering to Luke, followed by some not-so-quiet kissing. What did it feel like kissing that mouth? I had watched him while we ate last night: those full lips, dark eyebrows, blond hair. He kept jiggling his amazing legs under the table at dinner. Once, he raised his eyebrows at me after Kayla had called the hot dogs *wieners* for the thousandth time. Megan had already spewed out her lemonade when Kayla told us her uncle Dick played ball with himself with a machine in his backyard. Megan made a nonsensical joke about potato chips and laughed at herself. Finn, Luke, Drew, and I laughed really hard too. Kayla was all "I don't get it, guys." *That* made us all laugh even harder, except Tyler.

Much later in the night, Tyler climbed down from his bunk and walked over to the other side of the room where Megan slept. I heard some whispering, but afterward Tyler ran down the stairs. By himself. Guess Megan really was over him. I lay awake for a long time, imagining running after Tyler in the moonlight. *Forget her,* I'd say. *You've always got me.* I tried to picture him embracing me the way people do in movies, but instead I kept seeing that cold, hard look he'd given me on the dock. I also kept hearing Megan say that he was a mere speckle in the vast quantities of men. But he was a speckle who paid attention to me. Sometimes.

I finally fell asleep, feeling sorry for myself because Luke liked Kayla just because she was pretty, and Tyler liked Megan partly because they had stuff in common, but mostly because she was pretty. No one liked me. Even Wooster Tom had never asked for my phone number.

I woke early in spite of a lousy night of sleep, happy to have the night end, while Megan, Kayla, and Drew snored on, looking as beautiful as hand-drawn Disney characters while I resembled Medusa with my snaking, snarled hair.

For a few minutes I watched a beam of sunlight cross the white ceiling. Hunger pangs grumbled in my stomach; one night of real food had awakened a monster inside me. When I slid out of bed, I noticed that Tyler hadn't come back. Or maybe he'd woken up early. I paused and asked myself if I really cared. Or was it just a habit? A bad habit.

I tiptoed into the big open kitchen. Luke sat at the table reading an ancient issue of *Sports Illustrated* and drinking a big glass of water.

He raised his eyebrows at me. "Morning."

"Yeah, hi." I looked around at all the empty cups and glasses, the granite counter sticky with spilled margaritas. A big puddle of water on the floor showed where a bag of ice used to be. "Are you the only one awake?"

"Looks that way." He tipped his water back.

I opened a cupboard full of plastic cups. Where did they keep the cereal and pancake mix? Or bacon and eggs? My stomach rumbled as I opened the fridge, which was packed with beer and various mixers. No milk, no orange juice, though someone had stuck a plate of potato salad and a half-eaten hot dog on the top shelf.

"Don't bother looking for something to eat," Luke said. "Unless you want an old wiener." He laughed.

"This sucks." I slammed the fridge. "I'm starving."

"Tell me about it. I went on a run and I kept smelling people cooking bacon and my stomach hurt, and I thought I'd run back here and see one of the moms cooking in the kitchen. But then again, I've never really seen my mom eat much, and Mrs. Briggs looks like a skeleton, and Mrs. Dickenson and your mom—"

"Yeah, I know."

Luke put down the magazine. "Hey, I do know a place that makes killer doughnuts." He raised his eyebrows at me. "We could be total heroes to the hungry."

"Anything besides, you know—"

"Wieners?"

I smiled. "Yeah."

Luke snuck downstairs to grab his mom's keys while I ran and changed into a pair of shorts. As I braided my hair on the way down the stairs, I noticed Tyler sleeping on the sofa in the living room, but I followed Luke out to the green Lexus. License plate: SOCMOM.

Luke rolled down the windows and blasted the White Stripes.

"Do you like these guys?" he asked.

"Sure." *Oh, yeah. I'm such the conversationalist.*

I liked it that people in the doughnut shop looked at us as if we were a couple. I saw one girl do a double take at Luke, then glare at me. My new nose would have to get used to this, I thought.

"Nice," Luke said after I ordered plain doughnuts. "My favorites. Okay, we better add some with pink sprinkles for

Kayla, and Megan probably likes a classic, like a glazed, right? Our dads will all need something heavy, like bear claws."

"You sure know your doughnut personalities."

"My specialty." He raised his eyebrows. Twice.

We left with two dozen doughnuts and a cup of coffee for each of us.

"I'm not usually into caffeine," he said. "But I couldn't get to sleep last night."

"I heard."

Luke blushed. "I told her."

"It's no big deal. You guys are a real cute couple."

"Still, it's not cool to—" Luke turned the music up even louder and started beating out the rhythm on the steering wheel. I watched the lake sparkle with sunshine between the trees.

"Does the water look good for skiing?" Luke asked.

"I guess so." *Why can't I think of anything to say? No wonder no one is falling in love with my mind. I'm so boring.*

Megan was pacing on the front porch when we got back. Luke handed her the box of doughnuts and ran up to the sleeping porch, two steps at a time.

"So, when were you planning on heading back to town?" Megan set the doughnuts on the kitchen counter.

I shrugged. Let her suffer. I'd endured sitting through two stupid movies with them, sharing sodas, popcorn. So what if they had had a big fight? It wasn't *my* fault.

"Could you give me a ride?" Megan's voice sounded pleading.

"I guess." I bit into a cake doughnut. "But I kind of want to water-ski."

"What? You never want to do that kind of stuff. You're not exactly—"

Make her say it. "Athletic?"

Megan rubbed her temples. "Yeah, I guess. I really need to go home. Please."

"Maybe water-skiing could be my new passion. My passion is definitely not yoga. Or foreign cinema."

"Please, Jory." Megan looked at me with her big blue eyes. "Can't we just go home?" She lowered her voice to a whisper. "If you think you can score points with Tyler, don't bother." Her face shaded red, like a nasty sunburn.

"That's not it at all."

"Well, what then?"

"I'd like to try something new. What's the big deal?"

Megan blew her bangs. "God, Jory. Can't you see I'm in a bit of distress here?"

"I thought you thrived on it."

"That's *stress*." She looked over at Tyler, still sleeping on the couch. "This is *dis*tress."

"I'm not as stupid as you think I am, Megan."

"I don't think that." Megan stamped her foot. "I just want to go home." Her eyes filled with tears.

"Luke said he'd teach me to water-ski."

"So Luke's going to be your dreamboat now, huh? Correct me if I'm wrong, but he seems quite attached." Megan smoothed back her hair, regaining her composure. "Though I guess that's never bothered you, has it?"

Now my eyes stung. Megan stomped up to the sleeping porch as Kayla came downstairs wearing a baby-doll nightie with pink underwear showing through. Luke walked next to her, his hand on her butt.

"You got me pink sprinkles? You sweetie." She kissed his cheek. "Isn't he the greatest?" Luke kissed her mouth. "Ooh. You taste sweet," Kayla cooed as she kissed him back, as if I weren't standing right there.

Only to avoid the X-rated scene between Luke and Kayla, I followed Megan up to the sleeping porch and found her sitting on the edge of Finn's bed, talking low.

"Sure," I heard him say. "I'll see what I can do."

Was she using my own family against me? Megan hopped up when I came into the room and headed into the bathroom. She glanced at me kind of smug, but didn't say anything.

"Hey, Jor." Finn sat up. "I just remembered that I promised Coach I'd meet him and some of the guys to practice—"

"Don't let her play you, Finn." I gave the Look to the bathroom door the best I could. "Think with your head and not your dick."

"God, Jory. Chill." Finn stretched his arms above his head. "I'm only saying that Megan could drive the minivan, take me home, and get a ride from her mom. You can ride home with the parentals whenever."

"You actually think Mom will go for that so-called plan?" God. How could Megan be so selfish and ruin my entire family's day at the lake? I just hated her sometimes. So what if she was upset? It was her own stupid fault for going after the guy *I* liked. Now we had to rearrange our lives to make her feel better? I stomped around the room, wishing I had the courage to follow Megan into the bathroom and tell her what I really thought. Instead, I glared at Finn, the little traitor.

"What? Mom loves Megan." Finn got out of bed. "Plus she's responsible and has a sweet driving record."

"Whatever. Fine. Ruin your day."

"Spending time alone in a car with a girl like Megan." Finn grinned, making a crude gesture. "I'm up for that."

"You're disgusting!" I stomped downstairs and sat in the kitchen alone, eating part of Dad's bear claw.

❧

Of course Mom totally loved Finn's plan and eagerly handed Megan the keys to her minivan. When Barbara Briggs offered to take Mom and Dad home in her car, I thought Mom's face would crack from smiling like overdone cheesecake. I decided that I'd try my best to make water-skiing my passion. A day in a boat with cute guys could definitely work to my advantage.

Five hours, approximately twelve ski attempts, ten face-plants, six high-speed enemas, and one sunburn later, I found myself driving down the twisty Mount Rose highway with Tyler, listening to a dreary old Smiths album. I gripped the door handle as Tyler took yet another curve too fast. Forget getting hit by the Smiths' double-decker bus, I'd be dying in Tyler's Jeep.

I wanted to look out the window, but I kept seeing my Rudolph nose in the side mirror. So I stared straight ahead. So did Tyler. He hadn't said one word to me, or anyone else, all day. When his mom told him to take me home, he just shrugged. When his dad said something about "That's no way to treat your mother," he just shrugged. When his dad said, "How do you think this makes Jory feel?" he just shrugged.

"Thanks for the ride, I think," I said when I got out of the Jeep.

Tyler sped out of the driveway before I had time to grab my duffel bag. Three hours later, Finn found it on the porch.

No matter how much effort it took, I was going to be *so over* Tyler. Maybe my friendship with Megan was over too.

Chapter Fourteen

BUMPING AND BREAKING

I circled the block twice before I found a spot near the Jewel Café big enough to park the van. Parallel parking, still so not my passion. Why was it so crowded? I checked my watch: 12:45 P.M. Great—no lunch break for Incompetent Delivery Driver. I still had retirement flowers to deliver before—oh, God—1:00 P.M. I swung the van away from the curb and drove out toward some accountant's office on Lakeside.

The receptionist glared at me when I brought the flowers to her desk at 1:13 P.M. I'd driven by the place twice, stuck behind slow cars, unsure about the address.

"I hope you know that she's late for her retirement luncheon because we had to keep her here waiting for these flowers from her husband," she said. "I hope you know that I will be calling your boss to complain."

"I'm very sorry." My voice sounded mousy—timid, shy, fearful, wimpy, and self-conscious. Not in any way charming. If Hannah were doing my job, they'd be apologizing to her for making her come so early. Megan would simply never be late. My hands shook as I put the keys back in the ignition.

"Don't cry." I squeezed my eyes shut. I knew how to think of sad things when I didn't want to laugh, but what do you think about when you don't want to cry? I didn't have any recent happy memories, and somehow remembering myself as a little kid made me feel even more pitiful. The only thing that popped into my head was how I felt when Wooster Tom won that snake for me, but seeing him at the movies had been a total disaster, and I'd probably never see him again. My future: living alone in a seedy motel room, drinking a bottle of whiskey every night, passing out in bed next to my tattered carnival snake.

I pushed the gearshift into reverse and backed out. *Bump. Scrape. Oh, God, Jory. No!* I jumped out of the van and ran around the back.

"Oh, crap. I've killed a tree."

I had backed over the curb and onto the grass, hitting a slender young tree. Half its roots stuck out of the ground as it tilted at a distressingly acute angle. There was only a tiny little scratch in the middle of a yellow daisy painted on the van. Could've been there for ages. I tried to lift the tree up straight, but it only tipped closer to the ground, dumping loose dirt on my shoes. I glanced back at the glossy dark doors to the accountant's office.

"I can't do it. Not now."

I squeezed my eyes to block the tears, jumped into the van, and peeled out of there like an FTD Florist–sponsored racecar driver.

I had to drive around the block near the Jewel Café four times because my eyes looked so red; I ended up double-parking. Through the hedge around the courtyard I could hear people laughing and talking as I carried a cake box in each hand—Gideon's mom had doubled her order since last week. I pushed the door open with my hip; several ladies milled around the front room, looking over beads, putting them on little plastic trays.

One lady narrowed her eyes at me. "Helen, it looks like dessert has finally arrived."

Gideon's mom burst through the swinging doors to the beading room. "You're late, Jory! I expected you an hour ago."

Feeling like dirt, I started in on an apology, but she leaned down to whisper, "Thanks to you, several of the ladies have stuck around to buy beads." Helen took the boxes from me and hurried into the kitchen. I heard her call to Gideon to help me.

I went back outside and leaned into the van on my tippy-toes, reaching for a cake that had slid to the back of the shelf when I'd peeled out of the accountant's parking lot.

"I'll get it." Gideon reached around me. "Hand me a couple more."

"No, that's okay. I've got it."

"Fine by me." Gideon turned around and walked back into the café. What a weirdo: he wore holey socks on his feet in ninety-degree heat. He held the door open for me as I followed him inside, but he didn't say anything. He probably couldn't help his good manners.

Helen took the cakes out of the boxes and started slicing them up and then putting them on brightly painted pottery plates. "We just opened for lunch this week, and business is booming. Gideon did this whole e-mail campaign for me and, boy, did it work." She kissed his cheek. "My brilliant son!"

Gideon shook his hair and shuffled his feet. "Well, I better—"

His hairy big toe stuck out from his sock.

"You better offer Jory a sample of my pasta salad," Helen said. "Have you had your lunch break yet?"

"Oh, I don't know—" I peeked at Gideon to see his reaction, but he ignored me.

"I'll call Katie and cover for you. Stay a bit, have a bite." Helen handed me a bowl. "Go sit outside in the shade." Helen shooed us away with her hand, and Gideon picked up a plate with a slice of chocolate cake, rolled his eyes, and motioned for me to follow.

Helen had transformed the courtyard into a fairy garden. Lanterns hung in the trees; a whole wall of roses scented the air; and fairies seemed to be everywhere, sitting on branches, hiding behind bushes, perched on the tables. Cooling mist sprayed over several little umbrella-covered tables. A group of older ladies drank iced tea.

"I don't know why she thinks shade is cooler than the air conditioning inside," Gideon said.

I shrugged and stabbed a noodle with my fork. Everything around me looked so cheerful and happy, which made me feel worse about sitting next to a guy who tolerated me only because he wanted to please his mother. Total weirdo, right?

I tried not to touch his legs as we sat on a wrought-iron bench painted with wispy silver clouds. I watched the little waterfall that tumbled into a small pool with goldfish swimming in it. Gideon ate big forkfuls of cake while I nibbled on the pasta salad, trying to avoid getting dressing on my chin; I still managed to drop a greasy artichoke heart on my pants.

"I'll grab you a napkin," Gideon said. "Want something to drink?"

"Okay, I guess." I hadn't realized how hungry I'd been. Mom had been on the Raw Food Diet since feeling totally intimidated by Lindsey Dickenson's high-cut swimsuit. Plus, Mom swore she'd eaten a month's worth of calories on the Fourth. *Drank* would be more like it.

I hadn't eaten anything but fruits and vegetables for two days. Finn spent most of his allowance eating out; while I totally envied him, I'd stuck with whatever Mom served so I could save my nose-fund money. Gideon walked back out, carrying two glasses of iced tea and a few napkins.

I wiped my chin and, when Gideon wasn't looking, tried to wipe away any shine on my nose too.

"I liked the music you played the other night." The rush of carbs in my system made me feel strangely energetic and brave. "Violin sounds so good with, you know, rock music."

"Didn't think you'd noticed." He scraped frosting off his fork with his teeth. "You seemed a little busy."

I sighed. "That wasn't—"

"Whatever." Gideon flipped his hand back. "None of my business."

"Yeah, whatever." I balanced my bowl on my lap. My throat felt tight, so I took a drink of ice tea and had a big coughing fit. Tears dripped down my cheeks. The bowl wobbled on my lap. I watched the ladies who'd been having tea get up and go inside, leaving us alone.

Gideon put his hand on my back. "You okay?"

"I'm fine." I stared down at my chipped toenail polish and Gideon's holey socks. *Suck it up, Jory.*

"Trying to catch another glimpse of my toxic toenails?"

"No!" I whipped my head up and looked at him—for a second. *God, he's got long eyelashes.* "I didn't mean anything by that, I was just upset about, whatever, but I didn't want—And I noticed your toenails, like, glowing—" I scrunched my nose in spite of myself. "So, I just said something without thinking, and I'm sorry. Okay?" I regretted the sharp edge to my voice.

"All that laughing sure didn't do much for my confidence. Here I was freaked out about playing with the band for the first time, so when the crowd got into the song, I felt pretty good, and I got my courage up to come talk to you, even after you were all cozy with your man and all."

"Ass Grabber is *not* my man!" I jumped up and the bowl

fell from my lap, shattering on the patio. "Oh, God. I'm sorry." I knelt down and started to pick up the pieces. A few tears dripped onto the back of my hand.

"You'll cut yourself." Gideon took the shards of pottery from me like I was a little kid. "Let me get a broom."

As I sat on the ground with my head in my hands, my mood darkened like Mississippi mud cake. Why couldn't anything go right for me? I looked up at a wire fairy floating on a tree branch. Maybe an evil fairy had cursed me at birth as I lay in my crib, putting an ugly spell on me to ensure that I would never find my Prince Charming. I'd die alone in a motel room. The world's oldest virgin.

Gideon came back, swept up the pottery, and tossed it into the dumpster in the alley. I kept my head down and tried to think happy thoughts. Nothing. *Nada.* Zip.

Gideon sat next to me. "Guess I misunderstood. Want to talk about it?" He bumped my knee with his. "Come on. Helen always says you've got to talk it out or it'll eat you up."

What kind of weird guy wants to talk about problems and stuff? I wasn't about to spill my guts to some guy with glowing toenails and a big nose, even if he did have eyelashes to die for and amazingly dark hair. And great eyes. Great eyes that looked right at me. He kind of tilted his head, like, *Well, are you going to say something?*

"There's nothing to talk about, really." I looked straight ahead at a plump ceramic fairy with a mischievous grin sitting under a flowery shrub. She was the one who'd cursed me!

"Come on." Gideon's voice sounded soft.

"Some drunk guy came on to me. I'm supposed to be flattered, I guess?"

Hannah had tried to help me find the "positives in the situation," like she used to do for herself when people called her Hunchback Hannah in middle school. But getting attacked by a drunk guy at a party wasn't the same as having a medical condition. And it definitely wasn't flattering.

"He had you up against that wall," Gideon said. "It looked like—"

"Well, it wasn't."

"No, I know that now. I mean—he looked incredibly aggressive. That's reprehensible." Gideon shook his head. "Why are men such assholes?" He patted my knee. "Come on, you need a slice of cake."

"Oh, no. I can't. After working there, you know."

"Oh, yeah. That's why I don't wear many necklaces."

I smiled. "You're kind of funny."

"And you have beautiful hazel eyes."

"Thanks," I mumbled.

"Quit looking at my feet all the time." Gideon stepped one

foot over the other as he had the other night. "You're giving me a complex."

"Sorry." I looked up at his hair falling over one eye like a thundercloud. "You make me kind of nervous." *Oh, God. Why did I say that?* I looked down.

"I make *you* nervous." He laughed. "You're the one that's got me wearing socks when it's ninety-five degrees outside. I've even thought of inventing some kind of reverse toe sock. Everything would be open, except the toes. I'd market it to podiatrists and the foot-fungus-pharmaceuticals companies."

I kind of smiled, not sure if he was serious or joking.

"Okay, I guess I should shut up before I totally creep you out."

"Maybe." I risked looking into his eyes. Quick. He stared right at me. "I better get back to work." I glanced at my watch. "I've already got one lady threatening to call my boss."

"See you around." He pushed his toes into the ground. "Stop looking at my feet."

"Sorry. Again. Well, bye." I turned and ran through the kitchen, past all the ladies beading in the classroom, and out the front door.

As I pulled the van back into the street, I laughed hard for the first time in days.

Chapter Fifteen

POUTING AND PICNICS

The following Saturday, Hannah dragged me and Megan all the way out to Bower's Mansion Park so we could "refresh our friendship." Sounded more like a deodorant ad—and I still thought Megan stunk! We both refused until she e-mailed us a top-ten list of our Best Friendship Moments (so far!):

10. Our first slumber-not party

9. The Red Vines vs. Twizzlers survey

8. Popularity ploys (especially horrible-yet-hilarious cheerleading tryouts)

7. Sloppy slippy sledding (remember the sweater dudes?)

6. Worst first-day-of-school-outfit fashion show ("paging store security")

5. Rodeo Carnival roller coasters (spinning with fries!)

4. Operation Secret Locker Decorating

3. November 1 (you know the details!)

2. 3 A.M. breakfast at the Peppermill (the time ZZ was there!)

1. TBA—something from *this* summer!

After a long phone conversation about the "freeing feeling of forgiveness," I agreed to come along, but only because Hannah sounded so sad and pathetic, begging and everything.

"What do you guys think?" Hannah surveyed the picnic tables at the park. "I like the spirit this spot has. Plus, we'll have a view of the valley, plenty of sun, and it looks like we're near three family reunions and a couple of company picnics with good-looking guys close to our age."

I watched some guys tossing a Frisbee with a group of kids. They looked like dads.

"Whatever." Megan threw her towel in front of her and lay down, sticking her face into some definitely-not-a-beach-read novel. Typical Megan: always showing off.

"It's nice." I pulled on my frilly brimmed hat. No more nose freckles! After a week of nose peeling after the Fourth, I'd almost smeared that sticky white stuff all over my nose, except someone might've been tempted to mogul ski down it.

"Why don't you lay out by Megan?" Hannah asked.

I rummaged around in my tote bag for my magazines. With more than $1,400 in my bank account, I had to get serious about the new-nose search. Plus, Mom had asked me why I hadn't been spending any money on myself, so I showed her a few magazines and talked about looking for new fall looks (so what if she thought *fashion* while I thought *nose*).

"This is good," I said. "We can both talk to you."

"And not each other," Hannah mumbled. "Come on, guys. Let's stop this feud thingy." She held up her too-cute picnic basket. "We're on a summer picnic, making memories and stuff."

Megan sat up. "Maybe you need to convince Jory that I didn't steal the boyfriend she never had in the first place. Maybe you can explain that he's not exactly going out with me either. Three movies, one dinner, a walk around Virginia Lake, and a disastrous Fourth of July apparently doesn't make a boyfriend."

"You walked around Virginia Lake with him? You never told me that!"

"Because it didn't matter. Since when does feeding the ducks leftover popcorn equal a hot-and-heavy romance?" Megan stared at me through her dark sunglasses. Unnerving.

I glanced away and watched some kid cry over a dropped hot dog. *Just wait, kid,* I thought. *Life gets much worse.*

"This is so good." Hannah scooted back on her towel and wrapped her hands around her bent legs, nodding at us like some bikini-clad therapist. "At least you're talking."

Lately I'd been wishing that Hannah spent more time reading romance novels instead of all that self-improvement Zen stuff, because then she'd understand the severity of Megan's traitorous crimes.

"You guys seemed plenty chummy up at the lake." I narrowed my eyes at Megan's Darth Vader stare. "I heard him trying to get all cozy with you that night. All whispering and stuff."

"FYI, Jory, he was *not* whispering with me." Megan's voice wavered with tears.

"Was he trying to hook up with Kayla? Omigod, is that why he carried her off to the fireworks?"

"You want to know why he ran off with Kayla?" Megan's lip trembled slightly.

"Because she's as darling as teddy bears, cupcakes, and ladybugs put together? And she's got more moves than a porn star?"

"I really don't want to talk about this." Megan ran her hand through her glossy dark hair. "I kissed him. Okay—" She surrendered, her hands in the air. "Go ahead and scream at me."

"I'd expect nothing less from a traitor." No way would I scream *now*—that's what she expected. I bit my cheek hard instead.

"Jory, they *have* been hanging out and doing things together since school got out." Hannah put her hand on my shoulder. "They *do* work together."

"But I've liked him for over a year and we've had some moments. Actual moments. And I was trying to build on them." I shrugged her hand off me. "I'm not over at your church all of the time trying to get cozy with Alex. There are boundaries with friends' crushes, right?" I pulled my hat down tight around my ears until it hurt.

"You don't even go to my church." Hannah did that cute, scrunchy I-don't-understand thing with her nose. "You've never even met Alex."

Sometimes Hannah could be as dense as pound cake.

"That's not the point. The point is boundaries."

"You're not even listening to me," Megan said. "Forget it." She stuck her classically beautiful nose back into her book but wasn't turning any pages. I made a big show of flipping through my magazine. My eye caught a "Friend or Frenemy" article. Didn't need to read that one! I slapped the magazine shut. My head felt itchy and sweaty under my stupid hat.

"Come on," Hannah said. "We want to listen to you, Megan. Right, Jory?"

"Oh, God, Hannah." I ripped my hat off my head and flung it down by my feet.

Hannah gave me her don't-use-God's-name-in-vain-with-mine look.

"Okay, so I'm listening."

"Well, the issue is . . ." Megan's voice trembled. "He freaked out when I kissed him. He actually ran away, scooping that ridiculous sophomore into his arms, then sitting next to Drew at the fireworks. Ignoring me completely." Megan wiped underneath her dark glasses. "Talk about humiliation."

"So that's why you were so pissed," I said. "But later he tried to make up with you, so what's the big deal?"

"No, Jory. You're not hearing me. Later he climbed up onto the *top* bunk and tried to convince *Drew* to take a walk. To the *rocks*."

I sucked in my breath and clapped my hand over my mouth.

"That's weird," Hannah said. "But maybe he just wanted to talk. Get the male perspective."

"Han, I love ya, but hello?" Megan twisted her hair around and around her finger. "Drew isn't exactly the go-to guy about girl trouble. I should've been the one climbing into bed with Drew, asking him about boy trouble, if you know what I mean."

"Drew is—?" Hannah's brown eyes grew large. "Oh, my gosh!"

"Came out after graduation." I remembered Finn telling Mom. Drew had told the soccer team that he wanted to start the next phase of his life honestly.

"But he dated Claire for three years," Hannah said.

Megan picked at a loose thread on her shorts. "And apparently nothing ever happened."

"So?" A feeling of dread pushed through my body. "Does that really mean—"

"Think about it," Megan said. "Has Tyler ever had a serious girlfriend? Or even any serious rumors?"

I thought about his McQueen prom date, but didn't say anything.

"But he went home with that sleazy what's-her-name at the bonfire." Hannah bit her lip. "Everyone knows that she'll, you know, do whatever, with anyone."

"Maybe, but—" Megan looked over at the playground.

"What did he say at work?" I asked.

Megan pressed her fingers to her temples. "I don't know. I've called in sick three days in a row."

"That's *so* not like you." Hannah shot me a worried look.

"I know, but I didn't want to—couldn't—see him quite yet." Megan's voice sounded shaky again. "He tried to call me. Twice. I felt so stupid. Why couldn't he have simply told me so I didn't go and make a fool out of myself? And sorry, Jory, but I *did* like him. A lot. And I *did* think we were sort of going out."

All kinds of emotion flooded me: fear, anger, sadness, shock.

"I'm going to go for a swim." I jumped up and ran across the grass and through the gates to the pool, leaving my towel and everything behind. I dove into the deep end and sank to the bottom. I sat on the bottom screaming until I needed to breathe. I pushed up to the surface, choking on pool water, and swam hard, lap after lap. I heard the lifeguard ask if I was okay, but I just kept swimming and he left me alone. When my arms got so tired that I couldn't push them through the water any longer, I sank again and allowed myself to drift up into a dead-man's float. Finally, my mind felt empty. I rolled over and stared at the clear blue sky. What would it feel like to stand up there on the tiptop of Mount Rose and reach out to the sky? I breathed in the scent of chlorine, roasting hot dogs, and the teensy hint of pine trees as a breeze rippled the water around me. Maybe I'd take up hiking. I could become Solitary Nature Woman, writing poems about baby birds in spring and the death of leaves in autumn. When I turned forty, I could drink myself to death with my own homemade bootleg whiskey. Bears would eat my corpse. I stood up in the water and wrung out my hair.

"You swim fast, lady," a little kid said to me. "And you float good." His Popsicle dripped into the pool.

"Thanks." I smiled. "Keep practicing and you'll get fast too."

I shivered a bit in the breeze that swept down from the mountains as I walked back to our towels in the picnic area. Megan and Hannah sat on the swings in the playground and twisted. *Let Hannah play psychologist,* I thought as I lay down on my towel, enjoying the warmth of the sun soaking into my skin. All that swimming had made me hungry so I peeked into Hannah's picnic basket. The brownies were gone, which left carrot and celery sticks and peanut butter sandwiches. No, thanks.

I fished my wallet out of my tote, wrapped a sarong around my waist, tied my hair up in a big wet knot, and went searching for a vending machine or snack stand, anything but raw veggies or peanut butter.

"Jory!" Someone called my name as I walked past one of the pavilions. I turned around and saw Wooster Tom jogging toward me. He wore a light green IGT shirt and sported even more freckles than he'd had the last time I saw him.

"What are you doing here?" My voice sounded as sharp as one of Katie's pastry knives.

"Uh, sorry." He took a step backward. "My dad's company picnic."

"No, no. You surprised me. That's all." I tried to sound perky. "So, how are you doing?" I untwisted my hair and let it flap onto my bare back, all cold and wet. I shivered.

"The breeze is kind of cold, huh? Want to borrow a towel?"

"I've got one." Oh, God. Why was I so flirting challenged?

"Yeah, okay." He scooted back another step.

"I'm sorry." I wrapped my arms around my chest, feeling totally self-conscious in my swimsuit. "I'm just so starving and all my friends brought were peanut butter and raw foods and brownies, but they ate all the brownies while I was swimming and I don't think I'll ever eat peanut butter again—"

He smiled. "So let me guess. Your mom's wacky diets have made you hate everything but burgers and chips and maybe ice cream sundaes."

"Pretty much. How did you—?"

"You were a little bitter about peanut butter back when I met you at the carnival."

"Oh, yeah, right. Guess I've starved too many brain cells." I shivered as another gust of air blew through the valley. "It's July. Why is it so cold?"

"Wear this." Tom pulled off his shirt. "I'm not wet."

"I can't take your shirt." I tried not to stare at the curly blond hairs fluffing all around his big built-with-hours-of-free-weights muscles. I slipped the musky boy-smelling shirt over my head. The pit area was a tad damp, but when had a boy ever loaned me his shirt?

"Trust me. You're doing me a favor," Tom said. "It looks much better on you—brings out your eyes." Tom kind of flexed his muscles in a showing-off way. Again, I tried not to totally stare.

"Thanks, I guess." *Come on, Jory. Try to channel Kayla Neal, Hannah, anyone.* "I mean, thanks a whole bunch."

"Come on. We've got more burgers than all those skinny company wives will eat."

"Won't they know that I don't, you know, belong?" I glanced over at Hannah and Megan, deep in some conversation about the stupid Tyler issue.

"Naw, you're wearing the official shirt."

"I am starving." I followed Tom into the pavilion. A bunch of kids chased one another around, sticking their wet hands into various bags of chips. Thankfully, Tom opened a new bag and piled my plate with chips, a cheeseburger, and three brownies.

Tom nodded at me with approval. "Bet you're hungry after all that swimming."

"You saw me?" Hadn't I looked like a complete idiot? Did he see me screaming on the bottom of the pool like a mental patient? I glanced away to a group of dads by the barbecue, their beer bellies hanging out. The giant bald guy had to be Tom's dad.

"Yeah, I tried calling to you, but you were so focused," Tom said. "My coach would be impressed. You never told me you were a swimmer."

"I'm not. I was just, you know, upset." I twisted my wet hair into a knot again.

"Boy problems? I saw you leaving the movies with some guy and not looking too happy. That dandy giving you trouble? Is he here? I'll beat him up." He smacked his fist into his open palm.

I laughed, even though the thought of Tom hitting Tyler made a nervous shiver shoot through my stomach.

"What are you doing, spying on me?" I licked ketchup and mustard that had dripped down my chin. Great. I follow a half-decent comment with a disgusting tongue maneuver.

"You're the one stalking *me*. First the movies, now my dad's company picnic. I'm going to have to get a restraining order."

I giggled, sounding stupid to myself, but I noticed a couple of girls staring at us and whispering and that made me feel kind of good. But I couldn't help wondering if Tom had experience with restraining orders. Though·maybe he could help me out with Gold Dust West Stalker Guy.

"More like *friend* problems. My friend Hannah, the one from the carnival, dragged me and my other friend Megan out here to get us to start talking to each other again." I shook my head back and forth and rolled my eyes, hoping to look alluring, not demented.

"She trying to steal your boyfriend or something?"

"God, you're nosy!" I clapped my hand over my mouth. Oh, no. I used the *N* word. Jory Rule #1: Never draw attention to your nose in any manner, especially when talking to a guy who actually *has* six-pack abs, even if they are covered with curly blond hairs and freckles, which makes him look a little bit like a hairy slice of chocolate chip cake.

"What's wrong? You don't want to talk about it?"

I took another bite of my burger and shook my head while

I chewed. I'm sure I looked fabulous—like the cows in the pastures near Washoe Lake.

When my mouth was empty, I finally said, "It's a long story. Long and—"

"Jory! There you are. Tom! What are you doing here?" Hannah's eyes popped, but she quickly moved into adorable mode. "You've got to tell José that I'm still waiting for him to answer my text message. It's been, like, three whole days."

Hannah was still texting José? I had no idea. Tom mumbled something about José camping with his family but he'd be sure to tell him. He told Hannah that José talked about her all the time; the two girls who had whispered about me shot daggers at Hannah.

I munched handfuls of chips while Hannah engaged in the kind of darling banter I could never manage when talking to an actual human being. Finally, as I finished my first brownie, Hannah said, "Jory, we've got to go. Megan—" She bobbed her head and nodded toward the car. "I've got all your stuff packed up."

"I could give you a ride home," Tom said to me.

I hesitated for a moment. Maybe this was my chance. I imagined Tom pulling into my driveway; we'd sit in his car for an hour as I amazed him with my clever conversation; he'd take me in his arms and—Okay, maybe not. In reality,

I'd spend the whole drive trying to think of something to say besides "nice car" and "nice weather," plus Hannah would be mad at me for letting Megan down; my hair would dry in some crazy formation like meringue gone wild; and I wouldn't get any more details about Tyler. Not that I cared. That much. Really.

"No, thanks. I better go." As I followed Hannah back to Bugsy, I turned and waved goodbye to Tom, wishing I'd said something better, something that made me sound a little bit interested. I should have at least given him my phone number. I could've written it in mustard on a paper plate—or in sunscreen on his impressive muscles.

When we got to the parking lot, Megan sat in the back seat. *Hannah gets to drive Bugsy? Things must be bad.* It wasn't until we were passing Meadowood Mall that I realized I was still wearing Tom's shirt.

Chapter Sixteen

MARGARITA MADNESS

I pulled into the Mexican restaurant's parking lot in a bad mood, especially for a Wednesday. No Gideon. No luscious lips. No long lashes. No wild black curly hair. No toxic toenails. Helen had helped me carry the cakes into the kitchen, making small talk. A couple of older ladies whispered about me. I'd wanted to ask about him, but I didn't want to appear interested/desperate/stalkerish. After all, he pretty much thought I was a big-nosed freak who obsessed about feet.

Finally, after coming back into the kitchen for the third time, Helen said, "Gideon's studying music at Stanford for the next two weeks." She smiled. "I could tell by the way you kept looking back toward his room that you wanted to know."

Was I totally staring at his door? *Oh, God, Jory, get a grip. Why do I even like him? He's a total goofball who plays the violin. Dorky, right? And he's not all that good-looking because of the nose thing. We could never breed. Plus, he's some kind of delinquent because he got kicked out of school.* Hopefully, Megan would talk some sense into me over lunch. Though I had a feeling it would be all Tyler this and Tyler that. Hannah had been talking with Megan all week and bugging me a thousand times a day to talk to her myself. So here I was at the Mexican place. Ready to talk. Actually, I felt kind of relieved that Tyler didn't like me because he didn't like girls. That meant it wasn't a looks thing.

I didn't see Bugsy parked outside, but I went in to get a table anyway. Megan waved me over from a booth by the windows where she was sitting with two older guys in suits, all of them sharing a jumbo margarita with four straws. One of the guys scooted over and made room for me as Megan gushed, "Guys, this is my bestest friend Jory. Jory, these are the smartest law clerks ever. Tony and Michael. So finish your story, Tony." She looked up at him, practically batting her eyelashes.

I tried to catch Megan's eye, but she stared at Tony while sipping through her straw and nodding as if his legal mumbo jumbo were actually interesting.

I sat there feeling young and stupid with my childishly braided hair, Minnie Mouse T-shirt, and jeans. Then again, Megan acted a little *too* mature. What was she thinking?

"Isn't that amazing?" Megan asked. "Tony's working on

the big fraud case with—" Megan clapped her hands over her mouth. "I better not say too much."

"Don't worry. I don't understand any of it." I looked at my menu but couldn't focus on the words. The Michael guy jiggled his leg up and down next to me. Was this whole thing creeping him out too?

"I don't understand it either." Megan laughed and pushed the margarita over to me.

"No, thanks," I said. "I have enough trouble driving that floral atrocity of a van without any additional impairment." So now Megan was drinking not just after work but during her lunch break? "And we're only seventeen. It's kind of illegal, you know." I hated acting like a bitch, but she pissed me off. I had come prepared to talk, console, be a good friend. Not deal with uncharacteristically drunk Megan.

"Oh, come on, Jory. That's never stopped you before." Megan made a loud sucking sound with her straw, like a little kid getting every last bit of a milk shake. "It's yummy."

The waitress came, put down some chips, and took our orders. Tony ordered another jumbo margarita, but Michael ordered a Coke, and I asked for an ice water.

"So why didn't Tyler come to lunch with you?" I asked.

"Tyler's back kissing butt at the office." Megan broke into guffaws. "Get it, Jory?"

Megan ignored my dirty look, so I turned to Michael. "So you're in law school?"

"Yeah, I go to UCSF, and Tony's over at Hastings."

"So—" I crunched on a chip. "You must have to study a lot."

Tony reached around Megan's back to grab a chip, but she leaned forward and bit it out of his hand. He laughed and kept his arm around her. Michael jiggled his leg faster.

"I want to do real lawyer stuff and not all these copies, copies, copies." Megan pouted.

"You can help me with some of my cases," Tony said. "You're a smart cookie." He squeezed her shoulder.

When the waitress brought the second margarita, Megan flapped her straw in her mouth and aimed it toward the glass, missing twice.

"Maybe you'd better wait until you eat some more." I pushed the basket of chips toward her. "Try the guacamole."

Megan shook her hair into her face. "Nooo. I'm watching my figure." Since when did Megan turn down junk food?

I didn't exactly want to launch into the alcohol-has-so-many-empty-calories speech Mom had been mumbling for a week now. At least the Raw Food Diet had morphed into fruit for breakfast, veggies for lunch, and carbohydrates for dinner.

I could deal with spaghetti. Still, I looked forward to my carne asada burrito with extra sour cream.

"So, I kind of thought the whole two-martini-lunch thing was only in the movies—old cinema club–type movies." I looked at Michael, who glanced back at me.

"Should be," he mumbled.

"We're not drinking martinis. Gross! These are totally harmless." Megan sipped for several seconds, looking right at me, mascara smudged under her right eye.

"We thought we'd go by my condo after lunch before heading back to the office." Tony winked at Megan.

I glanced at my watch. I had another fifty minutes before Katie expected me back for the afternoon flower deliveries. "How long do you get for lunch?"

"We're taking an executive lunch." Tony sipped some of the margarita. "When the cat's away, the mice will play."

"Our boss is out of town." Michael filled me in, crunching on a piece of ice. "But I know that he still expects those cases to be researched when he gets back." More leg jiggles.

Tony ignored Michael while he and Megan had a sword fight with their straws, only calling a truce as the waitress set the food on the table. When my napkin dropped on the floor, I bent down and saw Tony play footsies with Megan. How old was he anyway? Twenty-two? Twenty-three? Older? He had a mustache. Ick!

Megan toyed with her food while Michael and Tony talked about different cases that could support a libel suit Michael had to write about for the *Law Review*. I silently devoured my burrito, wishing I could enjoy it more.

After Tony paid for lunch, Michael said he had to head back to the office.

"Watch out for your friend," he whispered to me as he held open the restaurant door.

I nodded. "Meg, maybe you should get back to work too," I said, trying to sound sensible. Actually, I tried to sound like *Megan!*

Ignored.

Megan tugged on Tony's arm. "Come on, I want to see where you live."

"We may even have time for a dip in the pool," said Tony, grabbing Megan's hand as she stumbled off the curb in the parking lot.

I looked at my watch. In twenty minutes Katie would be lining up flower arrangements and delivery directions by the back door. It took ten minutes to drive to Katie's shop from here.

Tony steered Megan toward a light blue Prius. "You can follow us."

I attempted a flirtatious hair flip, not very effective with braids. "Oh, can Megan please ride with me? I've got something to ask her. Just a few minutes of girl talk?"

"Jory, Jory, Jory," Megan said calmly. "Aren't you over Tyler yet? I'm sooo over him."

I hustled Megan to the front seat of the van, pushing her inside. "Meg, isn't this guy a little too old?"

Megan leaned across my lap and blew a kiss to Tony as he pulled in front of us. I grimaced as alcohol-and-bean breath wafted into my nose. I followed Tony's Prius down the street, feeling like an accessory to a crime.

"I'm so through with high school boys. Tyler can have them all. I'm sticking with men. Mature men."

If I'd said the same thing in this situation, nondrunk Megan would never have let me get away with it. How mature was it for a guy to get an underage girl drunk at lunch and take her to his condo? Sounds more like a recipe for date rape. Blah, blah, blah.

Instead, Megan said, "Do you think he means skinny-dipping?" Major giggles. "'Cause I didn't bring a bathing suit to work."

"Maybe I should take you back to work." I watched Tony's brake lights flash as he slowed around Virginia Lake. "Or you could call in sick. That would probably be best."

"I called in sick all last week." Megan pulled her hair over her face. "Plus, they saw me today so they won't believe me."

"Tell them your mom is sick."

"What, and my dog ate my homework too?" Megan brushed all her hair back. "We're going to Tony's. I'll sober up in the pool."

❧

Tony pulled into the condo parking lot, and Megan jumped out of the van before I'd even stopped all the way.

"Let's swim!" She yanked her blouse up, exposing her stomach.

Tony pushed her shirt down. "Not here. I've got a suit you can borrow inside."

I glanced at my watch. If I left right now, I could get back to Katie's with a few minutes to spare. Megan followed Tony into his condo, where he gave us the official tour: faux leather sofa, recliner, basic TV setup, clean kitchen, small glass-top table with four chairs, unmade bed, socks and underwear on the floor. Box of condoms on the bedside table!

"You can change in my room." Tony handed Megan a bikini and headed into the bathroom to change into his suit. "I wish I had another—"

"That's okay, I'm not much of a swimmer." My gaze caught

the clock on Tony's microwave. Ten minutes. Should I call? *Sorry, Katie, but I took an executive lunch with a couple of promising lawyers. Sorry, Katie, just had to take a swim break after an hour-long lunch. Sorry, Katie, but I've got to make sure my drunk friend doesn't get date-raped by her coworker.*

Why didn't Reno have more traffic? I should just leave. Megan deserved everything coming her way, right? But I thought about the frat party and how Hannah had appeared like an angel down in that smelly basement.

Megan came bouncing out of the bedroom, twirling around in the skimpy bikini. What kind of creep keeps a spare swimsuit handy? And who'd worn it before Megan? And what kinds of diseases did she have?

"What do you think?" Megan's long hair fanned across her back.

"Fits like a glove." Tony looked her up and down. "Just your size. Amazing."

"I'll be right out." My voice cracked. "I've got to make a call."

My stomach tightened into knots as I watched Tony and Megan jump into the pool, holding hands. Megan bounced back up, laughing and adjusting her skimpy top. Tony didn't take his eyes off her, or his hands.

I had no choice. I dialed Katie's number, even though part

of me considered dialing 911, or Megan's mom, or even *my* mom.

"Hello, Katie? I am so sorry, but there's a horrible accident blocking traffic. I'm stuck right behind it so I'm going to be a little late."

I felt my nose growing with every word.

Chapter Seventeen

CHEERS AND CHEETOS

I lay on my bed, paging through my July magazines for noses to put in my Nice Nose Notebook. I carefully cut around a brunette model's artfully blown hair, then pasted her into the notebook with a glue stick. Mom and Dad argued in the kitchen, probably about the Raw Food (With Pasta) Diet (day 11). Mom's knife slammed against the cutting board as she diced vegetables.

I turned my music down to listen: same old stuff. *Well, if you'd get that promotion, we could move up to one of those houses on Grubstake, Buckaroo, or Cutting Horse. Look, if I don't get that promotion, we may not be able to stay in this house. We moved too soon. Again, I bowed to your pressure so you could belong to the right book club. Speaking of clubs, you had no right to spend all that money on golf last month. That's business. Well, so is the book club. When those ladies tire of redecorating their houses,*

who do you think will finance their next mortgage? My social con-
nections are every bit as important as yours. Dad said something
really low. Mom stormed off into her bedroom. Dad slammed
the door to the garage. The lawn mower started up.

I cranked up the Yeah Yeah Yeahs louder than necessary
and cut the numbers *1, 8, 4,* and another *8* out of the magazine. The amount of money I'd saved for my new nose. The
tiny numbers stuck to my fingers as I tried to glue them near
a particularly cute girl with freckles. I figured my new nose
would be stuck with freckles, unless I could travel to Europe
for some special skin treatment. I imagined myself as Perky
Freckle-Nosed Model: I'd live in a cute townhouse somewhere
with a golden retriever that I'd walk through the town square
with my rugged outdoorsy boyfriend. We'd go hiking in the
mountains, and I'd have a whole wardrobe of soft sweaters.
What would my plaid-shirt-wearing guy look like? I flipped
right past a guy whose hair looked like Tyler's. Maybe someone with dark hair . . .

Mom flung her bedroom door open and yelled, "I'm going
to Port of Subs to get sandwiches to bring to the game. Who
wants one?"

Finn and I banged into each other in the hallway.

"How pathetic is this, huh?" Finn covered the phone receiver with his hand. "I'm so desperate for real food."

Finn and I both ordered Italian combo sandwiches and chips.

"So who's on the phone?"

"Who else?" He grinned. Kayla Neal's ditzy duplicate: Emily Wellington. "Sorry, babe. Hey, let me call you back. Buh-bye."

"How long have you been on the phone?" I asked. "Did you ignore any call-waitings?"

"Who calls you, Jor? Megan's pissed at you and Hannah doesn't really use the phone much because she likes to be present in the moment." Finn imitated Hannah's little nose-scrunch thing.

"Shouldn't you be in your room grunting and talking to yourself in the mirror to psych yourself up for your little game?"

Finn grunted and made a weird face. He still looked good. Genetic freak!

Back in my room, my stomach grumbled just because I was *imagining* sub sandwiches. Fresh-baked bread. Actual meat. Crunchy deep-fried Cheetos. I clipped out a photo of a hamburger and glued it next to a skinny model with a beautiful face but an even better evening gown.

"My elegant nose and I love to eat hamburgers," I said in a dramatic voice.

"What are you doing?" Megan stood in my doorway.

I flipped my notebook closed and shoved it under my

pillow. "Nothing. How did you get in here?" I sat on my pillow. *Please don't ask me about the notebook.* "What's up?"

Megan's eyes looked puffy and red.

"Fired." Megan put a wadded-up tissue to her nose and blew. "They fired me."

"Because of—Well, it was kind of stupid, right? To, you know, drink like that?" I sort of enjoyed watching her fall apart. Even her perfect hair looked messy as she ran her fingers through it again and again. Plus, she'd apparently forgotten that *I* nearly got fired for staying with her for over an hour, intervening every time Lusty Lawyer got extra friendly. I had to fake a majorly embarrassing case of menstrual cramps to get her out of his condo. And then when I'd tried to take her dripping-wet, drunk self home, she'd insisted on returning to the office. I called and called Hannah, but she never answered her cell. "You should've listened to me, maybe."

"I know." Megan flopped down on the end of my bed and sobbed into her arms. "I've completely screwed up. Now I'll never be a lawyer. They'll never give me a recommendation; they'll probably make sure that everyone knows I'm a total alcoholic screwup."

"What about what's-his-name?"

"Warning. He only got a warning."

"But he's an adult. Shouldn't he be responsible for, you know, corrupting a minor or something?" *At least* both *of them should get in trouble,* I thought.

"It's not like he forced me to drink, Jory." Megan slid off the mattress and sat with her back against my bed. "I knew exactly what I was doing. The thing is, I simply didn't care."

"I know. But he still ordered the drinks, right? And you *are* under age."

"Yeah, but I'm not a top student from the UCSF law school. Now I never will be." Tears poured down her face. "I'm going to end up living alone in a hotel room teaching piano and drinking too much whiskey every night, like that wretched Judith what's-her-face."

I moved next to Megan. "Oh, my God, Meg. That's totally my fear too."

"Really?" I watched a tear drip around her lip as she smiled. "God, that movie sucked. All during the movie I wanted Tyler to put his arm around me, or put his hand on my knee. I imagined how we would be during a movie and how afterward we would walk to the car, holding hands, and go out for nachos, or maybe walk along the river, talking and laughing about the movie. How stupid was that?"

A jealous twinge tightened my stomach. *Stop, Jory. This is*

191

Megan. Megan who got you through algebra, helped you make ex-
tra-credit español enchiladas from hell, and stood up for you when
Zoe Locke made fun of your bra during gym in ninth grade.

"Not stupid." I took a deep breath. "He's really, you know, good-looking and flirtatious."

"Oh, Jory. And I even almost ruined our friendship. Over a stupid guy! I knew you liked him, but did I care? No! I'm a bad, bad friend." Megan blew her nose. "He's not worth it."

I looked over to my mirror at the picture of Tyler smiling. I'd cut it out of a *Caughlin Rancher* article about his charity work at the animal shelter. Megan jumped up and tore the photo off the wall. A strange sensation relaxed my stomach as I watched Megan act out my *own* feelings.

"How could I not see that you weren't interested in me?" she yelled at the photo. "How stupid am I?"

"Meg. He's a big flirt." I channeled Megan as if I were starring in one of those body-switching movies.

"And it's a big lie. I'm going to tell everyone I know. I'll take an ad out in the paper. I'll spray-paint it on his car. I'll—" She crunched the newspaper clipping in her hand and tossed it on the bed.

I picked it up and smoothed it out. Maybe he'd just been trying to let Megan down easy. Maybe he made up all that stuff and faked it, so that Megan would leave him alone and he could be with me. He had touched my knee. He *had* been flirting with me practically all summer. But I kept seeing the cold expression on his face at the lake. Right after he'd spotted Drew's ski boat.

"Meg, just give it time. He's only one guy, remember? You said something about that at the lake."

"That was before I got fired." Megan took the clipping from me and tore it into little pieces. "You've ruined my life!" Megan wadded each torn piece into a little ball and flicked it off her hand. "You big loser!" *Flick. Flick.*

"Meg. I know you're upset about Tyler and all, but you're the one who decided to get drunk and go to work. Tyler really has nothing to do with the fact that you got fired." Again, I sounded like regular, sane Megan. "You did that to yourself."

"I know. I know. What am I going to do? I needed the recommendation, but I also needed the money. I don't live in a fancy house like you and Hannah. I need a scholarship."

I thought about all the overtime Mom put in at work and the fight she'd just had with Dad about money, but I didn't want to go into all that. "Getting fired doesn't show up on your transcript, you know."

"With my luck it probably will. The attorney will send a note or something to all the Ivy Leagues, UC schools—

everywhere but Truckee Meadows." Megan pouted. "Jory, be honest. Do you think I have alcohol issues?"

"Meg. Until that time before the movie, I'd never even seen you drink."

"Maybe it's like meth. You can get hooked the first time!" Megan's mouth twisted into a frown. "I'm just so sick of being a high school girl and losing the popularity game. I wanted to have a couple of drinks like a mature adult."

"I don't think it's working."

"Oh, God. It's totally not." Megan squeezed her head as if suppressing memories. "You should've seen me standing in front of Barnes with wet hair, getting a lecture that I totally would've given myself if I'd been sober. It was the worst thing ever." Tears fell down her cheeks as she told me the rest of the story—packing up her box of things while Lusty Lawyer ignored her. Refusing Tyler's help. Calling her mom out of a summer school class because she wasn't sober enough to drive. Refusing Tyler's help. Facing her mother's major wrath. Refusing Tyler's phone calls. More motherly wrath.

Megan wiped her eyes on her sleeve. "I'm grounded forever. But my mom really wanted me to apologize to you."

"Thanks," I said, surprised that I actually felt Hannah's silly freedom-of-forgiveness thing.

The door to the garage flung open. "Let's go!" Mom

shouted. Megan and I walked out into the kitchen. Grocery bags hung from Mom's hands. A frosted sugar cookie dangled in her mouth.

"Megan, dear!" she mumbled through a mouthful of cookie. Charming.

Mom's eyes had lit up like she had always secretly wanted Megan for a daughter; she'd probably even accept Megan's alcohol issues because they came with shiny hair and a beautiful classic nose.

Mom popped the rest of the cookie in her mouth and sneaked another one out of the package. "Won't you come to Finn's game with us? I bought subs and plenty of snacks." She put several bags on the counter.

Dad walked in. A look of shock froze on his face.

"Cookie?" Mom asked with her mouth full.

Megan and I sat on the ground next to my parents and their dedicated-and-experienced-soccer-mom-and-dad foldup chairs, umbrella, and cooler. I enjoyed the feeling of the cool grass against the backs of my legs. Megan ate only half a small sandwich, not even touching her Cheetos, while I ate an entire jumbo sub, picking every scrap of limp lettuce off the paper and popping it into my mouth. I also wet my finger and zapped up every little fragment of sour cream and onion potato chip in my bag. Who knew how long the junk food trend would last. Mom devoured her sandwich, plus another three cookies. Dad watched warily, as if some creature were about to erupt from Mom's body like in that old alien movie.

"Way to go, Finn!" Mom yelled as Finn scored a goal.

Megan waved when Finn looked in our direction. "Your brother is so amazing."

"Trust me. He's disgusting." I considered sticking my tongue into my chip bag and licking it clean but caught the gooey look on Megan's face. Did Megan like *Finn?* What did she mean by *amazing?* Soccer? Or looks? "Meg, he prides himself on belching the alphabet. And sometimes he and his buddies hold farting contests."

"All guys do that kind of thing."

"I doubt it." I couldn't imagine Tyler belching and farting in front of everyone. Would Gideon? No way. Too polite. Finn may have looked like an Adonis, but he acted like a barn animal.

"Finn is truly hopeless," I said. "My parents are going to have to send him away to some kind of training program for beastly brothers before any respectable woman will date him."

Megan raised her eyebrows at me and smirked. No one

needed to remind me that plenty of girls—respectable and otherwise—had already dated him.

"Pick someone else," I said.

We spent the rest of the game rating the players on various skills and qualities: Looks Best When He Runs (Mike Johnson); Best Butt Even in Ugly Nylon Shorts (#23 on the opposing team); Most Active Sweat Glands (poor Thomas Mason); Best Legs (#16); Loudest Grunter (#15); Nicest Smile (Ian Allen); Best Nose ("That's totally weird, Jory." Silent vote for #7); Best Sportsmanship (#5); Best Hair (Luke); Best Overall (Megan insisted it was Finn, but I gave Luke my vote).

After the game, we waited while the coach talked to the players, and Mom and Dad celebrated with the other parents. Luke and Finn kicked the ball back and forth. When they kicked the ball out-of-bounds, I picked it up and tossed it back, aiming right at Finn.

Wham.

The ball hit Luke in the back. *Oh, God. Just kill me now before I die of embarrassment.*

"Hey!" Luke sounded all offended, but he tossed the ball back to me.

"Throw it back to him," Megan whispered. "Now."

I faced Luke, let the ball fly, and watched it wobble through the air and land right in front of Finn.

"So that's the story, is it?" Luke ran up to Finn and stole the ball from him, kicking it so that it landed in front of me. I tried to kick it back but missed.

"Very funny," Luke said. "Kick it right here." He pointed to the ground right in front of him.

I pulled my leg way back. Connection! The ball lofted in the air and sailed right to Luke. *Yes! I'm a soccer goddess—Wham!*

Luke doubled over in pain. I stood there, mouth gaping, face blazing, not sure what to do.

"Oh, my God, Jory." Megan gasped. "You've put him out of commission. Maybe forever!"

What should I do? I can't exactly run over there and comfort the guy, right? Luke moaned and rolled on the ground.

"Nice one, klutz." Finn ran over and patted Luke on the back. "You okay, buddy?"

"I am so sorry!" I called out before running to the car, planning to peel out of the parking lot like a hit man in a mobster movie, forgetting that Mom had the keys. *Omigod. I've maimed the hottest guy at Reno High. Current chances of dying a virgin: 99.9 percent. And that's being charitable.*

Megan caught up with me. "Now *that's* what they mean by a ball breaker."

"Do you think I should apologize to Kayla?"

I meant it seriously, but Megan doubled over laughing. "Dear Kayla, I'm sorry to have ruined all your hopes for senior prom night. But think of all the benefits of castration." Megan laughed harder, making me laugh too.

"I don't think she'll understand *castration*," I said. "How about 'imagine a picnic without balls to play with or a wiener to roast.'"

Megan laughed until she couldn't breathe.

"It's not funny," Finn said in an angry voice as the door to the minivan slid open. "It hurts. Bad."

"Now I've blown it too." Megan held her lips closed for a split second before laughing again. Finn glared at her.

"Judith Hearne, here we come!" I yelled.

"To good old Judith." Megan high-fived me. "A bottle of whiskey is the only man we need."

In the rearview mirror, we saw Mom furrow her brows, but that just made us laugh until we snorted. *Everything is okay between Megan and me!* I felt as light as angel food cake.

Chapter Eighteen

SECRETS

The warm morning air blew through my shirt as I zipped around the speed bumps on Cashill, down Skyline, past the castle house and the golf course onto Arlington. All downhill: piece of cake. Pun intended. I dreaded the ride/walk while pushing my bike uphill at the end of the day in the hot, freckle-producing afternoon sun—pretty soon I'd look like a poppy seed cake. Katie had asked me to come to work early so I could drive out to the distribution place and pick up supplies.

SIX EASY STEPS TO PICKING UP SUPPLIES, JORY STYLE:

1. Park *near* loading-dock area but *not* near gigantic semi trucks. Smile when gum-snapping Warehouse Guy tells you to *back up* to the dock (even though you technically failed this portion of your driver's-license test).

2. Inch. Inch. Pause. Check to see how close you are to semi trucks. Too close.

3. Ignore the truck drivers handing one another money (yes, they *are* making bets).

4. Bump into loading dock. Straighten wheels? Ignore gleam from shiny red semi truck mere millimeters away. Ignore laughing, betting truckers. Do *not* ignore guy yelling, "Your wheels are crooked and that's my rig you're about to scrape up!"

5. Allow frantic trucker to guide you: "Inch a little way that way, no, too far. Go back. Why don't you just let me do it? No! Just a smidge this way. Too far. Listen to me, girl. Stop!"

6. Don't park *anywhere near* gigantic semi trucks. Thank truckers waddling all the way out to van with heavy boxes. Ignore guy counting his money.

❧

When I returned, Katie took one look at the boxes filling the van and muttered that she should have hired a man for my job. She kept asking me questions about why it had taken me so long. I swore that I hadn't gotten lost. Yes (nose growing), everything had gone well.

"It was really busy." I scratched my tingling nose. "I had to wait."

"Okay, okay. We'll manage, but we're kind of behind schedule. I've got to start baking so you're going to have to unload everything yourself."

I stared at the densely packed van. Several boxes had "Duncan Hines" printed in bold red letters. *Katie used a mix? If only all those brides knew!*

Katie rubbed her temples. "Don't just stand there. Get the box cutter, and bring them in one at a time if you have to. Why me?" she muttered on her way back inside.

By noon, sweat poured off the tip of my nose. Any makeup I'd put on that morning had run down my chin. My hair clung to the back of my neck with sweat. As I bunched my damp curls into a ponytail and fanned myself, Tyler's Jeep pulled up to the curb. I straightened my shirt and patted down my hair even as I thought, *Why?*

He pushed his sunglasses up. "Hey, Jory."

"I'm kind of busy." I hefted a bag of powdered sugar and carried it inside.

Tyler was leaning against the van looking down at his black loafers when I got back. He'd loosened his tie; it hung around his neck like a noose.

"I thought maybe I could take you to lunch." He looked up, then down at his feet again. "Maybe we could talk."

"I'm kind of in trouble for being so late today," I said,

glancing back toward the kitchen door. "I'm not sure she's going to give me a lunch break." And what could he possibly want to talk to *me* about anyway? Finn?

"I could help with your deliveries then." He looked at me with those blue eyes. "Like last time?" His voice sounded so shy and quiet.

"Let me go ask." I walked back in to see Katie pouring a box of Duncan Hines cake mix into a bowl. In spite of all the fans running at full speed, the kitchen shimmered with heat.

"Now you know my secret." She flushed. "I add things to improve it."

"Hey, they taste great, right?" I smiled. "And look gorgeous. Can I go to lunch now?"

Katie made me promise to get back by one, no calls about car accidents or backing-up troubles. "Chuck called from the distribution center. Guess you made quite a scene." Katie smiled reproachfully and turned the mixer on low.

"I guess I should've said something right away."

Katie shrugged.

Tyler drove me over to JJ's Pie Company for pizza. We ordered slices and sat in the dark dining room, not really looking at each other. My sweat-soaked shirt felt chilly in the air conditioning, and I'm sure I smelled great too. I lifted my hair up and tied it in a knot while looking around at all the posters hanging on the walls. Zane Zimmerman smiled at me from the Reno High basketball schedule. Maybe I'd have to revisit my ZZ obsession. So what if he was moving to California for college? Maybe I could go to boarding school. Or just skip senior year. My new nose and I could take California by storm. I could model, act, and maybe get my own sitcom. We'd have a fabulous beach house and a pool with waterfalls.

"So, about the lake." Tyler pushed the ice in his Coke around with his straw. "Um."

I looked up at Zane as if he'd whisk me away that very minute to my fabulous California-swimming-pool fantasy.

"Megan told me about—" I took a sip of my Coke and choked. As I coughed, I waited for Tyler to say something. *Anything.*

Tyler stared at me, making me nervous, so I stopped coughing and blabbed on. "We kind of—figured things out."

Even in the dark I could see Tyler blush deep crimson, but he still didn't say anything, so I blurted, "Megan kind of lost it, huh?"

Tyler stared down at the table. "About that."

"I know. It's so unlike her. I mean, if I had to vote for someone to be least likely to get drunk at work, it would be

Megan, right? But I don't know why they had to go and fire her. Shouldn't they fire the perv who paid for the drinks?"

The guy at the counter called my name, and I jumped up to grab our slices. Tyler's silence freaked me out. Usually he was the one joking around, flirting. I glanced up at a beer poster with a busty girl in a swimsuit. Pre–Fourth of July Tyler would've been making jokes about how he'd once dated her.

"Do you think Megan said anything at work—when she was drunk?" Tyler spoke so softly I had to lean toward him to hear.

"No. She totally covered for that jerk! As if the whole margarita incident were her idea. The guy actually keeps girls' bikinis in his condo. Can you believe it? I can't believe she found *anything* attractive about that guy. He seems so slimy."

Tyler looked up. "Did she say anything about *me?*" He hadn't even picked up his pizza.

"Why would she say anything about you?"

"Isn't she freaking out because of—?"

"Oh." I held my pizza slice midair. "She really liked you." My turn to blush as I took a bite of my pizza; the cheese felt rubbery in my mouth, so I set the rest of it down.

"Yeah. Right. I guess I kind of led her on. She's really cool and everything and I—" He put his head in his hands. "I'm such a screwup." His shoulders shook. Was Tyler crying?

I sat there like an idiot, not knowing what to do. *Say something comforting!* "Hey, look, lots of girls liked—like—you. You're really charming and cute, but—"

"Completely uninterested."

"But nobody really knows that."

"And they can't. Jory, they can't." He stared at me with wet eyes, twisting his napkin in his hand. "You've got to tell Megan that she can't say anything."

"Don't worry—" I reached out and touched his arm.

"Don't worry? If Megan starts telling people and my dad finds out, I'm over." A couple of girls at the table next to us turned their heads. Tyler glowered at the girls and leaned in closer. *"Over."*

"I'm sure your dad would understand. I mean—"

A flicker of panic crossed his face. "Jory, he can never know. He'd kill me. I'm not exaggerating. He'd rather see me dead than have a g-gay son. I've heard him say it."

I watched Tyler with his magazine-model face, thinking how he looked like the ideal son, the ideal boyfriend, the kind of guy always cast in ads and movies. I'd always thought his life was perfect: rich parents, nice car, gorgeous, popular, athletic. Tyler leaned toward me, picked up my hand, and squeezed hard.

"No one can find out," Tyler said in a low growl. "Ever."

He looked at me with an intense expression. An older woman passing by to pick up her order glanced at me with an ahh-young-love smile, as if I were having a romantic lunch with my boyfriend.

"I won't say anything." I tried to pull my aching hand away. "And I don't think you have to worry about Megan." I'd call her the minute I got home and make her promise not to do anything mean or stupid.

Tyler closed his eyes, nodded, and finally let go of my hand.

Questions whirred in my mind as if whipped by Katie's high-speed mixer. How did he know? *When* did he know? Why did he date that McQueen girl? What about Rachael Beal? Was he a hundred percent sure? Was he maybe just confused? Maybe it was a phase, like one of Mom's diets. No, that's stupid! Kids have killed themselves rather than admit that they're gay.

Tyler looked at me with wide eyes as if he were watching the questions churn in my mind. I reached over and touched his hand—quick—and he exhaled like a deflating balloon.

Neither of us finished the pizza or said much on the way back to Katie's. But later, when I left work and unlocked my bike, Tyler was there to give me a ride home.

Chapter Nineteen

DOLDRUMS, DELIVERIES, AND A DATE?

My nose twitched with pollen as I helped Katie sort new flowers into the black buckets in the cooler. A rose pricked my finger, and I sucked on it. Maybe it was a magic rose that could transport me back to the beginning of summer, back when everything and anything seemed possible. Back in June I'd had several new-nose possibilities picked out; Tyler Briggs had touched my knee, and that was just oh so close to other devirginizing areas; and I was going to become a hip film critic and hang out with famous intellectuals and movie stars. Yeah, right!

The phone rang and Katie went to take the order. I dropped a bunch of white carnations into water then opened another box of blooms. More roses. I drew in their deep, sweet scent. Who could I fantasize about now? Tom? I had managed to run into him twice, but he never seemed interested—just another flirt. Gideon? He wouldn't do anything for my social standing at school. Was I the dorky-rebel type? Wouldn't fit my new nose, for sure. He *did* make me feel kind of good about myself, though. I pushed the pink roses aside and placed the yellow roses next to them.

"That was strange," Katie said. "They insisted that *you* deliver the flowers."

"What? Was it a guy? Stalker Guy from the Gold Dust West?"

"No, it was a woman." Katie sat down, ripped open another box, and pulled out fern cuttings. "She said you'd recognize her."

"Oh?" Oh, no! That snippy receptionist was going to seek revenge for my ruining some old biddy's retirement luncheon and then knocking over that sapling. She'd drag me out to the desert and throw the flowers at me; I'd have to survive on the droplets of water left in the vase and whatever insects I could catch. That was two weeks ago to the day. Wednesday.

"Wait! Katie, I can't. I've got to take cakes to the Jewel Café."

"I'll take care of that." Katie smiled. "Helen has been bugging me to stop by and see the whole operation, so it'll give me a chance to catch up with her. We can just close up for an hour."

I let out a sigh. That had been the one thing I'd looked forward to this week: the possibility of seeing Gideon. Joking about his feet. Staring at his mouth when he wasn't looking. Imagining what all that dark hair would feel like if I dared to reach out and touch it.

"Time for frosting." Katie jumped up. "Will you wash up and help me mix a batch while I get some sheet cakes in the oven?"

I spread a wet towel over the mixer, turning it on low while the powdered sugar combined with the shortening. The thick smell of sugar and butter-flavored Crisco hung in the hot kitchen as I pulled the rubber-bandy part of my hairnet away from my forehead for a minute so a red line wouldn't form.

Katie pulled a hot cake pan from the oven and set it across from me to cool. Office-birthday-party cake. I turned the mixer on high and whipped the frosting into fluffy peaks. Katie separated the frosting into small bowls and added color to each one; watching her slather thick frosting across the cake, squeezing roses all around the edges, I wondered if I'd ever want to eat birthday cake again.

"Um," I said as Katie handed me a small bouquet of sunflowers and daisies for the mystery delivery. "If you're taking the van, I'm not sure how to get these flowers to wherever they're going."

"Take your car. I'll reimburse for the gas, if that's bothering you."

"Um." I rubbed the tip of my nose. "I don't have my car with me, exactly. I, um, rode my bike to work."

"Don't you live up off McCarren?"

"It's an easy ride down." I thought about how my stomach whooshed—the closest I'd ever get to feeling in love—when I'd flown down Skyline that morning. "It's the way home that's a bit rough."

Actually, Tyler had picked me up every day since Megan had been fired. It was as if my dream had finally come true. I had a boy who cared about me. Except it felt too much like blackmail and he had no desire for a girlfriend. Ever. Maybe I'd accidentally made one of those uncareful wishes where you leave out the crucial details, like a *heterosexual* boyfriend.

Katie looked at me. "Let me get this straight. You're a delivery girl, but you don't have a car?"

"Oh, it's mostly an exercise thing. You know, staying in shape." I smoothed my hands over my hips like Mom always did. "All that stuff."

Katie raised her eyebrows, shaking her head.

"Okay, drop me off at the Jewel and take the van, but come back and get me promptly—no traffic jams, coffee stops, or flash floods—at one."

My hands got sweaty as I put the key into the ignition. I hated the pressure of driving Katie, of having her watch me. Flashback to why I failed my driver's-license test four times: the big guy with the clipboard made me nervous (for that matter, so did the skinny woman with the clipboard, the old guy with the clipboard, and the bearded guy with the clipboard). Katie leaned back and closed her eyes, but I noticed her death grip on the door handle; I eased the van away from the curb and begged for green lights the whole way. At the Jewel Café I helped Katie carry the cakes into the kitchen. No Gideon. No violin. A bunch of gossiping ladies sat around wolfing down cake and saying mean things about their husbands.

"I told him the only foreplay I wanted was a clean kitchen floor," one woman said. All the others laughed.

As I left, Katie handed me the address for the flower delivery: the park rangers' house at San Rafael? Weird.

"Remember to pick me up by one," Katie called.

Fifteen minutes later, I pulled into San Rafael Park, locked up the van, and searched for the rangers' building. Wind blew my hair around my face; heavy clouds gathered around the mountains, but the sun still zoomed down to create massive nose freckles. A few petals blew off the bouquet. I imagined some burly ranger chewing me out like a rabid Smokey the Bear.

"Over here, Jory."

I looked around. Gideon stood under a tree. His hair puffed over his eyes in the strong breeze, but his luscious mouth smiled at me.

I froze like a wedding-reception ice sculpture. Confused. What was he doing at the park? Did Katie send him here to help me find the rangers' station?

He held up a basket. "Surprise!" He laughed at me. "I'm taking you on a picnic."

"Oh? But I have—" I felt really stupid holding the small bouquet of flowers. "The rangers' office?"

"They're for us. You can't have a picnic without flowers," Gideon said. "Come on."

He walked up the hill toward the duck pond. I hung back a bit, still holding on to the flowers, feeling like a total dork. I looked around to see if there was anyone I knew. Thank God. Just a bunch of little kids and moms with McDonald's bags rattling in the wind.

"You're staring at my ass, aren't you?" Gideon lurched ahead like Frankenstein. "Walk this way."

I laughed, but there was no way I was going to do anything like that in public, even if it was only in front of five-year-olds. My hair streamed out behind me as I followed Gideon through the blustery playground. He stopped by a tree fluttering its leaves, pulled a blanket out of his backpack, and put it on the ground, but it flapped up around his ankles.

"I ordered a sunny day, but damn if I didn't forget about the wind." He brushed his hair away from his face. "Hurry and sit down."

I knelt down on the blanket. "So you had this whole thing planned? Does Katie know?" *Is that why she insisted on having lunch at the Jewel Café?*

"Helen helped me." He handed me a cloth napkin. "I know, I know. A guy shouldn't need his mom to get a date."

This is a date? I felt my face flush, so I let my hair blow across my cheeks. Gideon reached over and pushed my hair away, then scrunched it behind my ear in a way that totally tickled my neck. I'm sure my face glowed like raspberry-glazed cheesecake.

"Blond hair does not go with chicken pesto sandwiches." He handed me a sandwich wrapped in paper. Our fingers touched.

"Did you make these yourself?"

"Of course. *Not.*" He smiled. "Helen. Again. She's afraid

I'm going to be a desperate old bachelor who will never leave home so she can finally listen to her disco music in peace."

I managed a giggle and bit into my sandwich, mostly because I couldn't think of anything to say. I felt funny chewing in front of him. Did it make my nose look strange? What if I got something stuck in my teeth?

"Oh, no. Not a courtesy laugh. Already."

"I'm just—surprised?" My voice sounded too squeaky. *Stick to eating.*

He shook his flip-flops off his feet and wiggled his toes. "In a good way or a bad way?"

"This is good." I took another bite, and then another, finishing the sandwich and going for some chips. "Really good."

"The picnic or the sandwich?"

"Both." Face. Red. Again.

He folded one knee so it touched mine. I stretched my legs out in front of me, tucked them back, sat cross-legged, then put them out, back, under, like some kind of weird Olympic floor routine.

"Ants in your pants?" Gideon licked a bit of avocado off his lip as he finished his sandwich. I stared at his mouth.

"What are your big brown eyes looking at?"

I threw my napkin at him. "Stop it. You're making me too nervous."

"But you're cute when you're nervous. Like a wiggly puppy."

He put his hand on my knee as I started to scoot my legs underneath my butt again. The tips of his fingers felt rough. Thank God I'd shaved my legs this morning! I left my legs out straight. He pushed *my* flip-flops off *my* feet and touched his toes to mine. A zing jolted through my body.

Gideon reached over and plucked a daisy out of the flower bouquet and stuck it behind my ear, leaning in close. "You smell like birthday cake," he whispered.

His black hair swept against my cheek. I reached up and touched his soft curls. He looked at me with his dark brown eyes, tilted his head, leaned closer, and kissed me. Our noses bumped. I pulled back and hid my nose with my hand.

Gideon laughed. "That's supposed to happen."

He took my hand in his, intertwining his fingers with mine, and kissed me again. Longer.

Chapter Twenty

ICE CREAM AND BIG QUESTIONS

After buying ice cream Megan, Hannah, and I drove to a deserted-at-ten-P.M. kiddie park near Hannah's house. Lying across the hood of her mom's BMW, Hannah posed like a swimsuit model, pouting her lips and making kissing noises.

I hadn't told them anything about Gideon yet.

I kind of liked keeping the moment to myself. No one could analyze it except me. I mostly just relived it, sometimes adding exotic variations like Gideon kissing me on the chairlift at Mount Rose; Gideon kissing me in a gondola in Venice; Gideon dressed as a knight sweeping me away on a white horse; Gideon kissing me in the park under a full moon. I looked over at the deserted playground.

Megan handed me a plastic spoon. I dug into the carton of Neapolitan ice cream, eating my section of chocolate. Megan always ate the vanilla and Hannah the strawberry. During our first-ever slumber-not party, we'd laughed about how we were meant to be friends because there was an ice cream flavor just for the three of us.

"I can't believe you're leaving us, Meggie." Hannah sucked ice cream off her spoon. "How long are you going to be gone?"

"Three weeks." Megan scooped ice cream at a rate that reminded me of Mom on day 3 of the Ice Cream, Cookie, Potato Chip, and Onion Dip Mad-at-Dad Diet. Finn and I loved it.

"My mom called my dad and begged him to take me," Megan said with a full mouth. "Pretty pathetic. I was listening, but she didn't know it. So she comes into my room and says, 'You'll never guess who called! Your dad wants you to come visit and he was hoping you could take time off work.'" Megan snorted. "As if *that* were an issue." She heaped more ice cream on her spoon, half of it from my chocolate, and rolled her eyes. "She has such issues with my dad, but at least I won't have to sit around here moping and thinking about Tyler's sexuality issues."

I took a tiny bite of chocolate ice cream. "He doesn't exactly have issues. He just *is,* you know. Gay."

"Well, I'm going to buy school clothes that will make him wish he were straight."

Hannah laughed. "Maybe he'll want to go shopping with you."

"That's kind of a stereotype, isn't it?" I sighed. "The whole shopping thing. I mean, Tyler doesn't really—" On the way home from work yesterday, Tyler had said something about how he hated all the expectations and stereotypes people felt they had to live up to. Like our moms thinking they had to be so skinny; men having to love watching sports and not being allowed to show emotion; girls always trying to act sexy, not intelligent. I thought he had a real and valid point.

"He totally dresses gay! All those silk shirts and expensive shoes." Megan waved her spoon around, and a drop of ice cream landed on my knee. "I should've noticed. He was the only guy at work whose socks matched."

"You know, he might be having a hard time with this too." I stuck my empty spoon in my mouth. Tyler told me he'd been feeling depressed but couldn't talk to a counselor because his parents might find out about *everything*. The look on his face had kind of scared me.

"Hard time!" Megan laughed. "That's what he's hoping for."

Hannah leaned over, laughing and spewing ice cream all over her legs.

"Wrong word choice." I sighed. "I really mean it, though.

Tyler said he'd die if anyone found out. He sounded so desperate. Not like Tyler at all."

"When did you talk to him?" Megan looked at me and pointed her spoon like a finger.

"He took me to lunch." I didn't want to say anything about the daily rides home, not yet.

"Oh, how cozy, Jory." Megan sounded snide. "You know he still doesn't want to be your little boyfriend."

"I know that," I said. "But he might need a friend." I brought all of my hair over my left shoulder and twisted it around my hand. "It's just that he's been feeling kind of alone with all of this."

Megan spooned a big glob of *my* chocolate into her mouth. "Sounds like quite a lunch."

"Well, actually, we've been talking more since then." I flipped my hair back. Forget it. I said it quickly: "He's been giving me rides home from work so I don't have to bike." I took a breath. "Uphill and all."

"I don't know, Jor. Your humongous crush and everything." Hannah tapped her spoon against her darling button nose. "You need to move on. Hey, Alex has a brother who's a sophomore. A total cutie—we could double-date."

Why couldn't they understand that I still liked Tyler as a person? All the reasons I had had a crush on him still existed.

He was still funny and smart and nice. And gorgeous, even though that one didn't matter so much anymore. I sighed. "I'm not going to date a sophomore. You're the one who told me to find more mature men, right?"

I nipped the inside of my cheek to stop myself from mentioning Gideon, even though I'd been dying to tell someone, anyone, besides my bathroom mirror and the diary I only wrote in a few times a year. I had exactly three entries:

August 25. First day of school. I'm going to write every day.

January 1. I'm going to write every day.

July 19. He kissed me! My first real kiss, not counting Spin the Bottle with icky Ian Lear. He took me on the most romantic picnic and it was like *Wuthering Heights* or something with the wind and all his dark hair blowing around, and his toes touched my toes. And he thought I smelled like cake. And then he leaned over and put his soft lips against mine and . . . am I in love? To be continued?

"Why are you smiling?" Megan asked. "Is there someone?"

"Not exactly." I scooped up a bite of ice cream that I didn't even want. "What?"

Hannah and Megan stared at me.

"Don't even tell me Tyler's not gay and you guys are now

an item." Megan's eyes narrowed. "That would give me major issues."

"No, of course not."

"Is it José's friend, with the fabulous body?" Hannah asked.

"No." I clacked the spoon against my teeth. "He doesn't even have my phone number."

"But he always pays a ton of attention to you."

"Only when I'm the only girl around." Jocks don't date big-nosed klutzes.

Hannah tapped her sticky spoon on my knee. "You've got to tell me, Jory."

"Yeah, tell us." Megan tapped her spoon on my knee too.

"I don't know if it's really anything." I couldn't stop the grin spreading across my face. "But there's this guy where I deliver cakes—"

"Not Gold Dust West Stalker guy?" Hannah shrieked. "You're totally losing it, Jory. Too, too desperate."

"No. Give me a break, Hannah." I leaned back against the windshield. "I'm not saying anything more."

"All right. Let me ask one question," Megan said. "Have I ever met him?"

I nodded and bit down on my spoon too hard; it broke in my mouth. I hopped off the car and ran to the garbage can across the parking lot. Hannah and Megan followed me, so I ran to the little merry-go-round and spun myself. Megan spun the merry-go-round so hard that I had to hold on tight. I started laughing and laughing.

"Jacob from Calc?" Megan called out guesses—all completely gorgeous, popular guys from school. "James Wick? Michael Patricks?" Guys who *never* noticed me.

"Oh-oh," Hannah said. "Blond guy from AP English."

"I'm not *in* AP English," I said.

"Oh, yeah. He's *my* alternative-to-Alex fantasy." Hannah giggled. "I know! Is it that Great-Legs Guy from Finn's soccer team?"

"You like Luke?" Megan stopped the merry-go-round. "You stole Luke from his little pink-sprinkle-cupcake girl?"

"They were doughnuts. And no."

My head and stomach felt almost as dizzy as they had after I'd left Gideon in San Rafael Park and drove back to pick up Katie. That whole afternoon I kept making mistakes and giggling to the point that Katie nearly sent me home early because I was driving her to distraction while she frosted a wedding cake that was shaped like a roll of paper towels. But I begged her to let me stay. I needed the money. On my next payday, I'd be about halfway to my new nose.

"But he did flirt with you the other day, before you maimed

him. And his little girlfriend was nowhere around." Megan gave me the Look. "Are you telling the truth?"

The merry-go-round finally slowed to a stop. "Don't you think I'd tell you if I'd snagged a guy like Luke?" I felt a little disloyal. "He's got, like, the whole package, even more than Tyler."

Megan stared at me, hands on her waist. "So what? He's not a whole-package guy?"

"That's not what I meant." I'm sure my cheeks glowed brighter than the moon peeking over the trees. "He's just not the kind of guy I usually go for, I guess."

"Come on. Tell us!" Hannah gripped the merry-go-round. "Or I'll spin you again."

"Please don't. We don't need another vomiting incident." Sprinklers kicked on across the park, separating us from Hannah's car. "I'll tell you, but you can't get all weird about it."

Hannah clapped her hands together and plopped down next to me, swinging the merry-go-round side to side. "Juicy details, *s'il vous plaît*."

"His name is Gideon and he works at the Jewel Café. I mean, his mom owns it, and he just transferred to Reno. I never saw him there, but he was at that frat party, you know, playing his violin."

Hannah gasped. "You like the guy with the big nose! The

one that you said made you laugh because he had, like, glowing toes?" Hannah paused. "And didn't he get all mad at you?"

"Yeah, but—"

"You should've seen his face, Jor." Hannah pursed her lips. "He's totally missing the humor vibe."

I picked at a fleck of peeling paint on the merry-go-round, not wanting to think about that awful frat party.

"Wait!" Megan said. "Is this the same freak who was playing the violin outside the movies? Did you know the police almost arrested him for loitering? Tyler said he got kicked out of several schools and even spent time at Wittenberg for his crimes. And he *does* have a big nose." Megan scrunched her own (small) nose for emphasis.

They both pounded me with a whole bunch of questions, but I was stuck on "big nose." Never mind all the stuff they said about social outcast, orchestra geek, juvenile delinquent, total rebel (but not in a good way), questionable foot hygiene, and his leading me down the wrong path. I wanted to shout at them, *So* what *if he has a big nose? Are you afraid we might breed and have children with noses so big that when we all sneeze a small town floods?*

Maybe they were right and dating a guy like Gideon *would* ruin me socially. We'd be the big-nosed freak outcasts. People would toss peanuts at us like we were elephants or something.

Did I really like him anyway? He kissed *me,* right? I didn't kiss him. And I never even said I'd go on a date or anything. He tricked me, right? *Any* girl who feared dying a virgin would kiss any guy, if only to make it seem less likely that she'd die alone with a bottle of whiskey in a sad hotel room.

I didn't say much on the ride home. Hannah and Megan talked to me like mothers, saying things like "Please don't commit social suicide," "You have to keep your moral standards high," and "We're concerned about your judgment, that's all."

What about your *judgment, Megan? You're the one who got drunk with a pervy coworker during lunch!* Hannah said that I'd "taken living in the moment way past too far." Megan worried that I was becoming "too desperate after too many unfulfilled boy-crazy years."

Maybe I was! Finding out that Finn had a better chance of snagging Tyler than I did had made me a little crazy. I was the one who had liked him for thirteen months, seven days . . . Whatever. How did I know that I wasn't the one who had made him want to be gay? Even though I knew he was born that way. Maybe I was the exception, the one that drove boys into the arms of men, like those super-ultra-religious people claimed.

"Megan, have fun at your dad's," I called out as I jumped out of Hannah's car. "Good luck with your yoga thingy tomorrow, Hannah." I tried to sound cheerful even as tears fuzzed up my vision. "Bye, guys. Promise to e-mail, Meg. Call me, Han. Promise."

I flung the door open, kicked it shut and gave it—them— the finger before running into my room, screaming, and slamming my door so hard it shook the walls. I didn't even care that Finn and a bunch of his friends totally gawked at me from the family room.

I flopped on my bed and screamed into my pillows like a million jilted brides. *I hate Megan! I hate Hannah!* The sharp corner of an envelope pressed into my cheek. I sat and picked up a small blue envelope with the initial *J* on the front. When I opened it, that flowery incense smell from the Jewel Café burst out. I sniffed the envelope right as Finn opened the door. Without knocking!

"Okay, that was a little nutso," Finn said. "And I don't even *want* to know what you're doing to that envelope, but I promised the guy who delivered it that I'd make sure to tell you to open it tonight." Finn started to close the door. "He didn't say anything about making out with it, though."

"Get out!" I threw a pillow across the room.

"Okay, then." Finn closed the door. "Jor's going mental, Mom. Might want to get the straitjacket out again."

His violent-movie-watching pals guffawed.

"Finn," Mom scolded. "Be nice." Then she laughed. *Nice support, Mom.*

There was no note in the envelope, only a bunch of beads. I poured them onto my bed and spread them with my fingers. Half of them were letters and the other half little pink flowers. I spent an hour putting the puzzle together, wishing I *had* been in AP English. With my heart beating so fast I thought it would jump out and dance around my room, I worked out: "Come to Bed Tuesday Night." Oh, my God! Burying my head in my pillow to hyperventilate, I found another little *a* bead tucked into a fold of my comforter. "Come to Bead Tuesday Night."

A few minutes later, after I calmed down a bit, I went into the kitchen for a glass of water.

Luke sat on the sofa next to Finn, watching some total gore-fest movie.

Oh, God, no! Luke would probably spread the word that not only did Finn's sister have the biggest nose in Reno, but she was mentally unstable. Cupcake Girl would send me sweet little not-meaning-to-be-sexual-innuendoes notes in the mental hospital. Hannah and Megan would spend all their visits nodding at me with concerned looks on their faces. "You should've listened to us and not kissed a dork/freak/rebel," they'd say.

Hoping to avoid further embarrassment, I snuck out of the kitchen during a big action scene, holding my glass of water to my smoldering cheek.

Luke raised his eyebrows. Twice. "Hey, Jory," he said with a chuckle.

Forget the mental hospital. Call the convent. Now.

Chapter Twenty-one

AUGUST: BEADS AND BONDING

I changed clothes about a million times on Tuesday night. I didn't want to look like I was trying too hard to be the new girlfriend or something, but I wanted to look very kissable. Did that mean snug jeans or a short skirt? Tank top or clever T-shirt? Gideon wore T-shirts from his favorite bands. All I had was an old Hannah Montana tee that I kept for sentimental reasons. Maybe I needed to listen to more serious music. I ran out to the family room and swiped one of Dad's classical CDs. Maybe that would get me in the mood. The whining strings and lumbering horns, however, just made me want to wear black and toss myself into a grave. Picked the wrong CD, I guess. I turned the radio on and set it to my favorite pop station. Love songs should get me in the mood, right?

After trying on nearly all of my clothes and tossing them in a heap on my bed, I skulked down the hall to Finn's room.

"Tight jeans or a miniskirt?" I asked.

"And the segue to this would be—"

"Please tell me. What makes you notice a girl?" The humiliation. Finn looked up from the book he was reading and stared at me.

Finn waggled his tongue. "Go naked. That'll get some attention."

"Oh, grow up." I slammed his door. "Thought I could ask a simple question without being totally humiliated!"

"Miniskirt with a tight shirt," Finn yelled through the door. "Show off your best *ass*-ets. Get it?" He laughed at his own pathetic joke. "That's no jug." More laughter.

What was I thinking, asking a fifteen-year-old, even if he did have far more extensive dating experience? Finn got asked to the senior prom last year as a freshman. He ended up hanging out with Zane Zimmerman and his date. Scary thought that keeps me awake at 3:17 A.M.: having to take my own brother to senior prom *and* having to make sure I asked him before someone else did.

I shimmied into a swirly-girlie miniskirt and put on my "Who Needs Boys?" T-shirt. Didn't want to appear desperate. Even though I totally was. I should've been wearing a "Kiss Me Now Before You Change Your Mind" T-shirt. Would he even kiss me?

After combing my hair for the tenth time and adding a little splash of eau de something from my mom's bathroom, I ran out to grab Mom's keys.

"Where are you going?" Mom stirred a pot of beet soup on the stove. A week of binging had suddenly morphed into the Cleansing Soup Diet (day 2). I had kind of liked the cool smoothie-esque blended-fruit breakfast soup.

"I'm trying out that jewelry-making class down, you know, where I deliver cakes on Wednesdays."

Could she totally tell that I was far more interested in kissing than beading? I tried to calm down and not look so eager, but I kept flapping my hands around while I talked.

"You know I'm trying to find my passion and all this summer, and—"

"Wait! Is it the Jewel Café? I've heard about that place! One of my coworkers ate lunch there and then Cynthia Simons mentioned it at book club. Maybe I'll join you." Mom turned off the burner. Bad sign. "Today's Tuesday, isn't it? I think this is exactly the class Cynthia's in. Wouldn't that be great?" Mom smoothed her hair.

"Oh, Mom. I'm really late." Nose growing. I pressed my thumb against the tip of my nose.

"Nonsense. Do you know you always touch your nose when you fib?" Mom smiled. "You've been doing it for years."

She shrugged. "How fun to do a mother-daughter bonding thing! Don't look so worried. Oh, God. What do I have to wear that still fits?"

Mom ran into her bedroom to put on her face and find something presentable to wear. Finn wandered out to the family room, munching on a power bar.

"Mother-daughter night? Bummer. Guess what that means for me, though."

"What?"

Finn stood in front of me with his perfectly tan legs, the right kind of wavy, blond hair, and blue eyes. No wonder every girl in Reno walked by our house.

"Pizza. Possibly a little alone time with Em." He blew me a kiss. "Thanks, Sis."

"Whatever."

Finn was on the verge of having an ultimate boy night. Cute girl, pizza, home alone. And I was about to show up to my not-really-a-date-right? *with my mother!* Gideon would never want to kiss, talk, or even acknowledge my existence again after a night in the presence of the desperate-to-live-on-Cutting-Horse-Circle Leah Michaels. Maybe I should pretend to get sick. Or run away and become some desperate homeless person in San Francisco who gets trapped in the illicit world of drugs (not sex, because no one will want me) and some TV

station will do an exposé on me: *Mother-Daughter Bonding:*
More Dangerous Than You Think!

❧

I ignored Mom's chitchat on the way to the café. *So Amanda*
Mullins isn't as bright as I thought she'd be; she didn't understand
the deeper themes in the book. Apparently having millions of dol-
lars doesn't substitute for a college degree. But you should have seen
her guest bathroom: candles, gorgeous big candles. Should I try
candles? You and your brother would probably just set the house
on fire. I may try her decorator, though. Unless it's too expensive,
but Dad thinks he might get that promotion—that's why he's been
working so late. They plan to announce in two weeks. Then maybe
I can cut back on my own hours. Or quit. Wouldn't that be great?

I grunted occasionally, which seemed to be enough for
her. Twice I thought about flinging myself out of the car. I
would end up in the hospital, and, of course, I'd need a nose
job. My eyes would look really pretty against all the bruis-
es and bandages, and Gideon could visit me in the hospital
and pledge his undying love. When the doctors unveiled the
new nose, I would awe everyone with my beauty. Or maybe
Zane Zimmerman would be in the next room recovering from
some knee injury or something and we could have a rehab
romance.

"Do I turn here?" Mom asked.

"I guess." I leaned forward. "My stomach doesn't feel so good." Major jitters.

"You're just hungry," Mom said. "I heard that her quiche is simply delicious."

"You're not going to make her blend it into some kind of soup, are you?"

"Jory, give me some credit, please." Mom smoothed her blouse over her capris. She looked better than I did. Her short hair framed her classic features, whereas I depended on my long hair like some literary heroine: my one beauty.

❧

Gideon opened the door and smiled really big, and then his eyes grew wide and his smile faded as my mother pushed in behind me.

"Cynthia!" She raced over to a skinny blonde who was gathering beads. "I'm here for a mother-daughter night. Jory, come here and meet Mrs. Simons."

Gideon kept holding the door open as my mom swept me into the room and introduced me all around.

"We're having a mother-daughter night," she bragged. "Jory practically *begged* me to come."

So not true! I tried to catch Gideon's eye, but he just stood there with a shocked expression. He wore nice jeans and a dark shirt that brought out his eyes. And his amazing hair. Mom gripped my arm with her manicured nails like she was some kind of socialite pro wrestler. I couldn't break away. I realized that I hadn't said a single word to Gideon. Not even *hi*. I smiled as Mom introduced me to another beading lady.

Helen brought us little trays on which to collect beads; Mom floated around the shop conducting a poll about which beads best matched her eyes. Gideon disappeared through a door in the back room without even looking in my direction. I swished my fingers through a box of round beads the color of Key lime pie, wondering what to do and trying not to let the tears in my eyes fall.

A few minutes later Helen found me in the corner searching through some jagged poke-your-neck-so-you-can-bleed-to-death beads.

"Your mother is quite a character," she said. "A force of nature."

"Tell me about it." I poked my finger on a bead, pressing until it hurt.

"These aren't good necklace material. Why don't you look for something more suitable. More Joryish."

"I don't really know what that is." I stared down at a shiny brown stone, blinking hard. *Don't cry*. Why couldn't Helen leave me alone? Why couldn't Mom find her own stupid hobby? She always gloms on to everyone else's passion. She's not interested in anything other than popularity. And I'm just as bad. I joined the film club because Megan likes that kind of thing. I did yoga because Hannah likes *that* kind of thing. I only listened to music that Tyler liked. I had no idea what *I* liked. I couldn't even decide if I liked Gideon or if I just liked the fact that he seemed to like me. Until tonight. A tear dripped out of my eye. I looked so dumb, standing there crying like a kid who'd lost her balloon.

"Now, now." Helen put her arm around me. "Why don't you look over by the door. Pick out eight to ten large beads and twice as many small beads. We're doing a string necklace tonight. Always good to practice those knots." Helen sashayed out of the room toward the group laughing in the classroom, leaving me alone.

Violin music now mixed with the New Age stuff Helen played; the sound made my heart hurt. I pulled the little blue envelope out of my purse and dropped those flower beads onto my tray, then searched for smaller beads to match the light green leaves on the flowers.

"Jory, hurry up." Mom swung through the door. "Helen is about to start."

On the way to the classroom we walked past Gideon's open

door. He stood in his bare feet playing the violin with his eyes closed. Sadness hunkered heavy in my stomach.

"Quite a musician, isn't he? Helen said he went to a very prestigious music camp this summer."

Mom positioned herself between Cynthia and me. Another woman kept giving Mom long nasty, jealous looks, but Mom didn't notice. Or didn't care.

"Oh, Cynthia. You're so naughty," Mom said as Cynthia went into far too much detail about her husband's vasectomy. I wanted to die when Mom started talking about how Dad had wanted another child, but she'd insisted that the skin on her stomach could *not* carry one more baby. Two had just about ruined her for swimwear.

"Oh, I thought your daughter was adopted," Jealous Woman said. "She doesn't look anything like your son, the soccer player, right?"

"What's wrong with adoption? *I* was adopted!" Cynthia spat.

Jealous Woman snapped her mouth shut and blushed a shade darker than her lipstick. But then Mom had to go and say, "Jory takes after the Lessinger side of the family. She's the spitting image of Evan's maternal grandfather."

How could she say that! Flustered, I bumped my tray, spilling my beads all over. While I crawled around on the floor looking at everyone's professionally polished toenails and expensive leather sandals and picking up beads, Gideon's bare feet padded through the room. Oh, God. Had he heard my mom tell everyone that I looked like Great-Grandpa Lessinger?

My face burned and I felt tears coming, so I sat on the floor under the table, hiding. Current chance of dying a virgin: 100 percent.

Mom peeked under the table. "Did you find them all, honey?"

"I'm missing one."

"Why don't you go get another one," Helen said. "I can't tell you how many beads I sweep up every night. I should make a necklace consisting only of lost beads." Everyone laughed.

I walked back into the front room and stood staring at all the bins of beads. I'd lost one of the flower beads from Gideon, and I hadn't seen any like it earlier. The door swung open.

Gideon.

"Helen said you lost a bead."

I nodded, not looking at his face.

"What did it look like?"

"You know." I turned around and stuck my hand in a box of red beads.

"Oh." Gideon paused. "Those are still in my room." He kind of tilted his head in that direction.

I followed him back to his room, even though I wasn't sure he wanted me to. His violin case lay open on his bed, next to the orange cat. *Starry Night* by van Gogh hung over the bed, but over his desk he had an Andrew Bird concert poster. A stack of books cluttered the floor. Gideon moved some papers on his desk, uncovering a bin of beads.

"Here." He put the little bead into my hand. "You better return to your classmates."

I wanted to say something, to explain, but he just glanced at my "Who Needs Boys?" T-shirt, made a snuffing sound, shook his head, and turned away. I wanted to make a joke, make him smile at me, something. *The shirt doesn't mean anything. I didn't want to come on too strong. Too desperate. Like I really am. And I for sure didn't invite my mom! She totally made that stuff up. You don't understand!*

"I'm sorry," I squeaked, then rushed out of the room.

By the time I got back, Helen had already shown everyone how to make knots. She came over to give me a private lesson, but I shook my head. Helen sighed and sent me into the kitchen to bring out the cake.

Gideon stayed in his room playing angry violin music.

Chapter Twenty-two

ROOM PARTY!

"Han, I'm not sure this is a good idea." The two of us rode up in the elevator to a suite at a non–cake-and-pie-delivery casino. José from Wooster had called Hannah to invite us. As we followed the squiggly patterns on the carpet down to the suite, I wondered if Wooster Tom would be there. Did I really care? Maybe. Or maybe I just needed someone to fill the guy slot in my ongoing fantasy of having an actual boyfriend. I imagined my life as one of those daytime soaps where they switch actors all of a sudden. The deep voice would say, *Tonight the role of Jory's Possible Boyfriend will be played by Wooster Tom.*

"Look, if Alex is going to be a total nun, I'm not waiting around. Especially after what happened to Megan." Hannah fluffed her short, newly highlighted strawberry-frosting-colored hair. "José's got quite the hot bod, plus he's sweet and adorable. He sends me the funniest text messages." Hannah skipped down the hall. "Do you have your ten bucks?"

Rap music boomed from the suite as we stood in front of the door.

"I bet Tom will be totally excited to see you," Hannah said. "José said he'd be here."

My stomach went *wah-wah-wah*. "Hannah, he's never even asked me for my number or anything." I said it more for my own benefit than Hannah's as I fanned my hair out behind me.

"Well, here goes." Hannah knocked on the door. Nothing. We both whacked the door. Nothing. The music beat out a fast rhythm. "They can't hear us."

"Hannah, let's go see a movie or something." My *wah-wah* stomach turned *whoa-whoa*. But I ignored any doubts as the door swung open. An older guy with a soul patch and a knit cap opened the door. "Ladies, welcome. Do you have your entry fee?" We each handed him ten bucks. "Go get yourself set up with drinks, and party on."

"Great!" Hannah smiled. I noticed she'd sprayed tons of glitter in her hair. The room smelled like a mixture of sweet marijuana smoke, lemon cleanser, and chlorine. I scratched my nose with the edge of my fingernail, trying not to mess up my nose-minimizing makeup.

People sat around in the living room on cushy little sofas and chairs. Two girls with long blond hair passed a joint between themselves; over by the bar, a few girls and a couple of guys sat in a hot tub.

"Hannah Banana!" José stood up in the middle of the hot tub. "Get yourself a drink and join us." He held up a bottle of beer. A few of the girls gave Hannah the evil eye, but she still waved, all cheerful.

"Hi, everyone!"

"Han? Did you bring a swimsuit?" I asked.

She giggled. "No, but I'm wearing a totally cute bra and matching panties."

Oh. My. God. My friends are out of control. First Megan freaks out over Tyler's big secret. Now Hannah is going crazy because Alex from Church refused to kiss her after driving her home from a youth-group dance. (He told her that he'd made an abstinence pledge and that kissing could lead to other temptations. Hannah tried to convince him that she had also made an abstinence pledge, but that didn't mean she would never kiss anyone good night. He called her a Jezebel, so she got out of the car and walked the rest of the way home. Two miles. At midnight. Her parents almost killed her.)

And here she was with her hair dyed pink, heading over to a fridge filled with alcohol, and wearing a cute bra to a party with a bunch of Wooster guys we didn't really know. Hannah handed me a bottle of hard lemonade, twisted the cap off hers, and drank it down in gulps. Lately, Hannah had been treating her body less like a temple and more like ancient ruins—tangling her morality with viny contradictions.

"Han—?"

"I'm just going to have a little," she said. "According to Alex, I'm a total sinner, so what's one little drink? I'm sick of always being the good girl. What good has it done me?"

Not knowing what to say, I twisted my hair around my hand, finally muttering, "Uh. Okay, I guess."

Hannah finished her drink, grabbed another one out of the fridge, and headed over to the hot tub, where she sat on the edge and dangled her legs in the water. Wooster José had his wet hands all over her knees.

I stood in the kitchen by myself, assessing my situation. Okay, it's August. Let's see. Summer goals:

- Not dying a virgin (Nope, still headed for the convent. Or, worse, Judith Hearne misery.)

- Finding a passion (Nope. Can't stand foreign films. Too klutzy for yoga. Mom ruined the whole jewelry thing for me. That leaves boys. Just boys. Pathetic boys. No good prospects.)

Tragedy of my young teen life: my only passion is boys, yet my big nose prevents any possibility of romance. I'm a doomed Cyrano without the clever wit. Another story I hate: man with big nose has to use good-looking guy to win girl. I could try using Hannah, but everyone would just fall in love with her. Yet:

- The nose fund: $2,568.00 (Appointment with plastic surgeon: Tuesday.)

A group of guys burst into the suite. "Munchies from the gift shop!" they yelled. My stomach fluttered when I spotted Tom wearing a T-shirt with the sleeves cut off, and long, baggy shorts. Nice arms. Nice legs.

"Hey!" He hugged me, lifting me off the ground. "Nice to see you."

I took a long drink of hard lemonade. "Hi!"

"I keep meaning to get your number—"

"No biggie." I finished my drink and turned around to get another bottle out of the fridge. Tom leaned over me and grabbed a beer.

"Come sit with me." Tom walked over to the group on the little sofas. He sat down and pulled me onto his lap, then reached around and put his hand on my leg. Warm. The guys played some car-chasing, shoot-everything-that-moves video game. Why hadn't I at least *tried* to play with Finn every once in a while? Who knew playing video games could be an important boyfriend-obtaining skill?

After dying in about forty-five seconds when I tried, I refused every time it was my turn, sipping my drink until I started to feel a little silly. I leaned back against Tom, and he put his arm around my stomach. He finished his beer and called for a guy to toss him another one, catching it in his hand as it flew across the room. Beer fizzed out of the can when he opened it.

"Get the foam." Tom laughed. "Hurry!"

I leaned down and slurped the bubbly beer off the edge of the can; Tom shared the rest with me. We took turns taking sips. Out of the corner of my eye, I watched Hannah pull off her T-shirt and shorts and slip into the water. One of the other girls got out. Then so did her friends; I watched the girl run into the bathroom in tears, but I didn't care. Live-in-the-moment Hannah always gets the cute guys. I felt warm all over. Tingly. The beer tasted bitter but kind of good. Better with each sip, at least. The girl sitting next to us got up and left, but I stayed on Tom's lap. A slow song played in the background. A few girls put their arms around one another, singing along.

"Tom! Come play quarters with us." A couple of guys waved Tom over to the little table near the windows.

"You want to?" Tom asked.

"Shurtainly." I laughed. "I mean—" More giggles. Everything seemed fuzzy and funny. I tried to stand up but fell against Tom's lap.

"You're not driving, are you?" Tom asked.

"Nope." I shook my head. "I drive for my job, even though I'm kind of a bad driver." I put my hand over my mouth. "Don't tell my boss."

Tom laughed. "We're going to pass on the quarters, guys."

One of them called him a chicken. Someone else made some kind of rude comment about me being Tom's chick. Someone else rhymed *that* with dick; I laughed even though the joke was about me.

Tom slid the balcony door open and took my hand. "Let's go outside."

"The lights look so pretty, like Christmas or something." I wobbled like a baby deer. A reindeer like Rudolph. Big red nose. Big Wooster Tom. Strange thoughts floated through my mind, bumping together like Katie's random helium-balloon messages. Everything seemed funny.

The hot air outside felt cozy, and the lights sparkling all around downtown looked pretty. Not the usual depressing old casinos with drunks begging for money. Everything seemed possible; I peered over the edge of the balcony and felt dizzy.

"Watch out." Tom put his arms around me from behind. I turned around and faced him.

"I kind of like you, Tom, even though I haven't obsessed about you for twelve months, six days, and however many minutes."

He played with my hair. "I'm not sure what that means, but I like you too."

I pressed my hand against his chest to steady myself. "Hey, I still have your shirt." I giggled. "I slept with it."

"Oh, yeah?" Tom's hand drifted a little below my waist.

"In it. I slept in it."

Through the window, I saw Hannah reach up and pull José into the hot tub. José splashed her, then pulled her close. I watched them kiss as if it were some kind of movie starring Hannah; she falls in love with the gorgeous football player, and I play the plain-but-sympathetic friend. I looked at Tom watching Hannah kiss José.

"José's been thinking about her since the Rodeo Carnival," Tom said. "I think he created this whole party just to invite her."

I pulled Tom's arms more tightly around me. I wanted to be the one kissing someone. Anyone. Why was it always Hannah, or Megan, or some skinny model on TV? It was supposed to be me when Gideon had kissed me at the park. It was finally going to be *my* turn.

"Let's go back inside," Tom said. "I feel like—"

"A peeping Tom?" I giggled.

"Haven't heard *that* one before." He slid the door open, walked over to the fridge, and grabbed another beer. "You ready for a soda or water, maybe?"

I slipped my hand up under his shirt; his stomach felt hard and warm. "Nah."

Tom glanced at Hannah and José alone in the hot tub. Most of the people had left the party, but I didn't care what time it was. Hannah's mom was out of town and I was spending the night at her house, so we had all kinds of time. Tonight was the night for magic.

"Come here." Tom pulled my hand out of his shirt and led me to a closed door. He knocked softly. No one answered, so he opened the door. A few of the guys playing quarters made rude comments. One cheered, something like "Tommy! Go for it!"

Tom led me over to the bed. The city lights twinkled through the big window, casting a soft glow in the room. As we sat down I noticed the bedspread was all messed up, but I didn't care. This was totally romantic, right? I reached up and knocked his baseball cap off.

"Hey," he said. "The hair."

I reached up and ran my hand through his spiky buzzcut. "That tickles."

He ran his hand through my long hair but got it stuck in my curls. "You're like Rapunzel."

"So kiss me." My head felt dizzy. But finally I knew what to say!

He leaned down and kissed me. The stale taste of beer filled my mouth as his tongue moved around mine. Kind of slobbery, but my whole body felt electric. I kissed him back, hoping I was doing things right. He pushed me down on the bed and lay next to me, kissing. He put his hand up under my shirt and under my bra. I copied him and put my hand under his shirt, rubbing the muscles on his chest.

We kissed for a long time, until my lips felt puffy and numb. Tom slid his hand down my pants. I pushed it back. He slid it down to the band of my panties. I pushed it back.

"What's wrong?" he asked.

"Nothing." I kissed him on the neck. He pushed my head down toward his boxers, which had slid up out of his baggy shorts. Or maybe his shorts had slid down. Something. My brain felt foggy. I pushed myself back up next to him and tried to kiss him again, but he took my hand and put it on his—his penis!

"What's that?" I started laughing. "Oh, my God! Is that your—"

I lay back down, laughing like I was watching the funniest movie ever. The whole thing seemed so silly, so not what I'd imagined as far as the romantic setting, the love-of-my-life guy, the lack of a curfew. I definitely hadn't imagined feeling so dizzy and a little sick to my stomach. Everything was wrong, but so funny!

"Stop laughing!" Tom pulled his shorts up and rolled off the bed.

"It's just so funny. Not you. This." I couldn't explain myself, so I kept laughing while Tom looked all over the floor in the dark for his baseball cap.

"You acted like you wanted it," he said. "Coming on so strong."

I stopped laughing and sat up. "I don't know what I want." My hair was shooting out in all directions; my shirt and bra were twisted all around. My stomach lurched as I stood up, straightened my shirt, rehooked my bra, sort of, and smoothed down my hair. "Not this," I said with a chuckle.

"I don't want *this* either." He spat the words at me. "You're not even that hot. Not even worth it."

People cheered as Tom walked out and shut the door on me. The slam of the heavy outer door followed, reverberating throughout the entire suite. I waited a few minutes, letting his words sink in: "Not even worth it." Translation: *ugly*.

The lights hurt my eyes as I entered the living room. Hannah snuggled with José on the sofa, playing footsies, but the guys playing quarters laughed at me. I reached up, felt my hair, which was all tangled and wild, and ran back into the bedroom. I found the bathroom and flipped on the lights.

Under the harsh fluorescent lights I looked like smooshed birthday cake. Mascara smudged around my eyes, cover-up swirled on my nose; my mouth looked puffy and red, and my hair was matted into knots. I didn't have a brush. Hannah knocked on the bathroom door as I took a long drink from the sink faucet and rubbed the makeup off my face with a wet towel.

"You okay, Jory?" She opened the door, glanced at me, and looked away.

"Yeah, but I *have* to get out of here."

"I'm not quite ready to leave," Hannah said, checking her teeth in the mirror. "José's such a sweetie. He's going to take me out to breakfast tomorrow since my mom's out of town and everything. Isn't that the sweetest?" Hannah looked so pretty—her skin was flushed a pale rose color that complemented her wet hair tied up in pigtails.

"What?" I stared at her, my mouth hanging open.

Hannah blinked at me. "It's just that I really want to savor this moment, Jor. This has been the best night of the summer. José planned it all for me."

"Can't you go home and call him and still go to breakfast or whatever?"

"Please, Jor?" Hannah smiled all coy. "Just this once."

"You want me to call my mom?" Empty threat, right?

"Will you? Oh, thanks! You're the best." Hannah hugged me. "I feel terrible, but—" She didn't even finish her sentence before running out and flopping next to José on the little couch.

"I can't believe this." I wiped my face clean, braided my hair, and stumbled out of the room without looking at anyone. Especially Hannah.

I left the suite and took the elevator down to the casino level. No one noticed me as I lost myself in the maze of jangling machines and blackjack tables. Everything seemed kind of hazy. My head hurt, and my stomach didn't feel much better. I wanted my mom. I clicked on my cell phone and looked at the time, blinking away the tears in my eyes. In seventeen years I'd never had to call my mom to come rescue me— especially not at three in the morning. I had no idea how she'd react, but it wouldn't be good. I *could* take a cab to Hannah's house. But then what? Wait on her front steps all night? How much did a cab cost, anyway? I opened my purse, rummaged around, found three dollars in change. Damn nose fund.

I staggered out of the casino into the flashy downtown lights. I could walk home. I turned around, blinking. That way! Or was it that direction? I'd lost my bearings. A drunk stumbled up to me, mumbling, staring at my boobs. I ran back inside and dialed home.

"Mom?" I couldn't stop myself from crying. "Come and get me."

Chapter Twenty-three

CAKES AND CRUSHES CRUSHED

What's wrong with me? It's 5:30 A.M. on a Saturday during my so-called summer of passion (yeah, right!), and I'm pedaling like crazy down Arlington to get to work on time. At least I'm feeling slightly warmer. What's with the clouds and wind in August?

Katie wanted me at work by 5:45 in the morning! Two weddings. After rubbing my arms and trying not to look like I'd biked to work, I helped Katie set the cake layers carefully into the van for the morning wedding at San Rafael Park. Don't even *think* about Gideon!

What's so romantic about sunrise? The bride would probably have puffy eyes; the groom would have bed head; all the guests would be crabby. And cake at six in the morning? Should've ordered a mega box of doughnuts, or a doughnut cake, or the world's biggest cinnamon roll.

I drove the van to do the initial setup while Katie stayed behind to put the finishing touches on the second cake. The second cake looked like a spaceship: oval layers covered with silver sugar crystals sat on top of the other, slightly offset, like something out of an old sci-fi movie. *When I get married, my cake*—I stopped the thought. Who would marry me? Boys only liked me in the dark. Drunk boys. All the others just played mind games or practiced their best flirting moves so they could use them on better girls, like Hannah and Megan. Megan had been at her dad's house for two weeks and had already gone out to a few parties with guys—high school guys—from her dad's surf school. Weirdest of all, she wrote long e-mails about finding her "authentic self" and had started to read the touchy-feely books that Hannah had been recommending for years. And Hannah? She hadn't been reading much besides José's text messages—about a million a day. He actually took her places—the beach, mountain biking, action movies, concerts in the park. She even joined his no-yoga-classes-available gym so they could lift weights together. Weights! Hannah barely apologized for the fact that her super-romantic breakfast had gotten me grounded "until further notice." That's a direct quote from Mom; it sounded more like something she stamped on bad mortgages. Jory Michaels's life will be denied until further notice.

I drove up through the quiet neighborhood to the park, just me, a few carousing cats, and some sunrise-loving bride, apparently. Light raindrops splattered against the windshield. The park was completely empty except for a couple with a baby playing Frisbee with their golden retriever at the dog park. If having a baby meant getting up at dawn with sunrise-obsessed brides, forget it—I'd die a virgin just to make sure that never happened to me.

Mom had "no immediate plans" to let me out of the house again anyway. She'd been talking to me with a tight mouth for the last week, and I don't think there was any Botox involved this time. Plus I saw a Krispy Kreme bag in her car. Not exactly an official item on the Caveman Diet (day 4). I could go out—but not in her car—to work, and to jewelry-making bonding time with the Mom Who's Pissed by Your Poor Choices and Lack of Responsibility—You Could Have Been Raped—and Though I'm Glad You Called Me, I Don't Know What to Do to Stop This Behavior.

No worries, Mom. I've sworn off boys. Forever. Bring on the *Guinness World Records* entry for World's Oldest Virgin.

Finally, I spotted a crew of people setting up a gazebo and chairs in the west end of the park. Nearby, a hot-air balloon heaved like an obscene phone caller. We'd had one couple drive off together on their Harleys at a wedding, but no one in a balloon. I carried the cake one layer at a time to a little table near the gazebo. Katie arrived with the fresh flowers and gauzy little butterflies on wires. I watched as she sank columns into the cake and placed flowers all around; early-bird guests had started to arrive by the time we set up the big vases of flowers around the gazebo. My hands itched after arranging so many prickly sunflower stems, among all the other weedy flowers, and my nose tingled with sneezes and my eyes watered a bit. My passion would not be flower arranging either.

"Jory, run back to the van for more floral tape." Katie leaned over, attaching flowers to the altar thing. If I ever *do* get married, I won't demand that weedy flowers be strapped to every stupid surface.

I jogged out to the van and sifted through Katie's big box for emergencies, finally finding a roll of tape. I turned around to run back to Katie, but froze. Gideon. Getting out of a girl's car. He wore a black tuxedo. Was he getting married? My heart raced. Should I run and hope he didn't see me? Act all cool and mature and say, *Good morning, Gideon. How are you?*

I ran.

I buried my nose in those weedy flowers, subtly wiping my runny nose on my sleeve and making those flowers stick to that altar like old chewing gum to a movie-theater seat. Behind me, I heard the injured-cat sound of a violin being tuned. I peeked through my hair over my shoulder and saw Gideon and the girl plus a couple of other guys sitting in a circle around music stands.

Katie tapped me on the shoulder. "That's enough. Let's go finish the cake table."

I stood up and rubbed my watery eyes. Gideon nudged Gorgeous Ski-Slope Nose Cello Player and laughed. *See? He's moved on. Just rustling up business for the jewelry-making trade with me. Probably flirted with different girls so his mom could start a teen bead club.* I stood at the cake table, randomly bunching flowers around the base of the cake. That's how it looks in nature, right?

"We're missing a butterfly," Katie said. "Jory, go look in the trunk of my car." She handed me the keys. "It's orange and yellow—a monarch."

I trudged off in search of butterflies. Would the bride collapse into tears without one more butterfly? My nose snuffled and I sneezed; she certainly could have survived without some of those flowers!

"Bless you." Gideon.

I turned around, wiping my nose against my sleeve again— real attractive, but better than staring at an ex–almost crush with snot running over my upper lip like I was a diseased four-year-old. Although I *felt* about four.

"You working?" My voice sounded jittery.

"Fourth wedding of the summer." Gideon shook his hair, covering half his face. "I've got to get some sheet music." His shiny black shoes looked out of place as I trailed after him, watching the footprints he made in the dewy grass. Why had Katie parked next to Cello Girl's car?

"I'm not following you. It's just that—" I fiddled with the button to open Katie's trunk. The horn started beeping so loud that I dropped the keys on the ground. Gideon and I bent down at the same time to pick them up; his hair brushed against my cheek, and our fingers almost touched, but I pulled my hand back fast and let him pick them up. He turned the alarm off and handed the keys back to me. I opened the trunk.

"You've got something stuck in your hair." Gideon pulled a yellow sunflower petal off the top of my head.

"Occupational hazard." I sounded so lame. "Look, about the other night—" I didn't know what to say next. That I couldn't say no to my mom, that I worry about her because all she does is diet and try to make friends with the fakest women in the neighborhood?

"Which night? The night you brought your mom over so you could avoid me? Or the night that you got grounded for staying out too late with your boyfriend?"

"What?" I shook my head, confused.

"I overheard your mom telling *the ladies* about some all-night casino party." Gideon turned around and slammed the door to Cello Girl's car. "You could've told me you weren't interested. You didn't need to advertise it on a T-shirt."

Gideon's remark prickled worse than the bride's thorny flowers. I wanted to have some kind of snappy comeback. Something clever, something that would hurt, something that would make him think about *me* for the rest of the day. But nothing came. I watched him take long strides back toward Cello Girl. I cringed, thinking about the stupid "Who Needs Boys?" T-shirt and the way Gideon's face had looked when my mom rushed into the shop. But I couldn't think of anything to say.

Dick in the Dark is not my boyfriend was the only thing that looped through my head, like a really bad song stuck on repeat. I wiped my eyes on my shirt, found the stupid little butterfly, delivered it to Katie, all while keeping my eyes on the ground so I wouldn't see Gideon. I only looked up when the quartet started playing as the guests found their seats. Gideon had a funny expression on his face. *Megan's right: he's just an orchestra geek with a big nose.*

I managed my best fake smile through the rest of the wedding ceremony, the cake-cutting, and the balloon takeoff.

Thank God they rushed things because of the rain clouds. Gideon kept playing as the balloon huffed and puffed in the air. I wished I too could float up, up, over the mountains, and away.

The bride tossed her bouquet from up in the sky. It landed near Cello Girl's feet, and the whole quartet started laughing. I caught Gideon's eye as he smiled. For a moment he smiled at me, but he tickled Cello Girl's waist. Let him have her and her well-shaped nose. Better for the gene pool.

A breeze was blowing my hair around my face by the time we packed things up. A few more raindrops splattered around us.

"Take some cake over to the musicians." Katie handed me four little plates with plastic forks. "They played beautifully, didn't they?"

"They didn't sound like sick cats, if that's what you mean."

Katie gave me a puzzled look.

I carried the plates over and handed one to each musician. I hesitated when I came to Gideon. Part of me wanted to smash it into his curly hair, but he stood and took the plate from me.

"Look." Gideon ducked his head and smiled with his lips closed. "I didn't mean to piss you off, really."

"Too late," I said. "And you're right. I'm *not* interested."

I grabbed the box Katie handed me to take back to the van and ran to the parking lot. Frosting-coated sunflowers and butterflies clattered around inside. I stopped short at the van. Great. The bride and groom's limo was parked at an angle in front me. All that trouble to park where I wouldn't have to back out. I looked at the fence behind me. Could I just wait till they returned? I looked at the tiny rainbow-colored dot of a balloon in the sky. Nope. Even though I'd be here for hours inching forward and back. How many modes of transportation did these people need? Why couldn't they float to their honeymoon? I decided to wait until Katie left for the shop so she wouldn't see what a pathetic driver she'd actually hired.

I got in the van and turned the key. Gideon walked by holding his violin case in one hand and the girl's cello in the other; she reached up and gave his hair a tousle. Keeping my eyes on Gideon, I threw the gear into reverse. *Wham.* I slammed against the fence. No biggie. That's what bumpers are for, right?

Gideon glanced over toward the sound but got into Cello Girl's car. I gave him the finger where he couldn't see it, yanked the gear into first, and pulled forward with a big lurch. The sickening crunch of metal ripping metal vibrated through the van. I lifted my foot off the clutch, pulled the key out of the ignition, and jumped out of the van. Katie's car had disappeared down the road, followed by Cello Girl's car.

I ran around to the passenger side—a short metal post, not attached to the fence, had ripped through the sliding door. A gash tore through the painted roses, gaping like a laughing mouth with giant pink lips. My legs shook. I leaned against the van with my head on my arms. Just suck it up. You can explain. Explain *what? Gosh, Katie, I was staring at the guy I thought I might like who might have actually liked me, but you see my friends think he's got a big nose and my mom insisted on coming to jewelry-making and I said something mean. And I couldn't stand to see him with that girl with the cello and the perfect nose. And . . .*

I drove back to the cake shop with tears and snot streaming down my face. Katie cried harder than I did when she saw the van.

Even though the van door wouldn't open, we still had another wedding to set up. Katie didn't look at me as she told me to carefully and *I really mean it*, goddamn it, lift the cake layers over the passenger seat and place them on the racks. Sugar crystals slid off the cake every time I tilted it even a little. Will the bride completely freak out if her cake isn't quite so sugar-sparkly? While packing the third layer, I scraped my leg against some metal part on the seat, but I kept that cake straight, goddamn it.

Katie didn't say one word to me as *she* drove to the Lakeridge Country Club. I sat in the passenger seat, surrounded by all the silvery purple roses that we couldn't get into the flower storage in the back, thanks to me. I'd probably never drive again. Ever. I'd just hunker down with my bus pass, my world-renowned virginity, and the love of my life: a bottle of whiskey. I blinked away more tears. How had I managed to screw up my entire summer in one stupid morning? I took a deep breath of rose-scented air and let one of the silvery purple roses prick my leg.

The reception room was a mass of silver balloons and mirrors; even the tables had mirrors on them. Everywhere I turned, I spotted my giant red-from-crying nose. I fluffed my hair close to my face so I'd see less of myself as I placed three roses in each table vase. Katie brought in the cake layers while the worried wedding planner squawked about having everything ready on time.

"Do you have extra sugar crystals?" Worried Wedding Planner asked. "These cakes do not sparkle like we'd agreed."

"Some blew off in all that wind, but I've got more in the

van." Katie sounded exhausted, because of me. She headed back out.

"Oh, dear." Worried Wedding Planner tapped a clipboard and stared at the oval cake layers spread out on the table. "The bridal party will arrive in twenty minutes."

I didn't want Katie to get in any more trouble, so I walked over and scooted the bottom layer into the center of the cake table. I stuck the short pillars into the cake. I'd done this how many times this summer? Well, I'd watched Katie do it, anyway. I set the middle oval on top, steadying it until it wasn't wobbly. So far, so good. I pressed the second set of pillars into the cake, and added the top layer. Gorgeous spaceship.

Worried Wedding Planner sighed. "Much better."

I picked up the empty flower buckets and headed out to the van. Katie didn't meet my eyes as she ran past, carrying a bottle of sparkly sugar crystals. Thick clouds darkened the sky.

I heard Katie's scream from the parking lot. I dropped the buckets next to the van and ran back inside. Had the freaked-out wedding planner gone ballistic and stabbed Katie?

No. Worse. Much, much worse.

The top layer of the cake had slid off, leaving a trail of sparkly silver frosting on the tablecloth before crashing to the floor like a thwarted alien invasion. I started hyperventilating. *All my fault. It's all my fault.*

"Run and get the extra layer!" Katie said.

"Extra layer?" I'd seen only three cake layers. The cake only had three layers. I brought all three layers. My heart beat fast.

Katie blinked fast. "You *did* pack the extra layer? The one I created in case of disaster?"

"Sorry," I peeped.

"Give me twenty minutes." Katie ran out the door. As I followed, Worried Wedding Planner shrieked about the bridal party, *the bridal party!*

Katie drove back to the shop as if she were starring in one of Finn's video games. We slammed around corners, peeled away from stoplights, and sped through quiet neighborhoods at freeway speeds. I gripped my door handle and closed my eyes. I was about to die: vehicular homicide.

I held the door open for her as she raced inside and grabbed the extra layer out of the big fridge in the back. How would I have known about that?

Katie placed the cake in a box on the floor of the passenger seat.

"Should I hold it in my lap?" I leaned over to pick up the box. How could I make this better? I'd be the best employee ever. I'd try my hardest to do everything exactly right.

"Uh-uh." Katie shook her head. "I'm going to have to let

you go." She closed her eyes as if she couldn't stand the sight of me. "Now."

"I'm fired?" My throat constricted as I tried to swallow back tears. I was only trying to help. Except I'm such a loser that everything I touch gets ruined.

"Oh, yeah. You're fired. I'll be lucky to book another wedding after this disaster." Katie rubbed her temples, jumped into the van, and screeched out of the driveway.

I rode my bike home. As I pedaled uphill against the wind, grit flew against my legs, and I nearly blew over a few times. It started to rain big, warm, puddly drops. I could hardly see ahead of me; my crying didn't help. By the time I got home, my clothes were splotchy with mud.

I looked just how I felt.

Chapter Twenty-four

SENIOR PHOTOS, NOSY MOM, BIG FIGHT

Mom insisted on coming to my senior class photo shoot—part of my bonding-with-Mother imprisonment punishment. What did she think I was going to do? Get drunk with the photographer and start taking nude photos to post on the Internet? I told her I could just ride my bike and get it over with. (I was completely grounded from driving after the delivery-van incident.) Plus, Mom and Dad insisted that I use my summer savings to pay for the repairs. Goodbye, nose fund. I still planned to finance the surgery without their help. Or knowledge. Somehow.

"Welcome, Reno High Seniors" was written on a whiteboard on an easel as we walked in the door. The shop smelled like cinnamon apple candles—that fake, make-your-nose-itch scent common at Christmastime. Did the guy know it was August?

Mom motioned for me to sit next to her in the little chairs in the waiting area. She dug in her oversize purse for a makeup bag and brushes.

"Stop it!" I pushed Mom's hand away from my nose. She kept trying to apply more "shading" to the sides of my nose even though I was wearing enough makeup to make a Circus Circus clown jealous.

Mom dabbed more junk on my nose. "Models use shading all the time to create the illusion of beauty."

"You're the one suffering from the *de*lusion that I have any so-called beauty to work with."

"Now, that's not the proper attitude." Mom pushed at my stiff-with-too-much-product hair, but it didn't budge. "This is a special day. You will look back on this photo with fond memories for the rest of your life." Mom smiled at me.

"Oh, yeah. I'm sure I'll have really fond memories of my mom trying to bring my nose down to an acceptable size with magical makeup."

"I guarantee you every one of your classmates is wearing makeup." Mom examined her well-manicured nails, frowning at a bit of chipped polish. "There's nothing wrong with trying to make the best of what you have."

"What I have is Great-Grandpa Lessinger's nose."

"Your face has such *character*." Mom couldn't keep herself from dabbing at my nose again with her makeup brush. "Your great-grandpa was quite a man. He was a war hero, you know."

"Whatever." I should just go with the "Photo Unavailable" spot in the yearbook. I stuck a magazine in front of my face. Thin models with flowing hair and perfect little noses scowled at me. Only four more days until I presented my Nice Nose Notebook to Dr. Lawrence, plastic surgeon extraordinaire, and we selected a beautiful nice nose together. I did have to figure out the money thing, but they'd have payment plans, right? Maybe I could still baby-sit or something. Maybe model with my nice new nose. I'm tall. Maybe we'd get a group discount if I could talk Mom into getting her few remaining fat cells sucked out of her body. We'd all be one happy, beautiful family. My grades would improve; I'd have a fabulous new boyfriend, or several new boyfriends. Maybe Zane Zimmerman would want me to fly out and visit him at college. It all depended upon the nice new nose.

Inside the studio, the photographer ohhed and ahhed over his subject. "Gorgeous! You belong in the pages of *Teen Vogue*." Was he lying to make some plain girl feel good, or did he actually have the next great teen model in his studio? Was I going to have to smile through a bunch of fake compliments?

"I think it's almost our turn." Mom attacked again with her

brush. "Let's touch up a few spots." She crinkled her cute little nose and examined me like some kind of redecorating project gone wrong.

"Mom. You're going to make me look like a zebra! Stop it." I turned away. "I'm sorry I'm not the gorgeous daughter you want me to be."

"Why would you say something like that?" Mom set down her brush and looked at me with wide eyes, as if I'd actually hurt her feelings. *Give me a break.*

"Because it's true. You think I don't notice the ratio of beautiful Adonis Finn photos compared to mine? It's obvious you don't want to have to look at me."

"I don't understand. What photos?"

"In the nice-nose hallway of fame. The gazillion photos of Finn?"

"What?" Mom looked totally confused. "Our hallway? I put all those sports photos up to be supportive."

"Face it. He's good-looking."

"Well, yes, but so are you."

"Yes, in my unique, special way. But what exactly is special about me? I don't do anything *special*. I'm not smart in any special way. I'm not pretty. I don't have anything that makes me unique. Except a big nose that you're always trying to hide."

Mom didn't have time to answer because Ashley Winters

swept out of the photo room, beaming like she'd just won the Miss Reno High Best Senior Photo Session Ever Pageant. Her skeleton-thin mother followed behind her.

"Can you believe how grown up our girls are?" she cooed.

Mom transitioned right into aren't-we-all-having-so-much-fun social mode. "I was just saying the same thing to Jory," Mom gushed. "Next thing I know, Finn will be graduating."

"He's such a gorgeous young man," Mrs. Winters said. "Even the senior girls are after him." She tilted her head toward Ashley.

Ashley acknowledged me—for the first time *ever*, I might add—with a slight finger wiggle. "Can you believe that we're seniors? I don't even *feel* like a senior." She sighed and shook her long red hair around her shoulders, actually looking like someone who had stepped out of the pages of *Teen Vogue*. Great. Ashley Winters is going to want to be nice to me so I can hook her up with my little brother.

"Come on in," the photographer said.

"Guess I gotta go." I rolled my eyes.

"You'll totally feel like a supermodel." Ashley giggled. "Say hi to Finn for me."

"You betcha." Maybe I could run a dating service for my brother and make up my missing nose money. I could put an ad in the *Caughlin Rancher:* "Desperate super-schnozzed senior will rent gorgeous brother for reasonable fee. Call 555-1891."

Mom pushed her nails into my back and scootched me into the photo studio. The photographer was mostly bald but had a long greasy ponytail slinking down his back, like a gray snake. He wore a black T-shirt that said "Photographers Do It in the Dark." So classy! Maybe I was kind of glad my mom tagged along. He handed me a little velvety shirt thing.

"For the formal shot." When he smiled, I saw that he had two gold teeth.

All the seniors had to match. In the photos, it looks like a glamorous evening gown; in reality, it looks like one of my grandma's sofa-armrest-protector thingies. And it was black. If there's one color that does not flatter my blond hair and freckled complexion, it's black. I went behind the little changing curtain, wondering if the guy had secret perv cams hidden in the walls. He looked the type. I heard Mom making small talk. "She's pretty nervous. Not very confident, you know. Also, we don't want any profile shots taken." I imagined her tapping her nose. *Great-Grandpa Lessinger,* she'd whisper in a low tone.

I flipped Mom off behind the curtain. Yeah, Mom, tell Perv Photographer that I'm an insecure big-nosed freak.

I walked out from behind the curtain wearing the velvety

little top thing over my jeans. The photographer pointed to a stool in front of a big camera.

"Now, relax. You're a beautiful girl." He winked at Mom. "One, two, three."

I stuck out my tongue.

"Jory!" Mom exclaimed. "I can't believe you did that!" She turned to the photographer. "I am so sorry. I'm simply shocked. She doesn't usually act like this."

"It was just a joke," I said.

"No funny photos. The yearbook editor made that very clear." The photographer stood behind his camera. "Now, smile like you're looking at the cutest boy in your class." This time he winked at me.

I leaned my head down by my shoulder, rolled my eyes up to the ceiling, and made a dreamy closed-mouth smile.

"Jory! What are you doing?" Mom stomped her foot. "You're embarrassing me."

"So what else is new, Mom?"

The photographer took a deep breath. "We'll try one more. Smile in the way you'd like to appear in the yearbook."

I put my hands over my face. *Click. Flash.*

"That's great." I jumped off the stool. "Ready, Mom?"

"No, it's not great. Sit," Mom hissed. "This photo isn't just for you. It's for me. It's for posterity. It's for the whole community."

The photographer nodded. What did he know?

"Who are you trying to impress, Mom? Maybe you could just put Finn in my place. It's not like Jory is a real name anyway. Just pretend you have two *gorgeous* sons," I said, mimicking Ashley Winters's mom. "I can just go live in a cave and give you the real scoop on the Caveman Diet. I'll hook you up with some dead rabbits."

The photographer turned around and pretended to adjust his camera.

"I don't know what's gotten into you." Mom spoke low. "Where did all your self-confidence go?"

"Where did it go?" I spoke loud. "When did I ever have any? You've been slathering my face with nose-minimizing makeup ever since I was twelve. You think I didn't get the message?

"That's ridiculous."

"No, it's not. Obviously I'm a total embarrassment. I'm probably the reason it took so long for you to be invited to that stupid book club, and now I'm keeping you and Dad out of the Mullinses' snobby wine club. Maybe if I were a cute cheerleader or a studly jock, you'd get in. But, no, I'm a big-nosed freak with absolutely no talent whatsoever." I yanked the scratchy little top off and threw it on the floor, standing there in my bra. "I don't even want to be in the yearbook."

The photographer guy slinked out of the room.

"Too bad there isn't a Nose Shrinking Diet, huh, Mom?"

"Is this about my dieting?" Mom looked small as she crossed her thin arms. "I'm only trying to improve myself."

"Why? You're gorgeous. If you don't like the way you look, how am I supposed to like the way *I* look? I'm never going to be as pretty as *you*. Never!" I ran behind the curtain and threw my inside-out T-shirt over my head. "I'm never going to be good enough for you!"

I ran out of the room, then looked back at Mom, who stood there crying.

Wham! I tripped over some guy's feet and went sprawling onto the dirty red carpet. I blinked back tears and pushed myself up to sitting. My elbow hurt and my knees felt raw. The guy pulled me up by my armpits as if I were a toddler learning to walk.

Gideon.

He didn't say anything, but his expression drooped like wilted flowers.

"What are you looking at?" I ran out, even though my scraped knees hurt. I dug in the bottom of my purse for my set of keys. Ha! She hadn't thought to confiscate them. After I jumped into the minivan, I looked back through the window of the photographer's shop. Helen embraced Mom in a big hug. Gideon watched me. I lifted both hands up high and flipped them all off where they *could* see it. I was sick of soaking up everything like a sponge cake! I sped away from the curb. Where should I go? No way would I go home to Mr. So Gorgeous All the Senior Girls Go Wild for Me Finn. Plus, I didn't want to see Mom again until all her hair turned gray and her perfect nose disappeared under a million wrinkles.

Maybe the plastic surgeon would see me today? I pulled into the plastic surgeon's parking lot over by the hospital, but I didn't have my Nice Nose Notebook and I didn't want to appear insane, with tears down my face and my hair all stiff and crazy. I yanked at my hair. Stupid hair. That's all anyone ever complimented me about. Anyone could grow hair!

I spotted Mom's beading accessory box. "I'll show them!" I rummaged through the various beads and wires until I found a pair of tiny scissors—and snipped away at my hair, one chunk at a time. My hair floated all around me in little wisps. I cut one side, but then my fingers got sore, so I stopped. I looked at my reflection in the rearview mirror. Ugly. My minimizing makeup smeared all around my nose like fudge marble cake batter. In the light I looked like some hideous old showgirl trying to look young again. Or one of those sad old prostitutes they interview on the local news sometimes. I wiped the makeup away with the wet wipes Mom kept in her ultimate soccer-mom minivan, scraping at my face until it hurt. And drove again.

I ended up at Virginia Lake, watching pairs of geese float around in the murky water. *Would anyone ever want to mate for life with me? Not the way I am now.* Only a new nose could rescue me from my miserable life.

I got out of the van and ran around the lake, once, twice, three times. Wouldn't Mr. Jock PE Teacher be proud? Jory Michaels ran three miles. I bent over, breathing hard. A mom with a double stroller pushed her children to the very edge of the sidewalk to avoid the crazy girl with half long, half short hair. Maybe if I ran long enough I'd just die. *Such a tragedy,* people would whisper at my funeral. *She destroys her best feature then dies.* Kids would ask, *Can people die from being ugly, Mommy?* I ran around a fourth time, finally stepping into the van with quivering legs. I didn't have the energy to cry.

I drove home to an empty house and cut off the rest of my hair.

Chapter Twenty-five

NOSE DOCTORS, WITCHES (ME), AND BIG TROUBLE

I smoothed my prickly short hair while looking at a blurry version of myself in the shiny elevator doors. My backpack with my Nice Nose Notebook hung heavy on my shoulder as I tried to calm my breathing. *Don't look like a crazy teenager who just cut off all her hair,* I told myself. I fanned my shirt over my stomach to dry off some of the sweat from biking all the way to the doctor's office—my armpits weren't exactly fragrant either.

I should've begged Mom for the minivan, but she wasn't talking to me. I did find the phone book open to "Psychologists," though, and I was pretty certain that she wasn't finally seeking help for her social-climbing, a-diet-will-cure-anything attitude. Plus, I'd overheard several hushed conversations between Mom, Dad, and even oh-so-sane-and-beautiful Finn. That's okay. Me and my new nose will go tour the world as a fashion model, purchase some private island inhabited only by gorgeous musclemen—who also have great personalities—and live happily ever after.

The doctor's waiting room smelled like alcohol wipes. Clean. Several large photographs of mountains decorated the walls. An older woman sat in a chair, reading a fat paperback novel. Face-lift? A younger woman flipped through magazines across from me. Definite boob job; she had a great nose. Everyone could tell what I was there for, right? Super Schnozz. I sat down in one of the plush little chairs and picked up a *Business Weekly* magazine; I wanted to appear older and mature.

The receptionist peered out at me from a little window in the corner. "Are you here for an appointment, miss?"

"Oh, yes." Boob-Job Woman glanced at me as I stood up and walked over to the little window. I felt really stupid. Whenever I went to the doctor, Mom did this part.

She handed me a clipboard of forms. "Fill these out."

I sat back down in the little cushy chair. High blood pressure? Does right now count? I checked *no* to everything, lingering on "Sexual Dysfunction" for a moment. Does being ugly and completely unattractive to boys count? I put a big fat *X* in the "no" box next to "Sexually Active" and brought the clipboard back to the receptionist.

"I need a copy of your insurance card," she said.

Insurance card? I opened my wallet and pretended to look for it. What on earth had possessed me to buy a Hello Kitty wallet? I looked like such a third-grader.

"Oh, I must have left it in my other wallet." Nose growing, but, hey, I was in the right place. "Can I send you a copy?" I envisioned sneaking into Mom's purse on a stealth mission late at night. *Caughlin Rancher* headline: "Desperate Big-Nosed Girl Bilks Mother's Insurance Company."

"Well, that's usually not our policy, but since this *is* just a consultation." The receptionist tapped her pen against her head. "Can you at least tell me your carrier? What's your copay?"

"Oh, it's a popular insurance. I know that." I saw my nose expanding past the woman's head until it hit the copy machine against the back wall. *Doctor! We have an emergency,* the receptionist would scream. *Hurry! This nose is going to take over the world.*

The receptionist's pen hung in mid-tap. "Would you like to phone your mother and ask?"

"Oh, no. No. My mother would kill me if she knew—I mean, if I disturbed her at work," I squeaked like a mouse. "I mean, she knows about my big nose and everything." Oh, God. Why hadn't I been practicing lying skills all these years? I sucked at lying. Sucked.

"Maybe you should pay up front today."

"Certainly." The receptionist's eyes grew wide as I pulled the wad of hundred-dollar bills out of my notebook covered with magazine cutouts of models with ideal noses. "How much is it?"

"Eighty-five."

My cheeks burned as I handed her a hundred-dollar bill. I tossed my head to fan my hair around my shoulders. Nothing moved. Oh, God. I forgot. I'd become Big-Nosed Butchered-Hair Girl. I put my hand up to my hair to smooth it out. It still stood up in little clumps. Mom had begged her hairdresser—begged—but he couldn't get me in until tomorrow and I wouldn't let Mom come near me with her scissors. She might decide it wasn't even worth it to have a daughter like me. *Caughlin Rancher* headline: "Mother Kills Desperate Big-Nosed Daughter." The article would go on: "'At least the embarrassment is over,' mother sighs. It turns out beautiful Adonis-like son is enough for Michaels family."

Both of the women in the waiting room tracked me with their eyes as I returned to my seat. This time I picked up *Teen People* magazine. I'd blown the whole maturity thing. The page I opened had a quote from a guy with soulful eyes and a totally kissable mouth who said that what he likes best about a girl is hair. "Longer the better." Not my type. Maybe I'd have to move to a forest and date a hedgehog. I paged through the rest of the magazine, feeling like a crumbly dirt clod, ugly and ready to fall apart. *Don't cry. You can't cry. Not now. Maybe you even needed to cut your hair before surgery.*

"Jory Michaels?" A woman in purple scrubs opened the doctor-area door. "Follow me, please."

I followed her into a little room that had big posters of the insides of a breast. They should bring tours of boys in here and show them that! Definitely not sexy. I looked at an old copy of *Better Homes and Gardens.* Total Mom mag. The fluffy frosted cake on page 43 reminded me of what a loser I'd become by getting fired from my summer job. That was one thing I'd actually had over Megan: my summer job. Now I was back to being Loser #1. I hadn't answered Hannah's calls (in spite of her long rambling apology messages about "selfishly living in the moment") or Megan's e-mails since wedding-disaster day; I did let Tyler take me out for a "comforting" cheeseburger and fries at Juicy's—I'd called him so he wouldn't come looking to give me a ride home after work. I hadn't minded, really, telling him all the gruesome details (minus the stuff about Gideon), but now I was ignoring his calls too.

About a million years later, a nurse came in to go over my

medical history. I wanted to roll up and mummify myself in the crinkly examining-table paper when she asked me about my sexual activity. "None," I peeped. The nurse nodded like, *Of course, how could someone like you have a boyfriend?*

"And you're here because?"

"Isn't it obvious?" I watched the nurse jiggle her shiny white sneakers up and down over her crossed knee. Up. Down. Up. Down.

Her foot stopped moving. "Why don't you tell me in your own words."

"I need a new nose."

"Do you have any breathing problems? Sleep problems?"

I shook my head, hating the empty feeling of having nearly no hair.

"Okay. Dr. Lawrence will be in to see you in a few minutes."

I picked up the magazine and read a story about a woman who'd lost her arm fighting in Iraq but came home and started painting. She'd sold a self-portrait for $4,000 in some fancy-schmancy gallery. Now that's optimism. I'd lost my hair, and I hadn't left my room for two days. How pathetic was that?

Knock. Knock. The doctor came into the room. With her long black hair tied up in a ponytail, she looked too young to be a doctor—plus she had a largish, bumpy nose. Didn't she have a friend who could help her with that? I could see how you couldn't operate on yourself, but didn't all plastic surgeons try to look perfect? Wouldn't that be advertising or something?

"My nurse tells me you're looking to get a new nose?" The doctor sat down and flipped through pages in a folder. "No breathing issues? Sleep issues?" She sounded like Megan.

"No, but I have boy issues, family issues, and ugliness issues," I said. "With a new nose, all those problems could disappear. I'd fit into my family. Some boy might actually like me in the daylight and I'd feel good about myself." I fidgeted and wondered if I'd said too much, or not enough. I should've brought Hannah. She could have elbowed me when I started talking too much. One problem: I didn't want to tell Hannah that I thought I had a big nose.

"So," Dr. Lawrence said in measured tones. "You're looking for a new nose to solve your problems? Am I understanding you correctly?"

"Exactly. I've known it for some time now and I've been saving money from my summer job." I unzipped my backpack. "Also, I've been doing research." I pulled out the Nice Nose Notebook. "I've collected several different noses you can choose from."

The doctor took the notebook from me and flipped through the pages slowly. "You've put a lot of time into this project."

"Yes. I'm very serious." My heart stopped beating quite so fast. This was actually happening. "Just stop and point out any noses you think would work on me."

The doctor closed the notebook without looking further.

"You stopped too soon. I stuck one in there the other day that had freckles on it just like mine." I reached for the book.

"Why don't we go back to my office and chat?" The doctor stood and opened the door for me. I followed her to a posh little office cluttered with papers and boring-looking magazines. A framed photo showed Dr. Lawrence hugging some guy on top of a mountain somewhere.

"I want to talk about what plastic surgery can do for you and what it can't do." She sighed just like Mom had after she saw my hair. "As a surgeon, I can help you work with what you have. I cannot transform your face to look like the models in your notebook. You cannot order a new nose like a sweater from a catalog."

I turned my notebook over in my lap. Why had I glued photos on the back of it too? Blond actresses smiled back at me with cute little crinkled noses.

"I didn't want to order a nose, exactly." My voice sounded babyish.

"Plastic surgery cannot solve family problems, or boyfriend problems, or make you popular."

"I don't want to be popular—that's Megan," I protested. "I want to be beautiful. I want to like myself."

"Plastic surgery can help you feel better about yourself, sometimes, but only if you already feel pretty good about yourself. The way you feel about yourself comes from your *thinking,* not your appearance."

"You sound like some guidance counselor slash advice columnist slash mother." Maybe I hadn't chosen the right plastic surgeon. This one was too touchy-feely New Age psychobabbly.

Dr. Lawrence folded her arms across her rather small bosom. "What *does* your mother think about this?"

I looked down at a small scrap of paper on the ground. "She doesn't know." I looked up quickly. "But she'd totally approve. She's always fussing over my looks because the rest of my family is gorgeous and I'm not, and she really cares about appearances and things. She would totally approve. I think."

"So why haven't you told her?"

"I just wanted to surprise her with my new nose." I'd planned it all out: how I could forge Mom's signature for permission, stay with a friend (probably Megan—she'd be good at post-op care) until I'd healed and everything, then return home. Surprise! I'm beautiful too.

"Rhinoplasty is major surgery, Jory. You don't go home

with a brand-new nose like it's an outfit from the mall. You will have weeks of recovery time. It's also quite expensive."

"Oh, I have the money," I said. "Some of the money." My voice sounded more wobbly than I wanted it to. "I have to pay to fix the van I wrecked at work." A stupid tear fell out of my eye. "But I'll still have some left over."

"It sounds like you have a lot going on." The doctor rummaged around in her desk drawer. "You might want to talk to a psychologist."

"I'm not crazy. I'm ugly." More tears. *Don't sob. Keep your voice steady.* Tom's angry voice reverberated in my memory: "Not even worth it." *You can't do anything right, Jory,* I thought to myself. *You can't even buy beauty.*

"I'm ugly. Why won't you fix me?"

"Jory, you're not ugly. Your nose actually fits your face." She tapped her own nose. "Most of us will never look like the girls in magazines—and most of them wear a lot of makeup to achieve those looks."

"You're not going to tell me that nose-minimizing makeup will solve all my problems, because it won't."

"There's nothing wrong with using makeup to enhance your features." Imperfect Nose Doctor gave me a look of pity. "You can also show off your best features. You might want to think about growing your pretty blond hair out."

I lost it. Big, loud, make-the-nurse-come-running sobs. The doctor handed me tissue after tissue.

"But I have the money. Won't you just do it for the money?" I held out a wad of cash and waved it at her like a desperate idiot. "If you won't, I'll find someone who will."

"Jory, I won't ever operate on someone who has unrealistic expectations. No surgeon will. Not to mention you need parental consent." Her voice softened. "With maturity, you will discover that you possess beauty in a package uniquely yours."

I kept crying, filling tissue after tissue with wet globs of snot.

Dr. Lawrence called my mom (at work!), told her *absolutely everything*, and asked her to come pick me up. My whole plan came crashing down like that wedding cake, totaled like the delivery van.

Chapter Twenty-six

TANTRUMS, BEADING, BOYS?

With my face buried in my pillow, I screamed out another tirade of obscenities. If Mom was going to send me to my room like a five-year-old, I was going to act like one. It's all her fault! *She's* the one obsessed with her body! So what if I want a new nose? That stupid surgeon and her special adolescent psychologist! I'll just fly to an obscure country in South America and have some doctor who got kicked out of medical school do the surgery. Or maybe I'll go live in the Amazon with one of those weird ancient tribes we studied in Mrs. Currie's class. I will become a legend. Future generations will try to find Crazy Big-Nose Girl, the way people go to the northwest to look for Bigfoot. Big Nose. Has a ring to it, right? I could leave nose prints for people to find—or used tissues.

Mom opened my door. "I expect you to be ready for beading class in half an hour."

"I'm not doing your little bonding activity because I hate you and I'd rather be dead than go anywhere with you. What am I, anyway? Your special charity case of ugliness? I am never showing my face in public again. If you make me go, I'll just run away from home and join some whorehouse out in the desert. Guys with a thing for giant noses will request me."

I wept at the fact of my true ugliness. How sad to be so ugly, so unloved. It took Judith Hearne years to achieve the desperate state I'd reached at the young age of seventeen. I didn't even need much alcohol. Kind of impressive, really.

I gave in to one last good pillow-and-stuffed-rabbit-soaking cry. Fifteen minutes later, I peeled myself off my bed and walked into the hall bathroom. That's when I saw that Finn had a friend over playing computer games in his room. Just what I needed: a witness. The kid would go back to school in two weeks. *Yeah, Finn has a sister. She's really ugly and I was there, dude, when she lost it. Yeah, the dudes from the crazy farm came and hauled her off. No, Finn's not really upset. He likes having a bathroom to himself, and they're turning her old room into a museum for his trophies.*

My nose glowed in the bathroom mirror. Big. Red. Jurassic. My eyes looked like dirt clods in pools of blood; they'd need hours to recover. I'd have to wear sunglasses. Maybe I could wear a ski mask. It could become my fashion statement, the way some celebrities carry small dogs everywhere. I'd knit ski masks in different colors and become mysterious, interesting. I splashed water on my face. My eyes stung. Mom tapped on the door and handed me a bottle of eye drops; I doused my eyes until fake sticky tears ran down my cheeks.

My hair. I had refused to see Mom's stylist after the whole plastic-surgeon-psychologist-phone-call thing. My blond hair stuck up in punk-rockish tufts. Work with it, right? I sprayed tons of glitter in my hair (Mom thinks glitter makes girls look like streetwalkers). I spritzed a little more on my most likely candidates for bangs before adding dark lipstick and too much eyeshadow.

Mom could make me go beading, but I could certainly make her regret it.

On the drive down to the Jewel Café, Mom didn't talk much. Part of me wanted her to say something—*anything*—about the plastic surgeon incident, or the school photo shoot. All week she'd been unusually quiet—not silent-treatment quiet, but *thinking* quiet, and that made me nervous.

Like an old regular, Mom strutted into the classroom,

dragging her special jewelry-making supply case. Over the past three weeks Mom had purchased all the little pliers, wires, and magazines for the Enthusiast. Her love of jewelry-making pretty much ensured that I would despise it and suck at it. Yup, it was going to be a hell of an evening. I didn't even allow myself to think about Gideon; thankfully, his door was closed when we walked past. I didn't hear him playing his violin either. My hands got sweaty and my heart beat fast every time I thought about all the crap he overheard at the photo studio. Mom swore they couldn't hear anything, but I stood there waiting for her nose to grow. I think mine just grew for her. I'd heard the photographer gushing over Ashley, so I *know* Helen and Gideon heard everything I'd said at a much louder volume—every last pathetic, embarrassing syllable.

Mom patted the plastic chair next to her at the table.

"Hello, girls." Mom grinned. "Some of you know my daughter, Jory."

"Nice to see you again, Jory," said an older lady wearing so many beaded necklaces that she resembled the jewelry rack at Hannah's favorite secondhand store. They all knew. Every sordid detail. I could tell by their too-kind smiles of sympathy.

"I thought her daughter had long hair?" the lady next to her whispered.

"She cut it, Rita," Necklace Lady said. "Remember?"

Cynthia Simons from the Ranch made a *tsk-tsk* sound. My hands flew up to my head; I crunched a stiff clump with my fingers, dusting the table with purple glitter. I smashed the rest of my hair down with my hand. I don't know if it looked better. At least it *felt* better.

Helen swept into the room, carrying a tray of cake slices and a teapot.

"Here come the goodies, ladies! Jory, welcome back. I'll teach you how to knot, even if these other ladies insist on moving on."

Everyone laughed as if she'd made an actual joke. Old people!

Helen set the tray down at the end of the table. "Go pick out something special. Ten large beads, twenty small ones."

I tiptoed past Gideon's room. I might have heard music playing low, but it could've been my heart beating like a drum solo. I swung the door to the main room open, feeling exposed, like even the walls watched me, mocked me. I quickly chose several swirly orange-green-yellow beads. I wasn't going to wear anything I'd ever make anyway, right? I was only here for enforced mother-bonding-with-crazy-nose-obsessed-daughter night.

As I walked back down the hallway, I watched the beads roll around on the little tray, like jaundiced eyeballs. *Wham!* The beads flew up in the air as I sprawled flat on the floor.

"I am so sorry, Jory," Gideon said. "I keep tripping you like some kind of idiot."

I sat up, rubbing my stinging palms. "No, *I* keep *tripping* like some kind of idiot."

"Let me see." Gideon sat down next to me, taking my hands in his. I nearly jerked away, but his touch felt so warm. He blew ticklishly on my palms while I stared at the rip in the knee of his jeans. "You'll be okay." He gave each hand a little squeeze before dropping it. He stood, pulling me up with one hand. "Why did you choose the vomit beads? They're so ugly."

"Maybe I'm in an ugly mood." I reached down to pick up a couple of beads. Why couldn't he let me suffer in peace?

"Yeah, Helen said she'd be surprised if you showed up."

"Great. I'm a regular gossip item." I blinked to prevent tears, noticing glitter on my eyelashes. "Why can't my mom just shut up? Blabbing about every stupid, embarrassing thing I do and then you—" I stopped myself from saying something about Gideon eavesdropping and hearing stuff but getting half of it wrong—like his thinking I actually had a boyfriend.

"Give her a break," he said in a soft voice. "She's worried about you."

"Whatever." Figures he'd take her side, though I probably deserved it. I scanned the floor for my other beads. Gideon's big toe stuck out of a hole in his sock. "Where did the rest of my stupid beads go? I just want to get this over with."

Gideon held the door open for me. "Come on, I'll help you pick out some new ones."

I stood among the bins of beads with my arms crossed while the gray and white cat wound itself around my legs. Gideon held the little tray. What a dork. He plays the violin. Dorky. He knows how to make jewelry. Major dorky. He likes his mom. Freaky dorky. He was still being nice to me even after knowing *all* about me. Just plain freaky.

"What color do you want?"

"Black."

Gideon shook his head. "Not your color." He walked around the room picking up beads here and there. I concentrated on his feet. Wears socks in the summer. Super dorky. But I kept looking up at his face and glorious hair. I touched my hair. At least it didn't feel too stiff, but I probably looked like a raving lunatic/rejected showgirl/cheap whore.

Gideon glanced at me sideways. "I like your hair. You kind of hid behind that long hair."

"No, I didn't." I turned away from him. *Did I?* I'd had to develop a whole new set of gestures since I'd cut my hair. All that twisting, flipping, and tossing—gone. I'd even tried biting my nails, but it didn't do much for me.

Gideon stared at me with a half-smile. "Maybe I should cut my hair."

"No, don't!" I plunged my hand into a box of beads. "I mean, you can do whatever you want, right? You don't have an image-obsessed mother who'd be embarrassed by you."

"You don't embarrass your mother."

"Yeah, right."

"You may freak her out, but you don't embarrass her." Gideon came over and handed me the little tray of beads, all different shades of soft brown and green. "Trust me. I *do* hear more gossip than is good for a growing boy's gender identity. Your mom's proud of how you worked hard all summer."

"Did she mention that I wrecked the van?"

"Well, I think anyone who knows you knows that you're accident-prone." Gideon ruffled my hair. "Ooh, it's sparkly too." He showed his purple glitter–covered palm to me. "You better get back in there or Helen will come searching for you." He rested his hand on my cheek. Just briefly. "Hang in there, Jory."

I could still feel his handprint on my cheek as I walked back into the beading room. Everyone ohhed and ahhed over my beads when I set the tray down. Matches your eyes, suits your blond hair, sassy style. I put my hand to my cheek. When I took it away, it glittered.

"That stuff is getting on everything." Mom sighed. "Girls and their hair."

"Leah, remember that awful colored mousse we used to use?" Mrs. Caughlin Ranch said. "I once ruined one of my mom's shower curtains with that stuff." She fluffed her streaked hair. "Now I can pay to have it done properly."

Everyone laughed (pathetic, humor-starved old people!). Helen sat down next to me and showed me how to use the needle-nose pliers to crimp the clasp onto the end of the silk string. I put my beads in order. Each bead was a little bit different, but they all belonged together somehow.

Helen showed me how to make a knot. "Hold the silk like this; now, give God the finger." I couldn't help but giggle as she demonstrated. "Throw little Timmy in the well." She dropped the silk down the center. "Use your tweezers to send Lassie down for the rescue. And pull." She'd made a perfect knot.

I tried, and I did it on the first try! I picked up a green bead with a pink rose on it and strung it onto the silk.

Helen nodded. "Great. Now make another knot. Use your cutoff straw as a spacer. Add your next bead."

Helen watched me do the next few beads before moving

on to help one of the other ladies do something complicated with earrings.

I felt calm as I strung a little green bead on top of a new knot. My necklace actually looked pretty good! I half listened to the other ladies gossip. *Well, you know, she found out about the cancer only the week before. And he still left her! Oh, I did give her the name of a great lawyer. Speaking of lawyers, my son is changing his major yet again. Another year of tuition; my husband is about to disown him. Well, that's nothing. My daughter was out with her boyfriend and came home so drunk—she had actually driven her car home in that state. I don't know what to do.* All the other ladies chimed in with advice.

Mom leaned over to me. "Thanks for calling me that night from the casino," she whispered.

I threw little Timmy back into the well, thinking that just a couple of hours ago I had wanted to throw myself into a well.

On the way home, Mom suddenly pulled to the side of the road. "I'm not very good at this," she said. "You're my oldest and it's always taken me longer to figure things out with you." She turned the engine off. "I don't mean that as a criticism." Mom sighed, filling the silent car with a whoosh of breath. "What I want to say is that I love you. Just the way you are. It hurts so much to think that I've made you feel bad about yourself—bad enough to want surgery. Just thinking about your Nice Nose Notebook makes me cry." Mom wiped tears from her eyes. "I never thought that my feelings about myself would affect you—"

"You care so much about looks."

"Only my own." Mom slapped her hands on the steering wheel. "No, I'm sorry. I've established a standard of perfection that neither one of us can meet. And I'm sorry that I've hurt you. I love you so much, Jory. And I want you to love yourself too."

"I'll try, Mom."

She leaned over and hugged me tight. "I'm going to do better, Jory. That's a promise." A passing car honked, flashing its lights. "Get a room!" a guy screamed.

"I guess we'd better move along or we'll get arrested."

"Wouldn't be the worst thing that's happened this summer."

"Oh, come on, it hasn't been *that* bad." Then Mom giggled. "That poor bride's cake."

"What about the van? The surgeon?"

"That appalling photographer!" Mom burst into laughter. "You're right. It's been quite a summer!"

Chapter Twenty-seven

JEWELING

I have to get over my face. Rolling over in bed, I grimaced at the clothes and other junk scattered on my floor and noticed my Nice Nose Notebook half buried under a dirty T-shirt, supermodels grinning, like being on my floor was the best place ever. I don't look like those girls and, according to Dr. Lawrence, I never will. Maybe I don't even want to. Okay, I guess I'd *really* be crazy if I didn't want to look gorgeous and exotic. But those girls have problems too. How many of them suffer from eating disorders, or addictions, or just plain old insecurity?

I reached for the notebook, sat up, flipped through the pages, and mimicked a beaming model stepping off a train. Anyone can fake happiness in a photograph. I made several more model poses. Pouty lips. Kissy lips. Coy smile. Pissed-off diva. Laughing like I'm having the most fun in the world. Maybe I could walk around *pretending* like I'm self-confident.

No one is ever really satisfied anyway, right? Hannah complains about her hair, as much as she tries to live in the moment, and sometimes she gets completely frustrated by her back problems and not being able to ski and stuff. Megan hates her hands because she thinks she has stubby fingers. Whatever.

The photographs in my notebook looked so artificial—super-skinny models don't eat huge slices of pizza. *Rip.* I tore the page into tiny pieces. Three gorgeous guys offering a girl diamond bracelets? *Rip.* Not in my world. Walking a dog in those stilettos? *Rip.* Don't think so. Wearing that much makeup to the beach? *Rip. Rip. Rip.* Yeah, right. One by one, I tore the pages from the notebook, creating glossy confetti. Adios, fake-happy models—even if you do have fabulous little noses.

Before sweeping the whole mess into my wastebasket, I sifted my shredded notebook pages through my fingers, listening to Mom and Dad talk-argue in the kitchen. *Promotion this and promotion that. Just don't blame me when they give it to Jones. I would never blame you. Yet you're the one who wants to move into some fancy house. You're the one who wants to join all those country clubbers for their golf vacations. Not really. Roberts can be such a prick. So is his wife. She stopped beading because Helen wouldn't special order precious stones. I won't put anything against my skin that isn't natural, she said. Dirt is natural. So is elephant dung.*

Dad laughed. Mom laughed. They kissed. *Really, honey, our happy little home is enough for me. I think I just needed to be happy with myself. Well, if hell does freeze over and I get that promotion, I'm taking you on one hell of a second honeymoon.* More kissing.

I turned on my radio.

Kissing. Gideon talked to me. But would he ever kiss me again? I flopped on my bed and buried my face in my squishy pillow. I didn't want to jinx everything by thinking about it. Plus, Hannah and Megan kept saying he was too this and not enough that (the details changed daily). But they were wrong—about as wrong as Gideon had been about the casino-party disaster.

Mom knocked on my door. "I'm going to run down to the Jewel Café. Want to join me?" Mom came in and sat down on my bed, tucking her legs under her. "I love the necklace you made. Do you think you'll keep up with the beading?"

"Maybe." I rolled over and looked at her; her face looked rounder, but happier. No official diet, day 5. "I mean, I think so. It's actually kind of relaxing and not too hard even for a klutz like me."

"You're not a klutz."

"Mom. I got kicked off my fourth-grade soccer team."

"That coach was an ass."

"Well, you know. I'm not really good at anything. Not like Finn."

"Finn simply found his talent early." Mom reached over and brushed my hair back with her hand. "I think I kind of like your hair short. I can see you better." She leaned over and kissed my forehead.

"It *is* easier to take care of."

"Well, then. Hop in the shower so we can get going. Helen just got a new shipment of charms that I want to pick over before anyone else gets to them."

"Charms! That sounds fun." I couldn't help myself.

Helen greeted each of us with a hug.

"I haven't even put them out front yet," she told Mom. "Follow me." Helen pushed through the swinging door. Gideon's door was shut. "Still sleeping," she said, as if we'd asked for an explanation. "Teenagers."

Helen set little bags of charms all over the classroom tables for Mom to examine.

"I'd like to make myself a bracelet. Something inspirational." Mom held up a bag of flat silver charms with words written on them. "These might be just right."

Helen handed Mom a pair of little scissors. "Go ahead and open them up."

I sorted through different baggies. Ladybugs. Butterflies. Wine bottles. Cacti. Horses. Cake.

"I can't believe they make a cake charm!" I laughed. "That's so funny. Do they have a wrecked van?"

"No, but I did order a mixed-motor-vehicle pack." Helen dug around in a big box. "Here it is."

"Oh, my God. There's a little van!" A necklace strung itself in my mind. I'd create layers of colored beads with charms mixed in from things that reminded me of this summer. I spotted a little beer-bottle charm. Perfect. What else would I need? A chunk-of-long-blond-hair charm? No, but scissors would work. I found a little red, white, and blue flag: great for the Fourth of July. A French-fries charm, for Hannah and Megan. A tiny drama mask, for the cinema club. A little wiggly-looking guy would symbolize yoga. Sunglasses would represent Tyler. A baseball cap for Dick in the Dark. I wanted to remember everything. Good and bad. Two tiny dice for casino-cake deliveries. I picked up a little violin.

Helen reached for the charm. "Oh, I'd like to give that one to Gideon."

"That's okay, she can have it."

I looked up to see Gideon standing with his hair fluffed out in all directions. He wore pajama bottoms and a baggy Modest Mouse T-shirt.

"Well, good morning." Helen shook her head. "It's almost noon."

"I dragged Jory out of bed around eleven." Mom put her arm around me. "Teenagers."

I held the tiny golden violin out to Gideon.

"No, you can keep it." He folded my fingers around the charm. "Helen can order me another one."

"Helen, will you help me pick out some great glass beads for my bracelet?" Mom kind of raised her eyebrows at me as she followed Helen out of the room. Could she be more obvious?

"So, you like making jewelry?" Gideon yawned. Did I bore him? He just woke up, but still.

"Yeah, I guess I kind of do. Like it, I mean," I said. "At least I don't completely suck at it."

Gideon lifted the necklace I'd made from my neck. The rough tips of his fingers tickled my skin.

"Pretty good knots for your first time," he said.

I crinkled my face.

He backed away, covering his mouth. "Oops, sorry. Morning breath."

"No, it's not that." I grimaced. "I guess I have a hard time taking a compliment."

"Get used to it." Gideon put his hand on my shoulder. "You've obviously got something unique planned." He tilted his head toward the pile of charms I'd collected on the table.

"Not really."

Gideon gave me the Look. No wonder Mom liked him.

"Well, I guess I *do* have a couple of ideas." I ran my fingers through my hair. "I miss my long hair."

"I don't," Gideon said. "What are your ideas?"

And for some reason I told him. "Well, one is a necklace with charms from, you know, this summer. Oh, and I want to make a button necklace for Hannah because she's, you know, cute as a button. And something classic for Megan, maybe round beads. But I think I'll start with the charms." I hoped I didn't sound too dumb.

"Cool." Gideon nodded. "Should the violin make me hopeful, or did you spend a lot of time at the symphony?"

My stomach fluttered.

"When you blush, your freckles really stand out."

"Oh, God." I covered my face with my hands, but he tugged them away.

"Don't. It's cute."

"I hate that word." Why did I say that? I wished that I could say flirty, fun things.

"Would you prefer *dainty, adorable, darling, sweet* . . ." Gideon thought for a minute. "Or *precious?*"

"What are you, a thesaurus?"

"I prefer *wordsmith*. I like to play around with words." Gideon looked down, and his hair flopped over one eye. "I'm even trying to write some of my own songs. Wanna hear?"

"Sure."

I followed Gideon to his room while out front Mom and Helen debated different beading possibilities. Gideon sat on the chair in front of his computer. I stood behind him, reading the Fleet Foxes poster next to his desk. He'd left the door open, and I liked that.

"Okay, it's a little rough. I'm still getting the hang of my new software."

"Do you sing it?" I shifted from foot to foot, feeling weird being in his bedroom with my mom about to walk past any second.

"No, but I do play some strings. I got Ben, the guy who sang at the frat party, to do the vocals. He likes it. He may add it to the band's regular set."

I thought back to the frat party—I had barely heard the band because of Ass Grabber. Smiling to myself, I remembered Gideon's toenails.

"Please, don't tell me you're thinking of my toxic toes," Gideon said.

"I wasn't. Swear." I put my hand up like a defendant on one of those lawyer shows.

"You're a lousy liar." Gideon pushed my hand down. "I like that about you."

I could hardly believe it. Here I was in a boy's room, and he wasn't a Caughlin Ranch honor-student-star-athlete guy, but a beading violinist who got kicked out of his last high school. And I *did* like him.

"Okay, here goes." Gideon clicked play. The song started with strings, then Ben's voice joined in, singing about a girl. I focused on the lyrics about a girl who didn't know how special she was; she kept making mistakes, drinking too much, dating the wrong guys, and numbing her pain. The singer wanted to save her but didn't know how.

"So?" Gideon peeked up at me with most of his hair covering his face.

"Great," I said. "Maybe too familiar."

"I did kind of think of you when I saw you with that Tyler guy at the movies."

"I'm over that. It got complicated. Long story." I didn't want to give anything away.

"I know all about Tyler," Gideon said. "He hit on me at a party last year."

"He thought you were . . . ?"

"I do play the violin *and* make jewelry." He raised an eyebrow. "Not to mention, I suck at sports. All sports."

"Me too." I sat down on Gideon's bed and pet the cat curled up near his pillow. "I'm especially an embarrassment when it comes to volleyball. Last winter when the air got really smoggy, we got stuck playing the most evil sport for weeks."

"Same at McQueen. I called it the Never-ending Bad Air Quality Volleyball Tournament." He sat next to me on the bed, and I turned to face him, sitting cross-legged. Gideon did the same. "I solved the problem by releasing all of McQueen's volleyballs back into nature." He told me how he and a friend had snuck into the gym, stolen all the volleyballs, and dumped them in the Truckee River.

"That's so great." I laughed. "Didn't you get caught?"

"Suspended. Three days."

"Did your mom kill you?" Gideon's knee touched mine. I wasn't sure if I should move, even though I liked the way it felt.

"Actually, Helen appreciates a little creativity." He stuck his other leg out straight. Right next to me! "Though she did lecture me about littering and made me volunteer to clean up San Rafael Park with her for two weekends."

"Your mom's great."

"I think you're pretty great."

Gideon leaned forward and kissed me, even though the door was still open.

Chapter Twenty-eight

CHARMING

For the arts festival up at Tahoe, Mom spent hours making charm bracelets that seriously could've been sold in boutiques and catalogs—they looked that good. Just before seven in the morning, Helen picked us up in her ancient blue Volvo station wagon, license plate JEWEL. The back held stacks of jewelry display cases; Mom crammed her own box between them.

"Climb in, ladies." Helen held up a sack. "I brought muffins."

I slid into the back seat next to Gideon. He smiled at me, rubbing his eyes. "Getting up this early is torture."

I kind of shook my head back and forth, not wanting to look too excited.

"Don't tell me you're one of those extra-cheerful morning people."

"Just today."

"Mmm." Mom stuck her cute little nose into the muffin bag. "Banana-nut!" She handed one each to me and Gideon and lifted her own supersized muffin out of the bag. She didn't offer to split it with anyone and didn't complain about how many calories she'd have to work off at the gym; she simply took a big bite. I watched as she finished the whole thing, even plucking a sticky crumb off her shirt. I bit into my own muffin, sat back against the seat, and watched the pine trees whoosh past as we cruised along on the freeway. Every now and then we had a view of sunlight sparkling on the river. Gideon reached over and held my hand. Everything felt right in the world.

Gideon stayed with his mom until she got into a groove with her cash register and credit card machine and knew where all her extra supplies were stacked under the table. After a few early sales, Mom decided to make some more charm bracelets, so I helped.

"Will you hand me another 'dream' charm?" Mom reached across the table. "I almost put 'love' on twice."

"Can't have too much love."

"True." Mom reached over and touched my hand. "Can I

tell you just once more how much this means to me? To finally have something in common with you? I can't remember feeling so happy, even though things haven't happened exactly like I'd hoped." Dad had *not* gotten the promotion. Mom talked—happily—about downsizing to a townhouse, as long as she had space for her beading supplies. And she still planned to cut back on her own work hours.

"I guess sometimes you think you want something more than you really do," I said, thinking *Tyler Briggs, devirgination, nose job.*

"Only seventeen and so wise." Mom held up a finished bracelet. "I love the silver with the blue. Don't you?" Mom smiled, all dreamy. Her face looked younger since she'd gained a little weight back.

A classic I-have-a-waterfront-house-at-Tahoe-and-my-third-husband-will-do-anything-for-me lady went gaga watching "an artist at work." She custom-ordered three bracelets. When Mom offered to let the woman select her own beads, she wanted to pay double.

"Mom, you really know how to work with these people," I whispered.

"Three years of trying to get into Lindsey Dickenson's book club has taught me quite a bit about the rich but not so famous." Mom shrugged, satisfied.

Gideon tapped me on the shoulder. "Come on, let's look around."

Gideon and I wandered past the rows of booths, avoiding all the pottery stuff, both agreeing that we'd never, ever care about such boring things as dishes. We spent at least ten minutes looking through fancy kaleidoscopes at one booth, trying to outdo the other with the prettiest designs. *Look at this one with the purple swirls. Ah, but see mine has little mirrors so you can see the pine trees.*

"Oh, I want one like this." I held up one that made patterns with dried flowers.

Gideon showed me the price tag: $150. Maybe not. But I would have some post-van-wreck money saved from my job. Did I really want to spend it on clothes, like Hannah suggested? Finn wanted me to buy a car. Pretty fishy request from someone only three months from his learner's permit. Megan told me to save it for college.

"You're actually thinking about it, aren't you?" Gideon stared at me. "You *are* one of those rich girls from the fancy neighborhood."

"No, but I did save all my money from my job—while I had it—this summer."

"Impressive discipline."

"Not really. I was saving for something specific." I glanced away so he wouldn't try to read my expression. No way would I *ever* tell anyone about the potential nose job. Too embarrassing!

"Flashy ride? Fashionista clothes? Trip around the world?" Gideon spoke in an English accent.

"Not exactly." I attempted a Russian accent: "I had a deep, dark, mysterious secret."

We stopped to look at another jewelry display, the usual stuff: wineglass charms, basic beaded necklaces, and simple earrings.

"Oh, Fifi," Gideon said in *his* English accent. "Wouldn't our dear pussycat Mr. Sullivan just love this?" He held up a gaudy leather cat collar studded with fake diamonds and pearls.

"Didn't I tell you, darling? Mr. Sullivan died last week. Choked on his diamond ear stud."

"Oh, tragedy!" Gideon fake sobbed. "How will we ever again find a cat that's part mountain lion, part Siamese—from Siam—and part alley cat? Such beauty."

The woman in the booth rolled her eyes at us, and we burst into laughter.

"Dah-ling," he said. "Let us go find some bangers and chips."

I laughed. "Some what?"

"Hot dogs and fries." His breath tickled my ear as he whispered, "You're blowing my cover."

"What? Now you're some secret agent?" I asked, bumping my shoulder against his.

"You're the one who has some mysterious, expensive, deep, dark, secret. What is it?"

I shook my head. "Too embarrassing." I pretended to lock my lips with a key.

"I know that combination." He leaned over and kissed me. "Secret?"

I spotted a booth with crazy hats. "Look! Hats!" I ran over and started trying them on. I began with a chicken head. Gideon put on a "My Bitch Done Left Me for a Dawg" cap that had long stringy hair hanging down.

"Not you." I plopped a wizard hat on him instead. "They should totally remake *Harry Potter* starring you." I tipped up on my toes and kissed him.

"So you have a thing for the dark arts?"

I felt kind of flustered, thinking about Tom and that dark room and what a big mistake *that* had been. What made me think I could trust Gideon? Maybe he was just the same—a friendly flirt who wanted one thing. The thing I'd decided I wasn't ready to give. Not yet. Even if I did get into some freak accident and died a virgin. Current chance of dying a virgin: I don't care.

"I said something wrong."

"No, no. I just thought of something. Something stupid."

Gideon put his arm around me and we walked, banging our hips together, down another row. Gideon stopped to look at some photographs of street scenes in Reno and pointed to a photo of garbage heaped on a storm-drain grate. "Now, that's the ultimate photo for the chronic litterbug."

I stared at the crumpled fast-food bags, soda cups, soggy fliers, and dead leaves, feeling like the photo represented my life. Garbage heaped on garbage, secrets heaped on secrets, preventing the good stuff from getting through.

"Hey, Gideon. You know a minute ago—you didn't say anything wrong. I was just reminded of this guy who tried to—well, I was drunk and acting stupid. I wanted someone to like me. Even though nothing really happened, it still kind of freaked me out." I covered my face. "I wanted to tell you so you didn't think it was you."

"So that was the time you called your mom from the casino?" Gideon asked, scrunching up his face. "I kind of overheard her talking about it."

Feeling only a little bit irritated about Mom's big mouth, I nodded. "Yeah, about that night—" Gideon looked at me with such compassion, and his eyes showed so much concern, that I started talking and talking. The new me: blab about it all.

"I didn't even like him, really. But I just wanted to like someone and you were angry with me plus my—" I stopped myself from saying that my friends thought he was a freak/dork/delinquent with a Super Schnozz.

"That's okay." Gideon looked at me. "I'd never take advantage of you. Besides, Helen would take a carving knife to my manhood if I ever did anything remotely like that to a girl."

"It's just that it seems that guys only like me for that reason, only, you know, in the dark. I used to think that's what I wanted, like it would make me feel special." My stomach fluttered and I felt hot all over. God, why was I saying so much? Shut up, Jory! I imagined Gideon turning from me with a cold Tyler expression on his face. *This girl is crazy. Accuses all men of being potential rapists.*

Gideon *did* run! I stared at him as he sprinted through the trees toward the parking area. *Now I've wrecked everything. He's leaving. How am I going to explain to Mom and Helen that we have to walk back to Reno?*

"Come here," he called.

I walked slowly toward him, blinking in the bright sunlight.

"I like you in the blazing sunshine," he said. "I like you because—I don't really know. It's just a feeling, but I feel good when I'm with you. Talking with you. Crawling around looking for beads on the floor. Anything. I just like you." He shrugged.

"I like you too." My voice sounded shaky. "I'm sorry I weirded out."

"No, thanks for telling me. I would've stayed awake all night rereading the Harry Potter books to figure out what I'd said wrong."

"You're such a dork."

"I'll take that as a compliment." He brought my hand to his lips. "My lady, I feel compelled to purchase said print of garbage for you."

We walked back to the photographer's booth and Gideon paid twenty-five dollars for a small framed copy of the photograph.

"Let me repay you." I dug into my purse, but Gideon pushed my hand away.

"No, make me a bracelet, but make sure it's manly since I'm going to have to start enduring mandatory PE five days a week. Something that will remind me of you."

"Maybe I should just spill a bunch of beads in your backpack."

"Too easy," he said. "Plus, you really do have talent. I want one of your early works so I can be rich someday."

"Yeah, right."

❦

In the afternoon we took over running the booth while Mom and Helen grabbed lunch. Mom had sold all of her charm bracelets and started taking special orders. I liked working with Gideon; he kept making me, not to mention the customers, laugh.

And I liked that I could tell him things.

Chapter Twenty-nine

GIDEON

A few nights later, at beading, Helen leaned over a newbie and showed her how to throw little Timmy in the well. The lady giggled like a twelve-year-old even though she was most definitely menopausal. It felt kind of funny that these older women were becoming like friends to me—and that we actually had things in common. I never joined in the so-and-so-is-getting-divorced talk, but I felt like I could be myself around them, even with Mom listening. Hannah had commented the other night that I "vibrated with self-love." I teased her about sounding like something out of one of those sex-obsessed magazines—totally making her blush and stammer—but I kind of knew what she meant. I liked myself more now. Most of the time.

"That choker is so unique," Helen said.

"Is that bad?" I had seen something like it in a catalog, but

I'd added a dangly cluster of beads to the front, making it a true Jory Creation. Was it too different?

"Jory, Jory, Jory." Helen shook her head, smiling. "As Bette Midler says, 'Cherish forever what makes you unique 'cuz you're a real yawn if it goes.'"

"Who's—"

"Some old actress." Gideon stood in the doorway. "Don't ask or you'll get a fifteen-minute reminiscence of all her sappy movies."

Too late. Everyone broke into major sharing. *"Wind Beneath My Wings." Oh, yes, I went through a box of Kleenex and that was way before menopause. Oh, my gosh, wasn't she so funny in that movie with oh, what's her name again, she was in that—*

"We better get out of here fast," Gideon said. "Unless you want to get stuck watching one of those sappy DVDs. She owns all of them."

Gideon pulled my hand and led me down the hall to his room.

"Jory would love her movies," Helen protested. "Bring her back here."

"You're not infecting my girlfriend with sappy-movie syndrome," Gideon called.

Girlfriend? I smiled all the way to my toes.

"I'll have to rent them." Mom's voice echoed down the hall.

Funny how the thought of snuggling up with Mom and a bowl of popcorn didn't completely horrify me like it would have only a few weeks ago. Maybe I could surprise her with a movie some night? We could bead at the coffee table.

Gideon pushed me into his room. "Narrow escape." He leaned down and kissed me. His fingers played around my waist, my hair, the back of my neck, and my ears.

"You're naked."

"What?"

"No jewelry." He pushed his hair over his eye. "It's something my mom says. Okay, that's *so* not what I wanted to bring up in this moment."

"I was in a hurry and forgot." Did he expect me to wear my green necklace all the time? Even when it totally clashed? "Sorry."

"Why are you apologizing? You don't need to apologize to me." He shook his head. "Don't do that insecure girl thing." He twisted his mouth into a frown. "That's not you."

Oh, yes, it is, I almost said out loud, except it wasn't quite so true anymore. Not that I didn't worry—okay, occasionally obsess—about stuff. I looked down at the floor, watching Gideon tap his bare toes. What if he stopped liking me? I was already freaking out about school starting. Would Gideon still like me when he saw all the other girls strutting around the yellow-tiled hallways in their new clothes, sporting summer tans and confidence? What if we didn't have any classes together? What if we did? How would Hannah and Megan treat us? Did that really matter?

"Oh, no. Please don't start staring at my feet again."

"Sorry."

Gideon yelped like he was in pain and put his hands up to defend himself. "No more apologies." He fell to the floor in slow motion. "I'm melting."

"Get up." I yanked on his arm, but he pulled me down on top of him and we kissed, running our hands through each other's hair, and up under our shirts, until I felt completely tingly all over. Not sure, I put my hand down near the band of his shorts.

"We better slow down." He sat up and smoothed my hair. "Want to get ice cream?"

"Sounds great." I jumped up, relieved.

❧

We walked around Virginia Lake on the paved path, trying not to wake up the ducks, because Gideon insisted they'd want to eat our ice cream.

"They especially go nuts for chocolate." He leaned over and licked my cone. "I better help you eat it fast."

"That's just an excuse. Admit it, you're in a chocolate mood." Gideon had already finished his vanilla cone.

"Maybe." He kissed my nose with cold lips. "Quiet. You're waking the ducks." Several wings fluttered nearby, but most of the ducks floated in little groups with their heads tucked under their wings. We walked across the street and sat on the swings at the playground.

"So tell me your mystery reason for saving money," he said. "Let me guess. You were planning to run off to Spain because you're in love with a matador."

"No, I'm not into animal cruelty, plus I have no Spanish accent. At least that's what Señora Rogers says."

"You're going to listen to a lady who insists on being called Señora with a last name like Rogers?"

"She swears she visits Mexico every year."

"Probably drinks the whole time." Gideon slurred his words and held up his hand. *"Mas cerveza, por favor."*

"Interesting. You know how to order beer in Spanish."

"Last summer my friend Toby and I thought it would be a good idea to learn how to order beer in every language. Thought girls would find it impressive. Plus, we'd planned to backpack all over Europe and hook up with all kinds of girls."

I imagined beautiful girls swarming all over Gideon in

manicured parks and quaint sidewalk cafés. They would run their long fingernails through his wavy hair.

"What's wrong? Too dorky?"

I shook my head.

"You're jealous!" He laughed. "You're using your overly creative imagination to picture me with all kinds of girls, aren't you?" He bumped his swing into mine. "Well, don't. I'm right where I want to be. But I'm still figuring out where *you* want to be." He studied me in the dark. "So, let me guess. You're saving money to fly to New York where you'll be discovered by a famous fashion photographer who'll turn you into a supermodel."

I pushed back on the ground and swung into the air. Was Gideon just like every other guy on the planet, fantasizing about dating a beautiful model? "I could never model."

"Why not? You're tall, just the right amount of curvy, and you've got that attitude."

"What attitude?" I soared so high that the chain started squeaking. Gideon pushed off and matched me swing for swing.

"Mysterious." He stopped pumping and let himself slow down. "Sometimes you do this look."

The Look? "I'm the only one who *can't* do the Look," I muttered.

"You're doing it right now. I can feel it, even though I can't see it in the dark."

"Yeah, right." I jumped off the swing, landing so hard my feet hurt. "I'm not pretty enough to model. Not to mention I've got a bumpy banana for a nose." I put my hands over my face. "I was saving money for a nose job." There. I'd said it. Now he would know. And he could dump me and spread rumors all over school.

"Why?" Gideon came up behind me, wrapping his arms around my waist. I felt his breath on my neck; he smelled like vanilla. "You're so cute."

"I don't want to be cute." I turned around so fast that he backed away a couple of steps.

"Come here." Gideon hugged me to his chest. "You're just right."

"No, I'm not. The surgeon wouldn't even operate on me because it would be too hard."

"That can't be what he said." Gideon pushed my sort-of bangs back and kissed my forehead.

"It was a *she*. A condescending, go-see-a-psychologist-be-cause-I-think-you're-crazy *she* doctor." I sniffed back tears. "She said I had unrealistic expectations."

"What were you expecting?"

"I had this notebook. Oh, God. Why am I telling you

this?" I looked into his eyes for signs of disgust, but it was too dark to see. "Now you're going to think I'm crazy."

"What kind of notebook? Like a diary?"

"No, a notebook filled with pictures of nice noses that would make me look pretty so I'd fit in with my family. The only family trait I possess is my Great-Grandpa Lessinger's Super Schnozz."

"Super Schnozz?" Gideon laughed. "That's ridiculous. You totally look like your mother: the shape of your eyes, your long legs, perfect little earlobes, even your hands; maybe that's why you're both good at making jewelry."

"Earlobes?" My mouth hung open. "I want her delicate freckle-free nose, not her stupid earlobes."

"You might want to change your mind." Gideon reached into his pocket. "Here." He handed me a crumpled tissue.

I started to wipe my nose.

"No, open it." Gideon pushed my hand from my nose. "I tried to kind of wrap it."

I unfolded the paper. Inside, tiny pink hearts dangled at the ends of two delicate silver-chain earrings.

"I can't tell you how long it took me to get those little loops right." Gideon gently put the earrings on me. "And I thought playing the violin took finger work."

"You really made these? They're so cute. Beautiful, I mean."

"No, you're right, they're cute, and so are you." Gideon put his hands on my shoulders and looked into my eyes. "And that's good. Cute is good. Us guys with weird toenails like cute girls."

I actually kind of believed him.

Chapter Thirty

MORE ICE CREAM AND PHOTO SHOOTS

Sounding like a heavy smoker running a marathon, Bugsy struggled up the winding mountain road to Virginia City—an old 1800s ghost town now mining gold as a tourist attraction, complete with historical tours, Old West–themed casinos, gift shops galore, and old-timey photo places. I sat in the back seat trying not to get carsick as we rounded the curves. We'd have to go with the sepia-toned photo if I looked too green. Turns out all of us had suffered with our senior photos. Bald Ponytail Guy tried to hit on Megan (in front of her mom!), and Hannah had accidentally tinted her hair orange the night before her photo shoot. I hadn't given them every detail about my yelling-and-screaming-not-knowing-Gideon-sat-outside meltdown, but that didn't seem to matter so much anymore.

Although the fact remained that the only photo of me that would appear in the yearbook would be me with my hands over my face, me with my tongue sticking out, or me looking demented and lovey-dovey (the photographer refused to schedule a reshoot because I was, quote, "unstable"). So we'd all decided to get our own senior photo up at Silver Sadie's studio in Virginia City and pool our money to buy space in the yearbook. With only three days before the start of school, we also decided to make a day of it, gorging on chocolate at Grandma's Fudge Shop, riding the old steam train, and window-shopping. Megan wanted to tour some of the historic buildings, and we all agreed that it might get us back into learning mode.

"Check out those legs!" Megan veered away from a cyclist pumping his way up the mountain. "After spending time at the beach this summer, I think I'm definitely a leg woman."

"Looking at these guys makes me feel tired," I said. "I never want to ride a bike again." I scanned the hillsides, hoping to spot some wild horses.

"But you probably got so good at going uphill," Hannah said.

"No, I got good at reassuring Tyler that we wouldn't give away his secret while he drove me home." Actually, I'd really missed my daily Tyler talks since I'd gotten fired. Even though I hadn't told him about the whole nose thing, we'd had great discussions about appearances versus reality, mostly using our mothers as examples. It seemed a little crazy, but we'd become friends.

"Have you seen him since you—" Hannah turned around.

"Got fired? We've been to lunch a couple of times," I said. "I wish he didn't feel like he needed to keep something so important a secret. He really needs friends right now."

"I've actually talked to him a few times myself," Megan said. "That perverted law clerk started a massive affair with the temp who was answering phones. They both got fired. Sweet justice. Tyler's still pretty nervous about how I feel about his secret. I keep telling him that I don't care. I'm saving myself for *mature* college men."

"Like the ones we met at that frat party? Good luck." Hannah and I giggled.

"Yeah, I know. You've told me a million times." I watched Megan smile shyly in the rearview mirror. "I did kind of run into Will Fryer at the mall—summer has been very good to that boy, if you know what I mean." She raised an eyebrow. "And he *is* on the academic team."

"You should totally go for a serious guy like Will," Hannah said. "So beyond Tyler."

"Actually, I'm trying to convince Tyler to join the team too. He's super smart, but his dad wants him to stick with sports."

I leaned against the back seat, checking to see how I felt about Megan talking with Tyler. I felt okay. Not threatened. I wanted the best for Tyler. Maybe the three of us could go to lunch?

"Tyler's dad seems to be pretty tough on him," I said. "He has all these expectations for Tyler to be a man's man and date gorgeous girls, drive expensive cars, and learn the high-rolling casino business."

"Seems like he wants a clone." Megan swerved around a pair of cyclists. "That would totally suck."

I used to think my mom wanted me to be her clone. Turned out she was just too hard on herself. Maybe Tyler's dad should take up beading with Helen; it might give him a new perspective. I imagined Mr. Briggs, an Italian-suit-wearing, cigar-smoking gorilla, crouched down at the table, stringing beads with his ring-covered fingers. I chuckled.

"What?" Megan said. "I'm driving okay."

"No, I was just imagining Tyler's dad at the Jewel Café."

"You're really into that jewelry stuff, aren't you?" Megan said.

"I think it's cool that you finally found a passion—something unique for you." Hannah turned to smile at me. Again. At this rate she'd make herself motion sick like she had at the Rodeo Carnival. Megan would lose it if Hannah hurled in Bugsy.

"You've got to cherish what's unique because you're a real yawn if it goes." I tried to remember exactly how Helen had phrased it. "Or something like that."

"I like that. Did you make that up?" Megan asked.

"Some actress said it. Bette Midler?" I shrugged my shoulders.

"Red hair, big nose?" Hannah asked.

"I guess." I let the phrase *big nose* wash over me. So what? Let people describe other people like that. I didn't have to do it. I didn't have to criticize how other people dressed. I didn't have to talk about their hair, or make fun of their belly bulges, big boobs, or big or small anything. I could be positive, see the best in people. Maybe even see the best in me.

Gideon does.

I let out a wish-I-could-be-making-out-with-Gideon sigh. I hadn't seen him in two days because Mom insisted on driving to Sacramento for school shopping (only so she could totally check out a bead store) and I'd promised Hannah and Megan I'd spend the last Saturday before school started with them. Gideon said taking a little break would be good. Let us cool off a bit. The other night after beading, we'd been kissing and doing a little exploring when he made me stop.

"You've been really honest with me," he said. "So I should be honest with you."

He looked nervous, fiddling with the edge of his quilt; I braced myself for bad news. Even the cat had jumped off the bed.

"You see . . ." He paused.

I prickled with panic.

"I've kind of decided that I won't lose my virginity in high school." He said it so fast that it took me a while to figure out what he'd said. "I know that's so lame and dorky."

I laughed, even though I knew it was exactly the wrong response.

"I should tell you that one of my summer goals was not to die a virgin," I said, then waited while his eyes got wide. "But I've changed my mind. I think I confused sex with acceptance or self-worth or some other mumbo jumbo from the book my mom not so subtly left on my pillow last week." I wrapped my hand around his. "Anyway, I think that what I wanted from sex is something I need to discover for myself. I'm still trying to figure it out. So waiting is a good thing."

Gideon let out a big breath. "You scared me there for a minute. Want some ice cream?"

"We're going to be eating a lot of ice cream this year, aren't we?"

He kissed my hand in a kind of dorky, kind of charming way. "I fear so, my lady."

❧

Megan found a parking spot near the Silver Queen Hotel. We wandered inside to look at the huge portrait of the lady with the gown made from real silver dollars.

"How many school clothes do you think you could buy with all those silver dollars?" Hannah asked as we gazed at the sparkling coins.

"Almost as many as Ashley Winters will wear the first month of school," Megan said.

Afterward, we toured the Mackay Mansion, Piper's Opera House, the schoolhouse, and the old church, at Hannah's insistence. She loved the fact that it had survived the great fire that had destroyed most of the town in 1875. I liked the fact that they had completely rebuilt the *rest* of the town within eighteen months—it reminded me of how all of us can recover from the bad things that happen.

Everywhere we went, Megan soaked up the information about Mark Twain's time as a reporter in Virginia City while Hannah went on and on about the spirit of the old objects.

Sample conversation:

"What do you think they made for the last meal cooked in

this kitchen?" Hannah asked. "What did the person who last slept in this bed dream?"

"How did the last bowel movement taken in that chamber pot smell?" Megan asked.

"How did it feel to scrub that floor for the last time?" I asked.

Hannah scoffed. "You two have no sense of history."

I paid a lot of attention to the jewelry the women wore in the old photographs. Wouldn't it be fun to re-create period jewelry? In the Mackay Mansion, one woman wore a choker that was kind of like the one I'd just finished, except hers had a jeweled cross on the end and mine had a heart-shaped bead.

"Your choker sort of looks like that." Megan stood next to me. "Is it antique?"

I had hoped one of them would notice my necklace. "No, I made it."

"You *did?* It looks, like, totally professional." Hannah put her fingers on my neck. "Can you make something for me?"

I thought of the multistranded button necklace I'd designed for Hannah. "I'm working on something for you."

"And me?"

"I have something very classic planned."

"Black?" Megan flipped her hair up and looked at me.

"Of course." I smiled, thinking that finally I had something unique about me. An actual skill! "I'm also making a charm bracelet for Katie to send along with my check for the van— hopefully, it will smooth things over a bit." I made a face.

Megan sighed. "We weren't exactly superlative summer employees, were we?"

"I think I'll go down as the worst delivery driver in history."

"What about me?" Megan shook her head, speechless.

Hannah wrapped her arms around our shoulders. "Well, I still think you guys are the best."

Megan and I rolled our eyes and started laughing.

We popped into various gift shops as we walked down the old-fashioned wooden sidewalks toward the photo place. The air ahead of us smelled sweet with fudge. It reminded me of the sweet, sugary smell at Katie's, but with a more pleasing chocolate aroma. Tourists gathered outside the corral for the fake gunfight. Megan gawked at the cute cowboy guy selling tickets.

"You should've seen the real cowboys—I mean, cowmen— at the Rodeo Carnival," I said.

"Trust me. I know."

"Friends come before boys," Hannah said, as if she hadn't been spending all her time with José.

"Hello? I'm the only one without a boyfriend." Megan made an exaggerated pouty face. "That reminds me. I need fudge. Or maybe ice cream."

I smiled to myself, thinking, *Gideon, boyfriend, my boyfriend, Gideon.*

"It *is* super hot," Hannah said. "I don't think I'll wear my new sweater on Monday."

"Only freshmen wear their new clothes," I said. "We're seniors. We know better." I had actually started looking forward to school: going out to lunch with Gideon, stopping by Gideon's locker, maybe even releasing all the PE volleyballs back into nature . . .

The fan whirring in the sweetshop cooled us a bit as we looked around. Hannah and Megan pored over the ice cream flavors while I looked at the fudge. I'd been eating a lot of ice cream lately; the thought of eating it without Gideon and his chocolate jokes made me feel a little lonely for him.

"I've been meaning to tell you that I love those earrings," Megan said as we paid for the ice cream and fudge.

"Me too." Hannah swung one of the little hearts with her finger. "Did you make them to match your necklace?"

"Not exactly." I blushed. "Gideon made them for me."

"He makes jewelry? Isn't that a little—" Hannah scrunched up her tiny nose.

"Suspicious, if you catch my drift." Megan frowned.

Not again. Why couldn't they leave Gideon and me alone? So what if he wasn't on the approved-potential-boyfriend list? He liked me; he cared about me; he made me feel good— about myself. "Trust me. It means he's good with his hands, if you catch *my* drift." I raised my eyebrows and attempted the Look.

"Jory! That's so not like you." Hannah giggled. "So bold."

"Yeah, Junior Jory could never have pulled off a look like that." Megan handed me my bag of fudge. I'd bought extra for Gideon. Vanilla.

"Next thing we know you'll be selling your jewelry on late night TV like that old soap star." Megan launched into a sales pitch, using a nasally voice and exaggerated hand gestures that bordered on the obscene.

I started laughing so hard that I dribbled chocolaty fudge spit down my shirt. My white shirt.

"Ah, now *that's* the Jory I remember," Megan said. "Patented neatness issues." Megan took a delicate bite out of her waffle cone. "Maybe I should do your TV spots."

"You're gorgeous enough." I didn't usually compliment my friends, but it felt good.

"I am not." Megan swatted my knee with her hand.

"You know you are," Hannah and I said together.

"Well, maybe." Megan vamped up and down the wooden sidewalk, finishing her cone. "But I'd rather sell shoes, if I'll get an employee discount. Or maybe textbooks. Do you know how much college textbooks cost?" Hannah and I reminded Megan that we *still* had a year of high school left.

"I know," Megan said. "And I promise to enjoy it. Ninety-five percent of the time. Maybe only eighty-five percent of the time."

"Come on, Meg. We're going to have a great year. Go, Huskies!" I moved my hands like pompoms.

That got Hannah started on a discussion about whether she should sit on the Wooster or Reno side during the first football game. *Will I be a traitor? Should I wear red and white, but not blue? People will see me with José afterward anyway.*

Megan and I exchanged looks as Hannah debated herself. Finally, Megan held up her watch in front of Hannah's face.

"Oh, no! We're supposed to be at the photo shop—and I still have to brush my teeth!" Megan and I rolled our eyes, but Hannah simply hooked her arms through ours and we walked down the street side by side, giggling like crazy while tourists stared at us.

ᔭᕈ

Hannah drove the photographer nuts trying to decide between proper Victorian lady or lady of the evening. She tried on a long, old-timey dress with a fancy bonnet, then a teddy with a bustier, then the old-timey dress again.

"What's right for the moment? This exact moment?" she fretted.

I went with the teddy and fishnets. So did Megan.

"People are going to have their yearbooks for years," Megan said. "Plus my mom has always told me to appreciate my youthful body."

"My mom said the same thing." I gasped. "She was all, Go for it, Jory. Enjoy being young with all your possibilities ahead. Eating actual meals has sure changed that woman!"

"I don't think she meant for you to look like a hooker, though," Hannah said.

"Soiled Dove, thank you very much." I liked the thought of Gideon seeing this photo—he'd end up eating cartons of ice cream!

"Come on, guys." Hannah waved a Little Bo Peep staff at us. "Isn't this sweet?"

"Well, I'm certainly not going to herd sheep." I pushed up my boobs. "I'm herding men," I said in a low, sexy voice.

Megan burst out laughing. Hannah blushed. We finally convinced Hannah to wear a slinky red nightie after assuring her that José wouldn't get the wrong idea even though it was Wooster colors, and besides the yearbook doesn't come out until June and we're sure your future husband won't mind, and, of course, you can hide it from your future kids.

The photographer arranged us with guns, cards, cash, and fake bottles of booze. I sat on the bar with one leg dangling over the other, a spiky shoe hanging off my front toes. Megan stood sideways to my right, glancing over her shoulder, her long hair draped around her. Hannah insisted on leaning behind the bar to my left, for modesty reasons. I don't think she had any idea what that did for her ample cleavage. The photographer put a frilly showgirl headdress on her and stepped over to the camera.

"Ready? One, two, three."

I looked straight into the camera and smiled.

A SPECIAL DELIVERY OF THANKS

Big bouquets to my agent, Ted Malawer, and to my editor, Julie Tibbott.

Warm pie and coffee to my writing group, especially Kelley and Susan.

Dozens and dozens of cupcakes to my dad, David, stepmom, Stephanie, brother, Ethan, and sister-in-law, Colleen, with extra sprinkles to my daughters, Emma and Sophie.

A tiered wedding cake to my husband, Mike. Thanks for always believing.

And finally, a charm bracelet to my mom, Rondi, who always burns the cookies but provides endless inspiration and source material.

SYDNEY SALTER held a variety of jobs before becoming a full-time writer, including a brief stint delivering pies and flowers, wrecking vans, and destroying wedding cakes in Reno, Nevada. Sydney now lives in Utah with her husband, two daughters, two cats, and two big Bernese Mountain dogs. She loves reading, writing, traveling, and, of course, baking and decorating cakes (but not driving them anywhere).

www.sydneysalter.com
www.mybignose.blogspot.com